DATE DUE

THE DEVIL'S DELILAH

Also by Loretta Chase

VISCOUNT VAGABOND
THE ENGLISH WITCH
ISABELLA

The Devil's Delilah

Loretta Chase

Walker and Company
New York

First published in the United States of America in 1989
by Walker Publishing Company, Inc.

Published simultaneously in Canada by Thomas Allen & Son
Canada, Limited, Markham, Ontario.

Library of Congress Cataloging-in-Publication Data

Chase, Loretta Lynda, 1949–
The Devil's Delilah / Loretta Chase.
p.   cm.
ISBN 0-8027-1058-1
I. Title.
PS3553.H3347D48   1989
813'.54—dc19   88-35247
CIP

Printed in the United States of America

10   9   8   7   6   5   4   3   2   1

=== 1 ===

RAIN DRUMMED FURIOUSLY against the sturdy timbers of the Black Cat Inn. Within, its public dining parlour, tap-room, and coffee rooms overflowed with orphans of the storm. From time to time a flash of lightning set the rooms ablaze with glaring light, and the more timid of the company shrank in terror at the deafening cannonade of thunder which instantly followed.

"Filthy night, sir," said Mrs. Tabithy, approaching one of her guests. "There'll be a sight more of them"—she nodded toward the group crowding the main passageway— "unless I miss my guess. If you'd come but a quarter hour later I couldn't have given you a private parlour, not if my life depended on it."

"Very kind of you, I'm sure," said the guest, gazing absently about the room.

His hostess eyed the thick volume in his hands and smiled. His mien was that of a gentleman. The quality and cut of his attire, despite its untidiness, bespoke wealth. He was a good-looking young man—not yet thirty, she would guess—and, judging by both the book and the rather dazed expression of his grey eyes, one of those harmless scholar types. This fellow would offer no trouble at all.

"Just down that passage," she said aloud. "Third door on the left. I'll send Sairey along to you as soon as ever I can— but she has her hands full, as you can see."

The young man only gave a vague nod and wandered off in the direction she indicated.

His hostess had guessed aright. Mr. Jack Langdon was a quiet, bookish sort, too preoccupied with his own musings to take any note of the service accorded him. At present he was more preoccupied—or muddled, rather—than usual. This was because Mr. Langdon was recently disappointed in love.

Retiring by nature, he was now sorely tempted to betake himself to a monastery. Unfortunately, he had responsibilities. Therefore he was taking himself to the next best refuge, his Uncle Albert's peaceful estate in Yorkshire. His uncle, Viscount Rossing, was a recluse, even more bookminded than the nephew. Jack could spend the entire summer at Rossing Hall without once having to attempt a conversation. Better still, except for servants, he need never see a single female.

Sadly contemplating the particular female who had cast a blighting frost upon his budding hopes, Mr. Langdon lost count of doors and opened the fifth.

The room was exceedingly dim, which was annoying. He could not read comfortably by lightning bolts, frequent as they were. He'd scarcely formulated the thought when the lightning crackled again to reveal, lit like a scene upon the stage, a young woman pressing a pistol against the Earl of Streetham's breast.

Without pausing to reflect further, Mr. Langdon hurled himself at the young woman, knocking her to the floor and the earl against the wall. Lord Streetham's head cracked against the window frame and his lordship slid, unconscious, to the floor.

The young woman remained fully conscious though, and in full possession of the pistol. As Jack grabbed for it, she jammed an elbow into his chest and tried to shove him away. He thrust the elbow away, and went again for the weapon. Her free hand tore into his scalp. He tried to pull away, but she caught hold of his ear and yanked so hard that the pain made his eyes water. While he struggled to pry her fingers loose, she brought up the hand wielding the weapon behind his neck. Just as the pistol's butt was about to slam down on his skull, Jack seized her wrist. He squeezed hard and the weapon dropped to the floor a few inches from her head. He lunged for the pistol, but her nails ripped into his scalp once more, jerking him back.

Mr. Langdon was growing distraught. To have assaulted a woman in the first place was contrary to his nature. Now he seemed to have no choice but to render her unconscious. He knew he could, having been well-trained at Gentleman Jack's, yet the idea of driving his fist into a feminine jaw was appalling.

While he struggled with his sense of propriety, she struggled to better purpose, punctuating her blows with a stream of choked oaths that would have shocked Mr. Langdon to the core had he been able to pay full attention. He, however, had all he could do to keep her down. He prayed she'd tire soon and spare him the shame of having to beat her senseless. But she only writhed, elbowed, scratched, and pummelled with unabated ferocity.

Mr. Langdon's prodigious patience began to fail him. In desperation, he grabbed both her wrists and pinned them to the floor. She cursed vehemently now, but her heaving bosom showed she was finally weakening, though she continued twisting frantically beneath him. That is when his concentration began to fail.

The form beneath his was strong and lithe, and he became acutely aware of supple muscles and lush curves. As her writhings abated, a warmth more beckoning than the heat of combat began to steal over him. In a moment it had stolen into his brain, along with a host of other inappropriate sensations, all of which loudly demanded attention.

Mr. Langdon attended and—alarmed at what he found— hastily lifted his weight off her. His adversary promptly thrust her knee against a portion of his anatomy.

Jack gasped and rolled onto the floor, and the young

woman scrambled to her feet, grabbed her pistol, and dashed out of the room.

Moments later, as Jack was struggling to rise, he heard a low groan and saw the earl painfully raising his head from the floor. Jack crawled towards him. Blood trickled past Lord Streetham's ear along his jaw line.

"My Lord, you're hurt," said Jack. He fumbled in his coat for his handkerchief.

Lord Streetham pulled himself up to a sitting position, clutching his head. "Damned madwoman," he muttered. "How was I to know she wasn't—what are you doing?" he cried.

"Your head, My Lord—"

"Never mind that. Go find the she-devil. I'll teach her to —well, what are you waiting for?"

From his earliest childhood Jack Langdon had run tame in the earl's house, dealt with on the same terms as his lordship's son, Tony. Jack had played with Tony, studied with Tony and—periodically—been flogged with Tony. When, therefore, Tony's father told Jack to do a thing, Jack did it.

He stumbled to his feet and out of the room.

"Well, Delilah, and now what have you been up to?" said Mr. Desmond as he coolly studied his daughter's disheveled appearance.

Delilah glanced at the pudgy little man who stood, perspiring profusely, beside her papa. "Oh, nothing," she said, airily indifferent to the scene of carnage she'd recently left. "A misunderstanding with one of our fellow guests. Two, actually," she added, half to herself.

"Good heavens, Miss Desmond, it appears to have been a great deal more than that. I hope one of the gentlemen has not behaved uncivilly. A terrible thing, these public inns," said the damp fellow. "You really should not have come unattended. Your maid—"

"My maid has a sick headache, Mr. Atkins, though I

have told her repeatedly that only women of the upper classes are permitted the luxury of megrims. I fear she has aspirations above her station." Miss Desmond impatiently thrust her tangled black curls back from her face.

"Mr. Atkins is right, my love. You should not have come."

"Of course I should, Papa. The matter nearly concerns me—as I hope you've explained to Mr. Atkins." She turned to the small man. "I believe Papa has already informed you of his change of plans. Therefore I cannot think why you have travelled all this way on a fruitless errand."

"Oh, Miss Desmond, not fruitless, surely. As I was just explaining to your father—" Mr. Atkins stopped short because at that moment the door flew open.

The woman Jack sought stood with her back to the door, but as he drew on his remaining strength for a second assault, he heard a low, lazy voice say, "Ah, the guest in question, I believe."

Mr. Langdon stopped mid-lunge as his gaze swung towards the voice. There were others in the room. Two others.

One was a small, rather plump, exceedingly agitated creature with a moist, round face. At the moment he was nervously mopping his forehead with his handkerchief.

The other—the voice's owner—was a tall, powerfully built man with a darkly handsome face and riveting green eyes. He stood coolly, almost negligently, surveying the intruder, yet his very negligence was threatening.

It occurred to Mr. Langdon that when and if the Old Harry took human form, this was the form he must take. The man exuded force, danger, and something else Jack couldn't define.

"I beg your pardon for interrupting," said Jack, bracing himself for he knew not what, "but I've been sent to apprehend this woman."

5

"You apprehended me once already," said she. "This smacks of obstinacy."

"Ah, it *is* the guest," said the satanic-looking fellow. He took a step towards Jack and smiled. The gleam of his white teeth was not comforting. "My dear young man, you must give up your pursuit of my daughter. She objects to being pursued by gentlemen to whom she has not been introduced. Objects most strongly. She is likely to shoot you."

"I don't doubt it," said Jack. "She just tried to murder the Earl of Streetham."

"Dear heaven!" cried the small man. "Lord Streetham? Oh, Miss Desmond, this will never do!"

"No, it will not," the man who claimed to be her father agreed. "How many times have I told you, Delilah, not to murder earls? Really, my dear, it is a very bad habit. Steel yourself. Overcome it. Mr. Atkins is quite right. Won't do at all." He turned to Jack. "My dear chap, I'm terribly sorry, but this is a fiend we never have done wrestling with. Rest assured that I will speak very firmly to my daughter later. Pray don't trouble yourself further about it. Goodbye."

Though this response was hardly satisfactory, there was something so assured in the man's tones that for one eerie instant, Jack, half convinced he was acting in a comic play, very nearly took his cue. He had even begun to back out of the room when he felt the young woman's gaze upon him. He turned towards her and froze.

In the heat of battle he had become conscious of her lush person. Now he saw that her heavy black hair framed a perfect oval face startlingly white in contrast, smooth and clear as his mother's precious porcelain. Her eyes, the grey-green of a stormy sea, had a slight upward slant. As she watched his baffled face, her generous mouth curved slightly in an enigmatic, maddening smile that made his heart lurch within him. Jack suddenly needed air.

All the same, he could not retreat. This young Circe had attempted the worst of crimes.

6

"I'm very sorry, sir, but I'm obliged to be troubled," said Jack, attempting similar nonchalance. "I'm afraid this is a matter for the constable."

"Dear God!" Mr. Atkins sank into a chair.

"As you like," said Miss Desmond. "I wish to speak to a constable myself. Perhaps he can explain why your Lord Streetham is permitted to wander about public inns assaulting defenceless young women. He cannot be very successful at it, since he requires accomplices. I shall recommend he find a hobby better suited to his limited skills."

"Assaulted *you*! You were holding a pistol to his heart."

"Ah, now I understand. His lordship is a tall man?" Mr. Desmond enquired.

"Yes, but that—"

"There you have it. She could not hold the pistol to his head. Much too awkward. As you can see, Delilah is scarcely above middle height."

"This is hardly a time for humour," said Jack, much provoked. "Lord Streetham lies bleeding just a few doors away."

"There you are mistaken," said Delilah's father. "He is bleeding slightly, but he is standing right behind you."

Jack whipped around. Sure enough, there was his lordship, leaning weakly against the door frame and pressing a handkerchief to the side of his head.

Mr. Atkins scurried towards the earl. "My Lord, you are hurt. Here, take my handkerchief. Shall I send for a physician? Shall I send for water? Shall I send for brandy?" The man continued babbling as he alternately thrust his handkerchief in the earl's face and mopped his own moist brow.

"Who *is* this person?" the earl demanded. "Why does he wave that filthy rag in my face?" He nodded to Jack. "Remove him, Jack. This is a private matter."

Mr. Atkins did not wait for removal. He shot past the earl out of the room.

Lord Streetham's icy glare now fell upon the dark gentleman, who produced another gleaming grin. The earl's hauteur faltered slightly. "So it *is* you, Desmond," he said. "When I heard that voice I was certain I'd passed over. Where else but in Hades would one expect to see *you* again?"

"But not, surely, where you'd expect to find yourself, eh, Marcus?" Mr. Desmond returned. "You are, I promise, still in this sad world, and this poor hostelry is hardly the Other Place, though the Devil himself takes refuge here from the storm."

Lord Streetham manufactured a taut smile. "Then I may take it this young woman belongs to you?"

The green eyes glittered. "Young *lady*, if you please. This is my daughter, Delilah."

"Daughter?" the earl repeated weakly.

The tension in the air was palpable. Once more Jack braced himself.

To his amazement, the earl's hauteur vanished completely, replaced by a rather white expression of solicitude. "My dear young lady, a thousand apologies," he said. "The poor light—and my eyes are not what they used to be. I took you for that saucy maid. A terrible misunderstanding."

Miss Desmond stared coldly at him.

"Nearly fatal, actually," said her father. "Now I suppose I must call you out. How tiresome."

"Too tiresome, Papa," said Miss Desmond. "His lordship has apologised. I am unharmed." Obviously, his lordship was not, but the young lady tactfully forbore to mention this. "Now if his accomplice will apologise as well," she added with an amused glance at Jack, "we might all continue peaceably about our business."

Jack was certain that some sort of signal passed then from daughter to father, but he could not perceive what it was. A flicker of an eyelid . . . an infinitesimal movement . . . or even—impossible—no one could read another's mind.

He looked to the earl for guidance.

"A misunderstanding, Jack," said Lord Streetham. "That's all."

All. He, Jack Langdon, had violently assaulted an innocent young woman who had only been attempting to defend her honour. He wished the floor would open up and swallow him, but as floors are rarely accommodating in this way, he reddened with mortification instead.

"I—I do beg your pardon, Miss Desmond," he stammered. "I'm dreadfully sorry—and—and—" Abruptly he recalled the appalling urges she'd aroused. "I hope I caused you no injury."

"Oh, no," she answered soberly, though her eyes were lit with amusement. "And I trust I caused *you* none."

Mr. Langdon's colour deepened. "N—no. Of course not."

"Very well, Mr.—?"

"Langdon," the earl impatiently supplied. "Jack Langdon. Known him since he was a babe. Wouldn't hurt a fly."

"Very well, Mr. Langdon. Apology accepted."

Mr. Langdon begged pardon of the room at large, then fled.

He found the correct parlour this time and sat staring at the table for half an hour before he remembered that he'd dropped his book during his scuffle with Miss Desmond. Reluctant to risk bumping into any of the witnesses to his humiliation, he sent a servant to retrieve the volume.

Once it was safely in his hands, Jack relaxed somewhat, and even managed to order his dinner without stammering. This was about all he could manage. He ate his meal without tasting it, and read his book without comprehending a syllable. The storm continued with savage fury, and he noticed nothing. Hours later, when all was quiet within and without, he crept to his room and stared at the ceiling until daybreak.

While Mr. Langdon was trying in vain to find oblivion in his book, and Miss Desmond was recounting her adventure to her papa, Lord Streetham was relieving his own frustrations at the expense of the hapless Mr. Atkins. After berating the poor fellow unmercifully for nearly revealing their connexion, his lordship proceeded to an unkind analysis of said connexion.

The world knew Lord Streetham as an enthusiastic book collector. Mr. Atkins knew him as a secret partner in his publishing business. That this was a closely guarded secret was perhaps because of the firm's tendency to offer the British public some of the naughtiest volumes ever to be hidden under mattresses or tucked away in locked drawers. Despite readers' regrettable affinity for anatomy manuals, directories of prostitutes, reviews of *crim con* cases, and guides to seduction, the business had not done well of late—as the earl was at present pointing out.

Atkins was obviously a failure, his lordship observed, perhaps a fraud as well. Be that as it may, he now had leave to plunge into bankruptcy solo. In short, Lord Streetham proposed to cease tossing good money after bad.

"But, My Lord, to give up now—when a brilliant success is practically in my grasp—virtually in the printer's hands." Mr. Atkins squeezed his eyes shut and bit his lip. "Oh, my. I had not meant—oh, dear me."

Lord Streetham paused in the act of bringing his glass to his lips and studied his companion's face over the rim. Then he put the glass down and fixed his pale blue eyes on the publisher.

"What hadn't you meant?" he asked.

The man only stood speechless and terrified, gazing back.

"You'd better speak up, Atkins. My patience is quite at an end."

"My—My Lord, I c—cannot. I'm sworn to s—secrecy."

"You have no business secrets from me. Speak up at once."

The publisher swallowed. "The memoirs, My Lord."

"I am not in the mood to catechize you, Atkins, and you are provoking me."

"*His* memoirs," the publisher said miserably. "Mr. Desmond has written his memoirs and I have paid him— partially, I mean, as an incentive to complete them speedily. That is why I am here. I learned he was travelling to Rossingley to visit relatives, so I came up from Town to— to spare him the trouble of bringing them to me."

"Written his memoirs, has he?" Lord Streetham asked as he absently poured more wine into his still nearly full glass.

"Yes, My Lord. I saw them—at least part of them— myself. He had written to ask whether I had any interest, and naturally, being familiar with his reputation—as who is not?—I made all haste to examine the work. I had to travel all the way to Scotland, but the journey was well worth my while, I assure you. All of Society will be clamouring to read Devil Desmond's story. We'll issue it in installments, you see, and—"

"And have you got them?" his lordship asked.

Mr. Atkins was forced to admit he had not, because Mr. Desmond had raised difficulties.

"Of course he has," said the earl. "If you know his reputation, you should know better than to give Devil Desmond money before you have the goods in your hands. You are a fool. These memoirs do not exist. He showed you a few scraps of paper he'd got up for the purpose, and you were cozened."

The publisher protested that the manuscript must exist, or Miss Desmond would not have been so eager to interrupt the meeting with her father. "He's ready to publish," Atkins explained, "but she won't let him. She's afraid of the scandal. The girl's looking for a husband, you know. That's why Mr. Desmond has returned to England."

The earl sneered. "Devil Desmond's daughter? A husband? The wench must be addled in her wits. I suppose she means to find herself a lord—a duke, perhaps?" Lord

Streetham chuckled. "Silly chit. What's one more scandal to her? As it is—but no, ancient history bores me. Still, the public dotes on such sorry tales, and you are correct. These memoirs, if they truly exist, are certain to be popular. Unfortunately . . ." He paused and lightly drummed his fingers on the table.

"My Lord?"

"People change, Atkins," said the earl, without looking up. "Some of those with whom Desmond consorted in his wicked youth have died of their excesses. Those who survived are today men of prominence, highly respected. They will not take kindly to such an exposure of their youthful follies. If you are not careful, you will be sued for libel."

"My Lord, I assure you—"

Lord Streetham continued, unheeding, "Furthermore, libellous or not, there may be information that would destroy the peace of innocent families. We can't have that." His lordship sipped his wine with an air of piety.

Mr. Atkins panicked. "Oh, My Lord. For fear of a few domestic squabbles you are prepared to deprive the world of these recollections? I promise you, they'll be pounding at the doors every time a new installment is announced. I beg of you, My Lord, reconsider." Tears formed in the publisher's eyes.

Lord Streetham reflected for several agonising minutes while Mr. Atkins mopped his brow and waited.

"Very well," said the earl at last. "It would be wrong to deprive the public. He has lived an extraordinary life. You may publish, if you can—but on one condition."

"Anything, My Lord."

"I must approve the material first. A bit of editing here and there will do no harm, and may spare some of my colleagues considerable pain."

Having agreed to accept any condition, Mr. Atkins could hardly quarrel with this modest request. Some time later, however, as he took himself to bed, he bewailed the cruel fate that had brought Lord Streetham to this accursed inn. By the time his lordship had done "approving" Devil Desmond's memoirs, they'd look like a book of sermons, and Mr. Atkins would consider himself very fortunate if even the Methodists would buy them.

Lord Streetham took to his own bed in bad humour. He might have known this would be a night of ill omen from the start, when his mistress had failed to appear. Then, when Desmond's chit had entered his private parlour, he'd mistaken her for the tart, and nearly had his claret spilled. After that, he'd narrowly escaped certain death at Devil Desmond's hands, had had to truckle to the monster—with Jack Langdon, the soul of rectitude, a witness to the whole tawdry scene. Worst of all were these curst memoirs, whose pages must surely reveal secrets of his own to the unsympathetic London mob.

His lordship was not altogether easy in his mind about the publisher, either. The choice between certain success and certain ruin is not a difficult one, and a desperate man is not a patient one. Suppose Atkins betrayed him, and made off with the manuscript? Suppose, even if he didn't, the book was so scurrilous that editing would not be enough? Perhaps it were safest to destroy the work altogether. With these and hosts of other, equally unsettling questions did Lord Streetham while away the long, dreary night.

= 2 =

HOPING ONCE AGAIN to avoid his fellow travellers, Jack stole out of his room shortly after dawn. As he was about to turn the corner towards the stairs, there came a noise from a room nearby. Jack glanced back at the precise instant that another gentleman came hurrying around the corner. The two collided, and Mr. Langdon was sent staggering against the wall.

"Drat—so sorr—Jack!" exclaimed the gentleman. "Is it you, truly?"

He reached out a hand to help, but Jack had swiftly recovered his balance, though he was still rather dazed. He glanced up into what most women would have described as the face of an angel. It was a face that might have been painted by Botticelli, so classically beautiful were its proportions, so finely chiseled every feature, so clear, blue, and innocent its eyes, so golden the halo of curls that crowned it.

This, however, was not only the face of a mortal man, but of a most unseraphic member of that gender. Lord Streetham's son, the Viscount Berne, was well on his way to becoming the most dangerous libertine the British peerage had ever produced. He was also Jack's oldest friend.

"Yes, it's me—at least I think so," said Jack with a grimace as he rubbed the back of his head.

"What brings you here—up and about at this ungodly hour? And as usual, never looking where you went. Why, I nearly threw you down in my haste."

"That's quite all right, Tony," said Mr. Langdon. "I'm growing accustomed to falling on my face."

Lord Berne's innocent countenance immediately became pitying. "Oh, yes, I heard about that. Too bad about Miss Pelliston."

Mr. Langdon winced. He had not been aware that his failure was common gossip.

"Still, that's the way of love," the viscount consoled. "Plants you a facer every now and then. The secret is to pick yourself up and march on to the next battle. We civilians must take our lesson from Wellington."

He threw an arm about his friend's shoulder and led him down the stairs. "First, you want sustenance. We shall breakfast together. Then, you must return with me to the ancestral pile for a long visit. I'm forced to ruralise because I am obliged to court Lady Jane Gathers. Of course she'll make a paragon of a wife. My sire's judgement is infallible, as he incessantly reminds me."

Since Lord Berne had a tendency to run on wherever his fancy took him, his monologues could continue for hours if not ruthlessly interrupted and hauled back to the point.

Accordingly, Jack cut in. "You don't usually ruralise at inns—at least not so close to home. What brings you here?"

"A wench of course. What else? Perhaps you have not yet met the fair and saucy Sarah? No matter. I scarcely saw her either, for I'd no sooner stepped into the coffee room than I spied a high flyer sitting lonely and neglected amid the storm-tossed rabble. What choice had I but to come to the dark-haired damsel's aid?"

"Lady Jane will hardly appreciate that sort of knight errantry," said Jack as they stepped into the main passage.

"Lady Jane is determined to know nothing about such matters, which is most becoming in her. I only wish her face were more becoming. But no matter. We'll woo her together, you and I," Tony offered.

He deftly steered his preoccupied friend into the public dining room. "Perhaps you'll steal her away. Actually, Jack,

I wish you would. She's all very well, but I'm not ready—
Good God! Where did *she* come from? With my noble sire,
no less. Where in blazes did *he* come from?"

Mr. Langdon followed his companion's gaze past the
enormous communal table to a quiet corner near the fireplace. There Mr. Desmond and his daughter sat breakfast-
ing with the Earl of Streetham.

Though the last thing in this world Jack wanted was
interaction with any of the three, he could hardly expect
Tony to ignore his own father, particularly when that
parent was in the company of a beautiful young woman.
There was no escape, because Tony had a firm grip on his
friend's arm and was propelling him towards the table.

Jack employed the next few minutes examining with
apparent fascination a small landscape containing several
evil-looking sheep which hung upon the wall some inches
above Miss Desmond's head. Dimly he heard introductions
and a number of what he was certain were falsehoods as
the earl and his son respectively accounted for their appearance at the Black Cat.

Mr. Langdon nudged himself to proper attention when
he heard the earl renew his pleas that the Desmonds be his
guests at Streetham Close. Since his lordship addressed his
requests primarily to the daughter, Jack gathered that she
was the more reluctant of the pair. In the next moment,
however, Tony added his persuasions, and, as might be
expected, Miss Desmond capitulated.

Having completed their meal, the trio soon left, one of
them followed by a look of such languishing adoration from
Lord Berne that the waiter knocked over two chairs in his
haste to reach the table, so certain was he the young
gentleman was about to perish of hunger.

Mr. Langdon, being inured to his companion's fits of
romantic stupefaction, took no notice. Their breakfast was
speedily served, and while they ate, Jack calmly explained
why he could not visit Streetham Close. His uncle was
expecting him, he said. He was not in a humour to be

sociable. He had not read a book through in months. These and other lame excuses received short shrift from the Viscount Berne.

"You only want to go off to hide and feel sorry for yourself, Jack, and that's unhealthy. To wish to be elsewhere when this exotic flower will be under my roof is evidence of mental decay. We must make you well again. If those grey eyes of hers don't restore you to manhood, I don't know what will."

"They're green," said Jack.

"Grey."

"Green. And I don't need to be restored by anyone's *eyes*. I want peace and quiet, Tony, and I must tell you there's nothing peaceful about the pair of them." Jack was on the brink of revealing the previous night's adventure when his friend blithely cut in.

"I don't expect them to be peaceful," said Lord Berne. "Don't you know who that is? Devil Desmond, the most infamous rogue in Christendom. Adventurer, charlatan, and—at least until he wed—corrupter of feminine virtue the like of which has not been seen since Casanova. His conquests would populate—"

"Thank you, Tony. The broad outlines will do."

"He's a legend in his own time, I tell you. Never thought he'd return to England after that duel with Billings—but that's aeons ago, isn't it?"

Mr. Langdon scowled at his coffee. "Then I wonder at your father's taking him under the ancestral roof."

"His lordship grows pious in his dotage. Maybe he means to reform the Devil. Still, what do I care about the reasons? Delilah." Lord Berne sighed. "Even her name throbs with sinful promise. She has not touched a hair of my head, yet I feel the strength ebbing from my very sinews."

His friend sighed inwardly. Tony fell in love on a daily—sometime hourly—basis, and the results, in the view of some, amounted to a national tragedy. The pitiful remains of the feminine hearts Lord Berne had shattered lay strewn in a broad path from London to Carlisle. One more scrap of wreckage would not change the course of history—though, unless Jack much missed his guess, Miss Desmond's heart was made of sturdier material.

For the philosopher, their interchange would provide an interesting study, but Mr. Langdon was not in a philosophic mood. He stubbornly insisted on going to his uncle's.

Lord Berne played his trump card. "You must come, Jack, to save me from myself."

"Rescue is not in my style," was the irritated reply.

"But who else can keep me from straying beyond light dalliance into dangerous depths? Very dangerous, I promise you. You will not want to see the Devil put a bullet through my too-tender heart, will you?"

"Then keep your hands to yourself."

"But Jack." Lord Berne fixed his friend with a wide-eyed gaze. "You know I can't."

Mr. Desmond and his daughter travelled in their own carriage, the earl preceding them on horseback. After they had driven some time in silence, Mr. Desmond remarked, "That young man interests me."

"Which young man, Papa?"

"My dear, you can hardly think I find that fair-haired coxcomb interesting. I have met his type across the world, through several generations. I refer to the Guest in Question. The unhappy young man with the rumpled brown hair and poetic grey eyes."

"I did not find him poetic."

"You most certainly did. Also, you felt sorry for him. I nearly swooned with astonishment."

Miss Desmond gazed stonily ahead. "I did neither. Your eyesight is failing you, Papa, just like poor Lord Streetham's."

"You are very cross today, Delilah. Is it because the

poetic young man turns out to be heir presumptive to Viscount Rossing and you regret your decision?"

Miss Desmond's head snapped towards her father so abruptly that her gypsy bonnet tipped over her ear. As she straightened it she said angrily, "I am not going to force a man to marry me on some trumped up pretext of being compromised. It's absurd."

"He would have done it, though."

"Because he's an innocent babe. Oh, Papa, that's not how I wish to begin—yet there's no fresh beginning, is there? My feet scarcely touch English soil before I become embroiled in a dreadful scene. I *wish* I could act like a lady. I can act everything else, it seems," she added ruefully.

"Had you acted a helpless female—which I take is your definition of a lady—you would have been dishonoured by that sanctimonious old hypocrite."

"If I'd waited for my maid or kept to my room I should not have invited incivility."

Mr. Desmond smiled, a far gentler smile than the one Mr. Langdon had observed the previous evening. "You were concerned that Mr. Atkins's pleas would soften my susceptible heart. A natural anxiety, my dear, though quite unnecessary. In fact, I've given the matter a great deal of thought. Perhaps I should destroy those paltry literary efforts of mine, so we might proceed in this enterprise with easy minds. I made a great mistake in contacting Atkins, I know. But I wanted to ascertain the value of the work. Suppose I died suddenly?"

Delilah shuddered. "Don't say such things, Papa."

"It might have easily happened but a year ago. You and your mama would be left destitute, with no prospects of aid from either of our callous families. Insurance, I thought. A nest egg in case of calamity. Naturally I had to make sure the egg was a golden one."

"Of course you did. And not another word about destroying your wonderful story, after all your months of work. As you say, calamities happen. I may never find a husband."

"Or you may fall in love with a penniless young man."

Miss Desmond sniffed disdainfully. "I have no intention of falling in love with anybody. One cannot preserve a clear head and be in love at the same time. My marriage wants a clear head."

"You mean a cold, calculating one, I suppose." The parent sighed. "I fear your mama and I went sadly astray in your upbringing. We have failed you."

"Oh, Papa." Miss Desmond hugged her father, setting her bonnet askew again. "You have never failed me. I only hope I might be clear-headed enough to find a man half as splendid as you."

"That, my love, wants a muddled head. What a silly girl you are. But at least you have recovered your temper. I shall endure the silliness."

Whatever objections Lady Streetham had about entertaining the notorious Devil Desmond were ruthlessly crushed by her lord and master.

"I have reasons," said he, "of a highly confidential and political nature. You may treat him with civility or you may blight my Cabinet prospects. The choice is yours."

After subduing his wife, Lord Streetham called upon his most trusted servants and, again citing national security, ordered them to search the Desmonds' belongings.

While Lord Streetham and his minions laboured on behalf of the imperiled kingdom, Lord Berne took his guests on a riding circuit of the park. Mr. Langdon went as well, though he knew every stick, stone, and rabbit hole of every acre. He had his book with him, however, and whenever the group had occasion to pause, would take it out to stare blindly at the pages.

Miss Desmond found this behaviour most curious. As

they were returning to the house, she asked Lord Berne, "Does he *always* have a book with him?"

"Always," said her companion, glancing back at his friend, "even in Town, at the most magnificent balls, routs, musicales. There you'll unfailingly find Jack Langdon with a book, which he unfailingly loses at some point, and must of course go poking about for. Drives the ladies wild. Not that I blame them. It must be most exasperating when you're just commencing a bit of flirtation to see his eyes glaze over and then watch him wander off, talking to himself." His own appreciative gaze dropped from her eyes to her lips. "Though I cannot understand his behaviour in the present case."

"I find it perfectly understandable," Miss Desmond answered lightly. "What lady can compete with Plutarch?"

The viscount opened his mouth to answer, but she added quickly, "Pray, My Lord, do not say it is myself, when the facts contradict you. Besides, that is too easy a compliment. You cannot think I was angling for it."

"You need never *angle* for praise, Miss Desmond," was the prompt reply.

The exotic countenance grew blank with boredom, and Lord Berne was wise enough to revise his tactics.

"Actually," he said, dropping his voice, "Jack is more than usually abstracted because"—he paused dramatically—"he has had a disappointment."

Miss Desmond was intrigued. "Really? What sort? It cannot have been love, since you say he eludes feminine wiles. What can it be?"

"To disclose that would be dishonourable."

"Then you were dishonourable to mention it at all," she retorted, tossing her head. This tipped her beaver riding hat over her forehead, causing several black tendrils to escape from behind. She impatiently thrust these back under the hat while Lord Berne watched with every evidence of enchantment.

"As long as I am sunk beneath reproach, I suppose one

more indiscretion can scarcely matter," he said, when hat and hair had been jammed into order. "Yes, there was a lady in the case. Amazing, isn't it?"

"She must have been extraordinary to distract him from his books."

"Not at all. From what I've heard, she was a mousy little model of propriety—and a blue-stocking. I think he's had a narrow escape, though it wouldn't do to tell him so, of course. A friend is obliged to sympathise and console."

"Then I keep you from your obligations, My Lord. You must attend to Mr. Langdon, and leave Papa and me to make shift without you." So saying, she rode ahead to catch up with her father.

"Bored so soon?" asked Mr. Desmond. "I told you he was like everyone else."

"On the contrary, he's a wonderful gossip. In less than an hour I have learned the entire past Season's *on-dits*."

"Then doubtless the conversation grew too warm for your maidenly ears."

Delilah shot him a disbelieving glance. "His lordship was courteously amusing, no more. Still, if the prey is not elusive, the hunter soon loses his relish for the pursuit, as you have told me a thousand times."

The father grinned. "I am always right, of course. You've set your mind on Streetham's heir, then?"

Delilah shook her head. "His parents would never condone it. I was most surprised by his lordship's invitation. I don't think he likes you, Papa."

"Loathes me," the Devil replied easily. "Still, he wouldn't want his *faux pas* to be noised about—and even I am not so low a cur as to tattle on my gracious host, am I?"

"What an old hypocrite he is! Naturally his son is out of the question." She smiled into the sunlit distance. "As a husband, I mean. But as a pursuer, he could prove useful. It would be pleasant to have at least one suitor on hand when the Little Season begins. Let us hope he pursues me as far as London."

It was fortunate that Lord Streetham was not a superstitious man, else he had concluded a curse had fallen upon him from the moment he'd strayed past the Black Cat's portals. A diligent search of all of the Desmonds' belongings, including their carriage, had yielded nothing.

Lord Streetham now had two choices. He could offer Desmond an enormous sum for the memoirs. Though the earl was tight-fisted, he was prepared to pay in so urgent a case. The trouble was, he must pay Desmond, and to admit himself at that creature's mercy was unthinkable. The second choice—to seek his irresponsible son's help—was nearly as unthinkable. Yet this was one of the few enterprises in which Tony's narrow talents could be useful. Thus, as soon as the group had returned to the house, Lord Streetham sent for his son.

"I suppose you are on your way to making a conquest of Miss Desmond," said the earl, once the door was closed.

Tony shifted uneasily. "I was only trying to entertain them, sir. That is one's duty to one's guests."

"I'll tell you your duty," the earl snapped. "I didn't ask them here for their amusement or yours, and I mean to be rid of them as soon as possible. Your mother is still in fits, and she doesn't know the half of it." Lord Streetham proceeded to tell his son the whole of it—or most of it, for he did not reveal precisely what revelations he feared. He dwelt instead upon the ignorance of the public and the jealousy of political rivals. The latter, he insisted, would snatch at any straw that might discredit him.

"They will twist minor peccadillos out of all recognition and make me appear unfit to lead," he stiffly explained. "What you or I, as men of the world, would shrug off as youthful folly they will exaggerate into weakness of character. Mere boyish pranks will be transformed into heinous crimes."

He turned from the window in time to catch his son grinning. The grin was hastily suppressed.

"I'm delighted you find this so amusing," said Lord Streetham coldly. "Doubtless your mother will find it equally so, particularly when she grows reluctant to go about in public, for fear of hearing her former friends snickering behind their fans, or—and I'm sure this will be most humorous—enduring their expressions of pity."

Lord Berne became properly solemn. "I beg your pardon, My Lord. I did not mean—"

"I'll tell you what you mean, you rattle! You mean to relieve Desmond of that confounded manuscript."

"I?"

"The girl, you idiot. If you must dally with her, then do so with a purpose. I am unable to locate the memoirs. That does not surprise me. Desmond is cunning. She may be equally so—certainly her mother is—but she *is* a female, and all females can be managed."

Since Lord Berne had never met a young woman he couldn't manage, he could hardly find fault with this reasoning. Nor, being sufficiently intelligent, was he slow to grasp what his father wished him to do.

"You believe I might persuade her to turn this manuscript over to me, sir?" he asked.

Lord Streetham uttered a sigh of vexation. "Why else would I impose so on that depraved brain of yours? Of course that is what I wish. Now go away and *do* it," he ordered.

Lord Berne went away not altogether pleased with his assignment—which was rather odd, considering this was the first time his father had ever trusted him with any matter of importance. Furthermore, what was at stake was power, and the viscount had selfish reasons for preferring that his father's not be diminished in any way. Lord Streetham's influence had more than once saved his son from an undesirable marriage, not to mention tiresome interviews with constables.

The trouble was, the son was accustomed to pursue pleasure for its own sake. Though he would have been delighted to dally with the ravishing Miss Desmond, doing so as a means to an end was very like *work*, and his aristocratic soul shuddered at the prospect.

Still, he thought, his noble sire could not possibly expect him to begin this minute. Consequently, Lord Berne took himself to the water tower for a cold bath, and remained there, coolly meditating, for two hours.

=== 3 ===

THOUGH SHE HAD bathed and dressed leisurely, Miss Desmond discovered she had still the remainder of the afternoon to get through and no idea what to do with herself.

Lady Streetham, Delilah knew, was not eager for her company, and the feeling was mutual. Papa was having a nap. Her host was closeted with his steward. Lord Berne, according to her maid, had not yet returned to the house.

Clearly, Miss Desmond would have to provide her own amusement until tea. The prospect was not appealing. She could not play billiards, because that was unladylike. She doubted very much her hosts would approve her gambling with the servants. For the same reason, she could not spend the time in target practice. This enforced inactivity left her to her reflections, which were not agreeable.

Though she'd made light of it to her father, last night's contretemps preyed on her mind. It was no good telling herself, as her father had assured her, she hadn't had any choice. She might have attempted at least to reason with the earl before drawing out her pistol. Certainly she needn't have *wrestled*, for heaven's sake, with Mr. Langdon. She might have pretended to faint or burst into tears, but not one of these alternatives had occurred to her, though they would have been instinctive to any truly genteel young lady.

Delilah Desmond had a great deal to learn about ladylike behaviour, that was for certain. She hoped Lady Potterby would be up to the task of re-educating her grand-niece.

Otherwise that grand-niece would never attract the sort of gentleman she needed to marry.

Right now, for instance, she ought to make an effort to impress her stony hostess by conversing with her on some suitably dull subject, preferably while doing needlework. The trouble was, Delilah was heartily sick of Lady Streetham's condescension and would be more likely to plunge her needle into that lady's starched bosom.

Miss Desmond decided her wisest course was to take a stroll in the gardens. At least they were extensive enough to make the walk something like real exercise.

She crossed the terrace and followed one of the neat gravel paths bordered by low, scrupulously manicured hedges until she came to an enormous fountain where water spewed from the mouths of four enraged stone dolphins. Staring raptly at the carved monstrosity was Mr. Langdon, book clamped to his side. He seemed oblivious to her approach.

"I wonder if they bite," said Delilah.

He spun round to face her, his countenance colouring slightly.

Miss Desmond was surprised to feel her own cheeks grow warm. She wished she hadn't struck him quite so violently last night—or at least not in that unseemly way. She shook her head to drive off the recollection, and two pins flew out of her hair to drop with a faint tinkle upon the paving stones.

As his glance went from her hair to the pins, his eyes seemed to darken, but Delilah could not be certain because he immediately bent to retrieve the pins. In her experience, gentlemen invariably used the return of her hairpins as an excuse for squeezing her hand. Mr. Langdon, however, gingerly dropped them into her outstretched palm as though he were afraid of being contaminated.

"Thank you," she said with an inward twitch of irritation, "but you needn't have bothered. I'm forever losing them. Papa says he can always tell where I've been because I leave a trail of hairpins behind me."

"Then why pin your hair up at all?" he asked.

She glanced at him suspiciously, but his expression was innocently enquiring. Thrusting the pins back any which way, she said, "Little girls may leave their hair down, Mr. Langdon. A young lady who does so may be mistaken for a demi-rep. At least, so my abigail repeatedly tells me. I have enough problems being mistaken for what I am not," she found herself adding under his sober grey gaze.

He winced as though she had struck him. "Miss Desmond, no words can express my shame and sorrow regarding my behaviour last night," he said hurriedly. "I should have realised—I should have tried to think first at least—it might have been obvious to an imbecile—"

"That I was only demonstrating the use of a pistol to his lordship?" Delilah smiled in spite of her discomfort. "Even I must admit the circumstances were most incriminating."

"That hardly changes the fact that my behaviour was ungentlemanly, to say the least."

How unhappy he was! That rather took the sting out of her own embarrassment. "Mine was unladylike," she said. "That makes us quits, Mr. Langdon. Shall we forgive each other—and ourselves?" She held out her hand.

He hesitated a moment before accepting the handshake. His clasp lingered just an instant longer than pure sportsmanship required, but after the business with the hairpins this might be accounted a minor triumph, and Miss Desmond had never been one to quibble over instants.

"As long as you've given me your hand, may I have your arm as well?" she asked lightly. "Will you walk with me and talk amiable inanities, as though we'd only now met in these sedate circumstances?"

"With pleasure," said her companion. He did not look pleased, however. He looked as though he'd much prefer to run away.

Though common sense told her he had good reason to

avoid her, Miss Desmond had sufficient vanity to be piqued by this show of reluctance.

"If you think it a pleasure, oughtn't you smile at least?" she chided as she took his arm and they began to walk. "You look so grim, as though I had asked you to commit treason—" She caught herself up, struck with a disconcerting possibility. "Or have I stepped wrong again? Was it forward of me to ask for your company?"

"Forward?" he asked, plainly bewildered.

"Fast. Bold. Vulgar. I don't know. Was it wrong?"

He considered for a moment. "Not wrong certainly. I mean, it can't be a hanging offence," he said with a faint smile, "though there were over two hundred of them at last count. As to bold or forward or fast, I am the last man on earth who'd know. There are some subtleties of social behaviour that utterly elude me. My friend Max always says any behaviour that's pleasant can't be correct. If I employ his measure, I must conclude," he said, his smile broadening and lighting up the clean, straight lines of his profile, "that it is incorrect."

He turned the smile full upon her then, and Miss Desmond felt a tad breathless, but she answered sturdily enough. "Of course it must be. I fear the subtleties elude me also, Mr. Langdon, but I assure you I mean to learn them. In future I will not make such unseemly requests. Lud, I hope I commit no *faux pas* at tea. As it is, her ladyship seems in constant expectation of some outrage. I daresay she's certain that Papa and I will swing from the draperies or slide down banisters or, heaven help us, treat the servants like human beings."

"You had better not say 'lud' then, Miss Desmond. I distinctly recall my mother ringing a peal over my sister Gwendolyn on that account."

"Fast?"

"Vulgar."

"How tiresome."

"Then we shan't speak of it," said Mr. Langdon, and

29

immediately turned the subject. "I understand you plan to visit your aunt?"

"My great-aunt. Lady Potterby."

Her companion started. "Lady *Millicent* Potterby?"

"Yes. Do you know of her?" Delilah asked, wondering why he'd changed instantly from amiability to discomfiture. Was there some dreadful scandal about Mama's Aunt Mimsy as well?

"I know her very well. She is a near neighbour of my uncle. The properties adjoin, actually. What a small world it is," he added uneasily. "I was on my way to visit him."

They had reached the shrubbery, but instead of taking the narrow pathway between the tall hedges, he steered her along the outer border.

Miss Desmond did not at first notice the abrupt change in direction. She was too taken up with the unsettling news that Mr. Langdon would be her next door neighbour—if, that is, he persisted in his intention to visit with his uncle. Perhaps now he would change his mind—and why on earth were they circling the hedges instead of entering them?

"Oh, Mr. Langdon, is it not a maze? I should like ever so much—"

"Another time, perhaps," he said stiffly.

She felt the warmth rising in her cheeks. "Lud—I mean, good heavens—I had not thought—but these tall hedges would screen one from view of the house, and we are obliged to keep in plain sight, are we not?"

"Miss Desmond—" He hesitated. Then he drew a long breath and said, "It is not a true maze, and we are indeed so obliged, particularly as your maid is not with you."

"To protect me, you mean. But from what, sir?" she could not help asking. "Do wild animals lurk there? Or is the danger in your company?"

"No—at least—*no.*"

She felt the muscles of his arm tighten under her hand and wondered if he would bolt now. Instead, he bent a searching look upon her and after a moment's hesitation asked, "Miss Desmond, are you . . . *flirting* with me?"

"Yes," she answered in some surprise. "I believe I am."

"Then I am obliged to tell you that is a prodigious waste of time."

"You are impervious to my charms, of course," she said, as he steered her back to the rose garden.

His face instantly became shuttered. "You must be well aware no man can be that, so long as he is breathing."

"Then perhaps you do not approve of flirtation," she persisted, intrigued. "You consider it indecorous."

"I am only a book-worm, Miss Desmond, not, I hope, a prig. I make an excellent book-worm, I'm told, but a most disappointing flirt."

"Now who told you that, I wonder?"

"No one had to tell me. It's perfectly obvious."

Her pique gave way to curiosity. He meant what he said. What an odd man he was.

"Not to me, Mr. Langdon," she answered, "and I assure you I am an excellent judge. Ah, now I *have* shocked you at last."

She found that steady, studying look upon her again and once more felt rather short of breath.

"Miss Desmond, only your beauty shocks me," he said as though the words were wrung from him. "A man could look upon your face for the next one hundred years and never grow tired of it. But you would soon grow tired of that, I think," he added more briskly, "when he could not simultaneously amuse you with witty gallantries. Nor, surely, could you amuse yourself by fencing with an unarmed man."

"Unarmed?" she repeated, bemused.

A voice called out then, and Delilah turned to see Lord Berne, his golden hair in damp ringlets about his head, sauntering up the pathway toward them. She simultaneously felt her companion gently disengage her hand from his arm. When the viscount drew near, Mr. Langdon, with some vague remark about "letters to write," excused himself and quickly strode away.

Mr. Langdon must have had a great many letters to write—or perhaps only one very long and difficult one—because he did not emerge from the library again until it was time to dress for dinner.

He was there the next day as well, with even less prospect of completing his task, for he spent most of his time wandering aimlessly about the room or staring out the windows. At the moment, he was engaged in the latter occupation, and it was not an especially agreeable one.

Really, the situation was absurd, he thought. He could hardly dash out and haul Tony away from the shrubbery. If that's where the reckless fool wanted to take Miss Desmond, that was the fool's problem.

All the same, Mr. Langdon continued to watch. Just as the pair approached the perilous pathway, he saw Lady Streetham shoot out of the house like a rocket and draw Miss Desmond back to the terrace. Jack smiled. Now the countess would send Tony off on one of her errands, as she had been doing practically from the moment the Desmonds arrived.

That was not at all surprising. Lady Streetham had been snatching her son out of the jaws of romantic disaster for years, and an entanglement with the penniless daughter of the notorious Devil Desmond was obviously in that category.

Mr. Langdon left the window and reseated himself at the writing desk. Miss Desmond ought to have known better, he told himself, especially after he dropped his hint about the perils of the hedgerows to her yesterday. If she was so set on learning decorum, she really oughtn't encourage Tony. Surely by now she must have recognised what a rakehell he was. Or at least her father might have warned her. But no. In a mere twenty-four hours she had developed all the usual symptoms. True, Tony had needed to add a few coals to the blaze of his charm, but Miss Desmond appeared ready enough now to be consumed.

Jack threw down his pen and went in search of a book sufficiently taxing to occupy his brain more profitably. His fingers flicked over volumes of Euripides, Aristophanes, Aristotle, and Herodotus, but each was rejected as too familiar, even in Greek. Then he found a large, moroccan-bound, heavily gilded volume whose title and author were unknown to him. He drew it out, selected a capacious leather chair, and settled himself to read.

What he found within the covers was not exactly what he'd expected, but after an initial gasp of surprise and a few moments of confusion, he became entirely deaf, dumb, and blind to all else but what he found in those pages.

Utterly absorbed, Mr. Langdon continued reading as late morning warmed into early afternoon and luncheon passed unnoticed. The household being familiar with his ways, a modest array of sustenance was brought to him on a tray. It remained untouched and was later carried away by the same servant, who smiled indulgently as he closed the library doors behind him.

The servant speedily erased his smile a moment later when he met up in the hall with his mistress and Miss Desmond.

Lady Streetham frowned at the tray and then, more deeply, at the servant. "This will not do," she said. "You will bring him another, Nicholas, and this time be sure he is eating *before* you leave the room."

"I am sure I have told them a hundred times not to leave it to him," said Lady Streetham after the servant had bowed himself away. "One would think after all these years they would learn, but they do not. Of course that tiresome boy will neglect his tea as well, and what good dinner will do him I cannot think, when he only daydreams at the epergne."

Miss Desmond suppressed her own smile. "I hope Mr. Langdon is not ill," she said.

"It is a miracle if he is not. He is always engrossed in one book or another, to the exclusion of all else—friends, family, even his own health. I do what I can, because he is very like a son to me, but one cannot watch him every minute."

Especially not, Delilah added inwardly, when one is maintaining unwinking guard over one's actual offspring. She had no opportunity to make the obligatory sympathetic response because the butler now approached to inform the countess that Lady Gathers and her daughter had arrived.

"So soon?" said Lady Streetham. "But Tony is not yet retur— Well, no matter." She turned to her guest with an expression of cold resignation. "Miss Desmond, if you are not too fatigued, perhaps you would enjoy meeting my neighbours."

"I should like nothing better," Delilah answered.

Her hostess's features grew more rigid.

"Unfortunately," Miss Desmond went on, "I find myself unusually susceptible to the heat and am sure to make but poor company as a result. Would you think it unconscionably rude, My Lady, if I excused myself?"

"Not at all," said the countess with a shade of eagerness in her customary chilly tones. "Quite oppressive, the heat. Perhaps you will want a long nap before tea?"

"Actually, I had thought I would sit quietly in your cool library with a book. If Mr. Langdon is still there, I will certainly urge him to cease insulting your excellent chef."

Lady Streetham's frigid countenance thawed ever so slightly. "Very well," she said, and took herself away.

"Yes, it is very well, you stuck-up old battle-axe," said Delilah under her breath. "Far better than having to introduce Devil Desmond's daughter to your exalted friends." Not, Delilah told herself as she moved down the long hall towards the library, that she *wanted* to meet them. Lady Gathers was doubtless another battle-axe and her daughter a demurely proper nincompoop. The entire conversation would be devoted to tearing their friends' reputations to shreds.

All the same, it was rather hard to be treated like a leper, for heaven's sake, when one's blood was every bit as blue as theirs. Bluer. In Charles II's time, the Melgraves had been mere jumped-up squires, while her papa's family had been Norman barons long before the Conqueror was an illicit gleam in his father's eye.

Caught up in her angry reflections, Delilah neglected to knock. As soon as she entered she perceived that knocking would have been futile anyhow. Mr. Langdon did not even look up when she flounced into the room.

He ought to look up. He ought to have looked up at least once in the past twenty-four hours. She had not needed Lord Berne's lyrical compliments last night to be assured that her new amber gown became her. Even this simple sprigged muslin fit her to perfection, and it had cost Papa a substantial sum. Mr. Langdon might at least show some aesthetic interest.

What on earth was so fascinating about that stupid book? She crept noiselessly to his chair and glanced down over his shoulder at the volume that lay open on his lap. Then she gasped.

Mr. Langdon came abruptly to attention. "Miss Desmond," he began, but the look on her face stopped him.

"You!" she cried. "You—you *beast!*"

"Miss Desmond—"

"Don't you speak to me, you wretched man. How dare you?"

"I—I beg your pardon?" said Mr. Langdon, much taken aback. Bent over him was a flushed, furious, and blindingly beautiful countenance whose wrath seemed to set the very air throbbing. Certainly it had his senses reeling.

"A sneak. A horrid, sneaking thief. And I felt sorry for you. Oh, I wish Papa had killed you. No, I wish I had done it myself." Her hand went to the neckline of her frock, then halted.

It dawned on Mr. Langdon that he was for some unaccountable reason in very real danger. The gesture had puzzled him only for an instant, until he'd guessed that she'd gone for her pistol, which, luckily for him, was not at present upon her person. Quickly he stood up, the volume clutched under his arm.

"Miss Desmond, you are distressed. Shall I—"

"Distressed?" she echoed wrathfully. "You have stolen my father's manuscript and sit here coolly reading it, when anyone might come in and—and—" She paused. "Good Lord, are you mad?"

"I am not mad, Miss Desmond," he said in the soothing tones usually reserved for sufferers of delirium. "I fear, however, that you are hysterical. This volume belongs to your father?"

"No," she snapped. "It is the property of the Archbishop of York. Of course it's my papa's. Surely you noticed that the pages are handwritten—that it is a manuscript, in fact—that it is my father's?"

"Yes, I noticed all that."

"Well?"

"I also could hardly fail to notice that it was here on the shelves with the rest of our host's collection. I assumed your father had given it to Lord Streetham. My own collection contains some unpublished efforts by friends— though I must say this is far more worthy of publication."

The angry flush on her cheeks faded to a more becoming pink as her fury subsided, to be replaced by discomfiture. She did not answer, however, only gazed unhappily at the book he held.

"You are telling me, Miss Desmond, that this book does not belong to Lord Streetham?"

"No, it does not," she answered in a choked voice.

"Then why was it here, and enclosed in this odd binding?" He moved closer to show her the richly tooled cover. "This is supposed to be a work on horticulture."

"Yes, I know. I can read Greek," she said stiffly.

"You can?"

"Don't patronise me, sir."

"I beg your pardon. I meant no offence. It's just that young ladies—"

"Oh, *don't*, please."

To his surprise, Miss Desmond threw herself into the chair he'd vacated and clutched her head in her hands. Several pins flew out, and the gleaming black tresses they'd contained slipped out after them to dangle against her shoulders.

Jack politely looked away.

"Young ladies," she muttered. "Yes, a fine lady I am, don't you think? Make a fool of myself first, then think after. That's the way of it. Good grief." She looked up, her grey-green eyes clouded with remorse. "I'm sorry I called you those horrid names. In case you had any doubts, I have a beastly temper. And no one knows where I get it from because Mama and Papa both are so—oh, never mind."

Though he was unaccustomed to coping with over-wrought young women—that was more in Tony's line—Jack had lived with three short-tempered sisters. "I don't mind," he said, trying for the airy tone he often took with Gwendolyn. "It was all very exciting, actually—though I was grateful you hadn't a weapon handy. As the child's rhyme goes, names will never hurt me."

"Oh," she moaned, twisting herself into the corner of the chair and burying her face in her arms. "Now you're going to be gallant. I can't bear it."

"Shall I call *you* names, then, and make us even?"

"Yes," was the muffled response. "And you'd better not be gentle."

"Very well." Holding the volume against his breast, Jack recited calmly. "Virago. Hellcat. Beldam."

She winced.

"Is that enough?" he asked.

She shook her head.

Jack thought. "Termagant," he said.

"Yes."

"Shrew, fury, tigress, she-wolf. Ah, here's an excellent one: cross-patch."

Miss Desmond giggled weakly and raised her pale face towards him.

"Shall I commence in Latin or Greek, or is that sufficient?"

"That will do, Mr. Langdon. I feel much better." She rose. "Now if you will please to give me the book."

Jack's face fell and he backed away. He was, of course, a gentleman to the very core and would do anything to assist a damsel in distress. Anything, that is, except relinquish a book before he'd finished reading it. Especially this book, which was a revelation to him.

"But Miss Desmond, I'm scarcely halfway through it," he said uneasily. "Your father's hand is not always decipherable."

Her slanted eyes narrowed. "Sir, that work is not intended for public consumption," she responded with the exaggerated patience of one addressing a half-wit. "I am not certain why Papa placed it here, though I would guess it was his idea of a perfect hiding place. He has used that false binding before," she explained. "Greek is unenticing to the average person. The topic is even less inviting. The combination is guaranteed to drive off all potential readers. Except," she added with a small sigh, "*you.*"

"I see." He gazed disconsolately at the volume. "I had better put it back." He turned towards the shelves.

"No!" she cried. "You must give it to me. It's obviously not safe here."

"Of course it is," he said, growing stubborn. "Lord Streetham only collects books for show. He never reads anything but political tracts. Tony is interested only in sporting journals. The countess is addicted to gothics. As you said, no one but I would ever muster any interest in so forbidding a volume. Your father obviously knew what he was about. Besides, I might still finish it."

"No! I don't want you to read any more," she blurted out.

Though he was convinced Miss Desmond was a tad unbalanced at present, Mr. Langdon felt guilty. Unbalanced or not, she should not be tormented. He saw her eyes glisten then, and he was undone. He had never in his life made a woman cry, and he was certain this woman was not one to weep easily. He felt like a monster.

He took a step towards her, then paused. She wanted the book, not comforting, and it was not his place to comfort her anyhow—not at least in the way he'd instinctively wished to.

"I do beg your pardon," he said quietly. "I've been most inconsiderate. I'm afraid I thought only of finishing this wonderful story and not—"

"And not about entertaining the ladies, eh, Mr. Langdon?" came a low voice from the doorway.

= 4 =

MISS DESMOND WHIRLED round. "Papa," she breathed.

Her father was glancing over his shoulder into the hall. "In here, Marcus," he said in more carrying tones. "As her ladyship promised, Delilah has come to rescue Mr. Langdon from eyestrain."

Mr. Desmond stepped into the library. An instant later, Lord Streetham appeared.

"Ah, still here," said the earl to Jack. "My lady wife tells me you've been holed up all day, neglecting your meals. Won't do, you know. You must relinquish your books and tend to the ladies at least, if you will not attend to your victuals." He glanced at the volume Jack clasped to his breast. "What have you got there? Greek? You are a sorry rogue, indeed. What do you want with such dusty stuff?"

"Mr. Langdon does not find the work at all dull," said Delilah smoothly when Jack proved mute. "He's spent the last quarter hour explaining it to me. How remarkable, is it not, that he understands Greek so well, to be able to translate such complicated horticultural theories?"

The earl's eyes glazed over. "Yes, yes, I daresay. All the same, Jack, you must come off your hobby-horse and be sociable. No more reading. Take the book home with you when you go, if you like it so much. It's yours. I'm sure I'll never miss it, and Greek is not Tony's forte, as you know."

"You are too generous, My Lord," said Jack, nervously eying Mr. Desmond. "I can't possibly accept."

"Take it, take it," said the earl irritably as he moved to the door. "But mind you appear for tea or her ladyship will be most vexed with you."

"But My Lord—" Jack called after the earl's retreating back.

"Don't be ungrateful, Mr. Langdon," said Mr. Desmond. "Mustn't hurt his lordship's feelings, you know." He winked and followed the earl out of the room.

Delilah was just opening her mouth to speak when her papa put his head back in the door. "My dear, hadn't you better go upstairs and let Joan do something about your hair? I'm afraid you're all atumble again. You will not wish to outrage your hostess's sensibilities, I'm sure."

Miss Desmond shot Mr. Langdon a resentful glance and hastened from the room.

Mr. Langdon had scarcely a minute to recover his composure before Nicholas appeared, bearing a heavily laden tray. "If you please, sir," he said, "her ladyship has asked me to convey her wishes that you take a bite to sustain you until tea time."

"Yes, yes, of course," Jack muttered.

The servant deposited the tray upon a side table, drew out a chair, and stood waiting.

"Was there anything else, Nicholas?"

"I beg your pardon, sir, but she told me I was not to stir from the room until I actually saw you begin to eat," the servant said apologetically.

Jack sighed, placed the troublesome volume upon the writing desk, and sat down before the repast. He lifted a napkin, glared at it, and dropped it onto his lap. With the air of a man condemned to hard labour, he took up his silverware and began to eat.

Nicholas waited a few minutes, then bowed and exited.

"I shall not need to enter a monastery," Jack grumbled to himself when the door had closed. "By nightfall they'll have packed me off to Bedlam."

When he'd made a reasonable show of attending to his victuals, Mr. Langdon took up the so-called work on horticulture and went in search of Mr. Desmond. He finally ran that gentleman to ground in the billiard room, where a thick grey haze showed that Mr. Desmond had retired to enjoy a cheroot in solitude.

"I must speak with you, sir," said Jack without preamble.

"Yes, I thought so. Well, have a seat. Will you join me?" the older man asked as he offered his cigar case.

Jack, whose meal had not settled very well, shook his head. "I won't be but a moment," he said. "I only wanted to return your manuscript to you."

"Ah, but I'd much rather you didn't," said the Devil, sending up a lovely grey billowing cloud that curled about his head much as darker, more ominous smoke must hover about his namesake. "You see, it's no longer safe in my custody," he explained. "That is why I'm obliged to relinquish it to yours."

Mr. Langdon had already had one disagreeable experience in connexion with this volume. Now he began to scent danger, an aroma as palpable as that of Mr. Desmond's cigar. Jack also sensed that he'd have a very difficult time dissuading this gentleman from involving him.

Mr. Desmond's easy courtesy and low, drawling tones could not disguise a most formidable will. He was, Jack thought, the Irresistible Force personified. Obviously, more than the man's escapades had earned Desmond his nickname.

"I'm flattered you repose such trust in me," Jack said cautiously, "but I really don't deserve it. I'm not reliable. Ask anybody."

"I have," said the Devil, "and what I hear only confirms my belief that you are exactly the man for the job."

Jack sat down, taking the volume upon his lap. It had grown much heavier in the past few minutes.

"Perhaps I had better explain," said Mr. Desmond.

"Yes, thank you. I would appreciate that."

Mr. Desmond began by describing the near-fatal illness which had inspired him to write his recollections. He had intended that, in the event of calamity, their publication would obtain his wife and daughter a respectable sum. Invested wisely, the sum would earn them a modest but reliable annual income.

There being no calamity at the moment, Mr. Desmond was not inclined to stir up old animosities against himself and his family, particularly in the present circumstances. His daughter was unwed. As it was, she would have sufficient difficulty being accepted by a Great World which had decades ago shut its doors to her parents. To publish now was to eliminate any possibility of a respectable marriage to one of her own class.

"Delilah must marry into that class, of course, Mr. Langdon. Though her mama trod the boards for a brief time, she is still an Ornesby and Lord Stivling's niece. Nor am I precisely a parvenu. The barony my brother inherited is an ancient one. Besides, we cannot shackle Delilah to the blacksmith or the tavern-keeper. Their tastes run along more oxenlike lines, I think. Poor child. She's neither fish nor fowl. You have seen for yourself how unrefined her manners are. Not to mention that beastly temper of hers. She will not count to ten."

Without appearing to notice his listener's faint flush, Mr. Desmond went on, "Lady Potterby, my wife's aunt, has courageously agreed to transform Delilah into a Society miss and attempt to launch her in the Little Season."

Lady Potterby must be addled in her wits to take on this Augean task, Jack thought. Still, who was he to judge? What else could a young lady do but wed, especially if she is not a well-heeled young lady? The only gainful employment open to her was as governess, companion, or prostitute. For the former two Miss Desmond's personality appeared profoundly ill-suited. The third alternative was not to be contemplated.

"I understand your reasons for suppressing your story," said Jack, when he belatedly became aware that a response was awaited. "I simply don't understand the difficulty in doing so. Why did you say the manuscript was no longer safe in your custody?"

"Atkins wants it, apparently more desperately than I'd believed. He has hired confederates to invade this household and search our belongings. I made the discovery this morning. Fortunately, I'd already thought to store the manuscript in that false binding. Whoever examined my room did not trouble with a book left out in plain sight. After breakfast I took the book to the library, just as though I'd borrowed it. I had no fear of discovery. I knew that whatever Marcus pretended to be these days, he was no bibliophile. Further, his Greek and Latin were always abominable."

"This sounds so—so conspiratorial," said Jack uncomfortably. "Are you certain, sir, these intruders were not simply common burglars?"

"Then why has there been no general alarm? Why trouble with the belongings of obviously down-at-heel guests when there are richer pickings elsewhere? No, sir, I'm convinced Atkins is at the bottom of this. Admittedly, I did wonder at first whether our host had set his servants to search for deadly weapons. After all, we Desmonds might run amok and embark upon a murder spree." Mr. Desmond chuckled.

Mr. Langdon's sense of humour had deserted him. Nor were his spirits raised when Mr. Desmond went on to describe Mr. Atkins's grief in learning the book would not be his after all. This had upset the publisher far more than hearing he must be patient for his money.

"I had not expected such intrepidity from him, I must confess," Mr. Desmond continued. "But with your help we will keep this desperate fellow at bay until I come up with the blunt to repay him."

The reminder that he was to be the memoirs' guardian

made the hairs at the back of Jack's neck rise. Unfortunately, he could contrive no reason for declining the honour that did not sound discourteous or cowardly, especially after Mr. Desmond pointed out Jack's advantages as custodian.

Jack was fully aware that everyone in the world knew he was bookish. He always carried volumes about with him. He might carry this tome wherever he went and not arouse the least speculation. He was, in short, doomed.

"It was Destiny brought you to the Black Cat the other night, sir," said the Devil, as though he had read Jack's mind. "The gods knew we wanted help and wisely sent the perfect man for the job."

Having bent Mr. Langdon to his will, Mr. Desmond was next confronted with the more onerous task of pacifying his daughter, who appeared moments after Mr. Langdon had dazedly departed. In fact, judging from her high colour, she had probably collided with that young man in the hall.

"Oh, he is impossible!" she snapped, slamming the billiard room door behind her.

"Not at all. Mr. Langdon is most accommodating. He has agreed to assist us, Delilah, so I recommend you mind your manners with him. From his expression earlier, I guessed you had treated him to a tantrum, then apologised with the usual fit of self-flagellation. Never before has a young man seemed so relieved at my untimely entrance. I thought he would collapse, weeping, in my arms."

"He is stupid and obstinate. What on earth were you thinking of, to leave him with your book? He had it with him just now. How could you, Papa?"

Mr. Desmond unperturbedly explained precisely how he could, and turned an amiably deaf ear to all her ensuing protestations. He pointed out that Lord Streetham's was an enormous old house which would crumble to pieces if not constantly kept in repair. Of the hired labourers who frequently came on this mission, any one might be Atkins's accomplice. Until the Desmonds were securely housed at Lady Potterby's and could safeguard against further intrusions, Mr. Langdon must keep the manuscript.

His daughter replied that they had better leave immediately for Elmhurst, because she would not sleep a wink until the manuscript was back in her father's possession. Mr. Langdon would be sure to bring the book to dinner, where he would inevitably drop it into his soup. Miss Desmond had never met such a muddled, stupidly oblivious person in her whole life. With these closing remarks, she stormed out of the billiard room.

Mr. Atkins had been told he would not be welcome at Streetham Close while the earl's guests remained. The publisher had therefore taken rooms in a small, uncomfortable inn nearby. The inn's main asset was its tap-room, a gathering place for all the local idlers and gossips. Virtually all that occurred at Streetham Close was a matter of public information within hours.

Mr. Atkins was swallowing a mug of ale he was certain had been made with his hostess's laundry water when he learned the Desmonds had departed for Rossingley. An hour later, the publisher was in Lord Streetham's study, ostensibly to seek his lordship's advice regarding the memoirs.

His lordship was decidedly ungracious. This did not disturb Mr. Atkins, who was accustomed to be treated like the lowest species of insect. He knew less noble investors might be more amiable, but they were not likely to prove useful when a libel suit was imminent. In these litigious times, when a royal whim might land a man in prison for sedition, a wise businessman sought as backers not merely men of wealth, but men of influence. Lord Streetham being such a man, his lack of amiability might be overlooked.

What did disturb the publisher, however, was the earl's curt announcement that Mr. Atkins need not concern himself about the manuscript, since Lord Berne had been charged with "persuading" the Desmonds to relinquish the work.

"With all due respect, My Lord," said Mr. Atkins, "why should they do that? Lord Berne has not paid for it."

"One fool throwing away money is sufficient, I should think," said the earl. "We are dealing with an exceedingly devious man. In self-defence we must be devious as well. You've paid him for goods which he now refuses to deliver. In that case, someone must deliver them for him. Your ignorance of such simple economic logic is the reason you are on the brink of bankruptcy."

What Lord Streetham called "economic logic" sounded remarkably like theft to Mr. Atkins, but he held his tongue, endured a few more insults, and humbly took his leave.

He then took himself back to the inn, where he argued with his landlady for an hour over the reckoning. Finally, having paid his exorbitant shot, Mr. Atkins set out for Rossingley.

Rossingley, as Lord Berne pointed out to his father, was twenty-five miles away. The viscount could hardly visit Miss Desmond every day, claiming he was merely passing through the neighbourhood. He could not stay with Jack at Rossing Hall because Lord Rossing hated company, and Lord Berne's company especially.

"There won't be any need to stop every day if you would but apply yourself," the earl retorted. "You might have had the manuscript by now if you had not been gadding about the countryside."

This was grossly unfair. Lord Berne had tried to apply himself to Miss Desmond, but his officious mama had constantly interrupted, sending him on one cork-brained mission after another. That same mama, he now told the earl, would go off in an apoplexy if he commenced regular visits to Lady Potterby's house. "As it is she's prodigious displeased with my neglect of Lady Jane," said Tony.

"Lady Jane will not elope with one of the grooms while you are gone—and so I shall assure your mother. Nor need you blame her for your ineptitude. You were not on errands last evening, yet you allowed Miss Desmond to spend the whole time flirting with Langdon."

Lord Berne frowned. That had been most disconcerting. Jack had been totally oblivious to all Miss Desmond's efforts to draw him out, yet she'd persisted. She'd even resorted to Latin epigrams, for heaven's sake!

Since no woman in his vast experience had ever favoured dull Jack Langdon over himself, Lord Berne had assumed Miss Desmond was simply attempting to spur a rivalry. Still, it was rather lowering to find he could not understand a word of the Latin which had roused Jack from his reveries. What business had the chit knowing the language in the first place?

"You know, Father, she is a very strange girl," said the viscount thoughtfully.

"Of course she's strange. Look who her father is. And her mother an actress. What do you expect?"

The frown deepened. Desmond behaved very oddly, too. Most fathers of young women instinctively viewed Lord Berne with a wary eye, if not outright hostility. But Devil Desmond was not remotely hostile. He appeared to regard the viscount as an endlessly amusing joke. Whenever and whatever the Devil was about, Tony always felt as though the man were laughing at him, even when there wasn't the faintest flicker of a smile on his satanic face. Desmond would not, Tony reflected, be quite so amused when his memoirs disappeared.

"Well?" said Lord Streetham. "Do you mean to stand there sulking all day?"

"I can hardly run after them this very moment, sir. They've scarcely left. And it would look too particular if I did so tomorrow—unless they've left something behind?"

"No," was the curt reply. "I had their rooms sear— inspected shortly after they left."

"Doubtless Jack's forgotten something. He always does when his valet isn't by to look after him. I'll go to Rossingley in a day or two to return whatever it is, then call on Lady Potterby. I hope that's satisfactory?"

Lord Streetham was about to voice his opinion that it was *not*, but a moment's reflection stopped him, for he did not want to awaken any suspicions at Lady Potterby's. Oddly enough, there was some sense in Tony's arguments. Thus the earl answered sarcastically that he must, by all means, patiently await his son's convenience.

= 5 =

HER RESTLESS HANDS folded tightly before her, Miss Desmond stood listening with increasing dismay to her great-aunt. It was late afternoon and the still air which hung like a thick blanket over the countryside hung heavier still in her luxuriously appointed guest chamber. Lady Potterby flitted about the room like a fussy little white-capped bird, taking up one after another the garments draped upon the bed, shaking her head and twitting unhappily. At the moment, she was frowning at the beloved amber silk.

"Good heavens, child, were you so distant from civilisation that you could not obtain a copy of *La Belle Assemblée*? When girls straight from the schoolroom bare their bosoms in public it is absurd for a woman of twenty to be swathed up to the neck. I realise your endowments are excessive," she added, flicking a reproving glance at her grand-niece's bosom, "but if you hide them, the world will think you hide some deformity. That is, if they do not conclude you are a strumpet trying to pass as a chaste maiden."

"Then the world," said Miss Desmond irritably, "is an ass."

"Even if that is so, it is most impolite to mention it, particularly in those terms. Where did you learn such language? But why do I ask? Your papa never troubles to curb his tongue, regardless who is present. Don't slouch, Delilah. Poor posture is both unbecoming and vulgar, and it will only draw added attention to your figure."

Certainly there was no hint of vulgarity about Lady

Potterby. Her lace cap was immaculately white. Her grey afternoon gown was the epitome of tidy elegance. She might flutter, but she did so with all the dignity appropriate to her station. Everything about her was exactly *comme il faut*. As a consequence, she made Delilah feel too large, too clumsy, too noisy, and altogether too much of everything.

"I'm sorry, Aunt, that my figure is so unfashionable, but I'm afraid there is no way to amend it."

"Sadly true," said her ladyship with a sigh. "Yet we must not be cast down. In that matter at least, the gentlemen are not such slaves to fashion as ourselves." She brightened and patted the amber silk with something like satisfaction. "Mrs. Archer can drop the neckline an inch or so, and when we get to London, we will leave everything to Madame Germaine. She is frightfully dear, but her taste is impeccable. As to workmanship, there is scarce another dressmaker in Town who can touch her."

"Aunt, I do hope you are not saying I need a new wardrobe," said Delilah with alarm. "Papa really cannot afford—"

"Well, who asked him?" Lady Potterby now took up a light green muslin frock. "This will do for church, I think—at least in Rossingley," she muttered to herself. Then more distinctly she said, "Your papa has nothing to do with it. I told your mama I would move heaven and earth to see you wed. I should hardly stop at a trifle such as a wardrobe. Besides, there is my late elder sister's bequest. She urged me to use it on your behalf. The poor dear had so many regrets towards the end. We always doted upon your mama, you know, but neither of us wished to stir up more ill-will in the family. Really, sometimes it is very difficult to know what is right."

This Delilah understood too well, in spite of her irritation. Her great-aunt's fault-finding, which had commenced the instant Delilah had alit from the carriage, had continued almost unceasingly since. Still, one was forced to admit the elder lady had the right of it most of the time, and certainly she meant well. One ought to strive for patience, considering the risks her ladyship was prepared to run. The entire Beau Monde was certain to believe Lady Potterby had lost her mind, and the Ornesbys had already ceased communicating with her.

The best return Delilah could make was in striving to be a credit to her great-aunt. Only thus could she hope to overcome the world's prejudices.

"I understand, Aunt," Delilah said, "and I'm deeply grateful for your kindness. I only wish this business were not so expensive."

"Frankly, child, expense is the least of our problems," her aunt answered as she put the green frock aside. "With a mama once an actress and a papa a notorious adventurer— and of course with such a face and figure—you will be prey to every evil-minded man in the kingdom. They will be endlessly casting out lures. I hope you are prepared."

"Yes, Aunt, I know my position is precarious, to say the least. I only wonder," Delilah added dolefully, "if it can ever be made secure. If the men are so busy casting out lures, they may not have time to consider offering marriage."

"It is up to you to behave in such a way to force them to consider it," was the brisk reply. "That wicked Letty Lade got herself a title. Lord Berwick married Harriette Wilson's sister, Sophia, only last year. If noblemen wed demi-reps, why should they not marry a good-looking, blue-blooded maiden?"

"Yes, there must be some senile lord or ambitious Cit who'll be sufficiently blinded by my looks to tumble onto his knees."

"You will not even contemplate marrying into trade, miss," said Lady Potterby sternly as she took up a dark green riding habit. "This is better," she murmured. "Quite dashing."

Then she recollected her grand-niece. "Good heavens,

why that long face?" she asked, putting her head to one side like a puzzled sparrow to study the girl. "I hope my frank speech has not lowered your spirits. I only wanted us to face the obstacles squarely, not be overcome by them. Ornesbys are never overcome by obstacles, and certainly not the Desmonds, either." She glanced at the watch dangling from her waist. "Gracious, how late it grows. No wonder you are cross. It is past time for tea."

Tea, it turned out, was an opportunity for a lesson in deportment. Delilah was called upon to pour, so that her great-aunt could size up her command of common etiquette and ability to take instruction. In Lady Potterby's opinion, few exercises so clearly demonstrated a lady's character as her manner in presiding at the tea table.

"Doubtless you observed how Lady Streetham conducted herself," said the great-aunt, watching narrowly as her niece lifted the delicate teapot. "I suppose you were shocked, so stiff she is and lacking in grace."

"My daughter was too busy talking at Mr. Langdon to remark Lady Streetham's skills," said Mr. Desmond as he accepted his cup with a gracious nod. "I am sure Delilah never even glanced at the tea tray—if she did, I cannot think why such an innocent object should cause her to blush so prettily."

"I am vastly relieved to hear she can blush at all," her ladyship returned tartly, "considering your notions of parental guidance. I distinctly heard her utter two oaths when Joan was pinning up her hair."

She turned to Delilah, who was fuming at the teapot. "In future, my dear, you will confine your exclamations to 'good grief' or 'dear me.' But what is this of Mr. Langdon? What on earth could that diffident boy have said to put you to the blush?"

"Perhaps I blushed at my own forwardness in attempting to draw him into conversation, Aunt," said Delilah, darting a quelling glance at her parent. He knew perfectly well why she'd been talking frantically at Mr. Langdon. She'd been terrified the muddled creature would blurt out some quote from her papa's memoirs. She would not have been placed in so awkward and frustrating a position if her papa had not been so obstinate.

Delilah's scowl turned into an expression of dismay as she recollected that Mr. Langdon still had the book. Where *was* the stupid man? He should have returned it immediately. He'd left Streetham Close hours before they had—and without so much as a farewell.

"What on earth is the matter, miss? Have you spilled tea on your skirt? Did I not just tell you to keep an easy, amiable countenance, as though the activity required no effort or concentration whatsoever?"

"I fear we must look deeper than the teapot, Millicent. Obviously, Delilah is pining for Mr. Langdon." Mr. Desmond turned to his daughter. "I beg your pardon, my dear. I should not have brought his name into the conversation."

"Certainly not in so absurd a way," said Delilah indignantly. "Pining for him, indeed. What nonsense. I hope you will pay Papa no mind, Aunt. He is an incorrigible tease." She picked up a plate of pastries. "Will you try the seed-cake, My Lady?"

Lady Potterby smiled approvingly. "Very well done, my dear. Just the right air. Is it not, Darryl? Could Queen Charlotte do any better, I ask you?"

"Not when His Majesty is by. I understand he has long, bawdy conversations with the cucumber sandwiches," was the irreverent reply.

"That is cruel, Darryl, and possibly seditious. You cannot know how the poor man suffers."

"Of course I know. Am I not acquainted with his sons? It's a wonder to me he went on producing offspring. Surely the first half dozen must have shown him his seed was cursed."

"You will not speak of such topics before the girl, sir. If

she has had a steady diet of such conversation, it is a miracle she can blush as you claim. A young lady must be capable of blushing," Lady Potterby pointed out to her grand-niece, "or she will appear hardened in iniquity."

"No fear of that," said Mr. Desmond. "She colours very nicely when a certain gentleman who must remain name-less is by, I assure you."

"Papa, you are most tiresome today," said Delilah, putting down her cup and saucer with a clatter that made her great-aunt frown.

"Indeed you are, Darryl. Why do you tease so about poor Mr. Langdon? I cannot believe he has been making sheep's eyes at Delilah—or any young lady, for that matter. Lord Berne is another case altogether," the lady went on, instantly reverting to an earlier bone of contention with her male relative. "You should never have stopped there when that wicked young man was at home. I could not rest easy a moment after I got your message. Do you know the dreadful boy took Annabelle Carstairs into the hedge-rows—on his own father's property—and now she calls herself Mrs. Johnson and lives in Dublin, and there never was a Mr. Johnson, not that ever stood before the parson with her."

"Oh, not that rattle," said Desmond. "Delilah took his measure quickly enough. Didn't you, my precious?"

Miss Desmond's cheeks were tingling. The hedgerows. No wonder Mr. Langdon had steered her away so firmly. If Lady Streetham had not rushed out of the house . . . but that was absurd. Delilah Desmond was no naïve Annabelle Carstairs. She was not about to be seduced in *bushes*, for heaven's sake.

"He is obviously a rake," she said primly.

"He most certainly is—and that is the kindest name one can give him," Lady Potterby agreed. "You did well to devote your attention to Mr. Langdon instead."

"I did not—"

"I admit he's excessively shy," the great-aunt went on

unheedingly. "But he at least is a perfect gentleman. I am sure he subjected you to no over-warm compliments."

"Well, he must have said something to raise her temperature. I am sure she turned pink every time she was in his company," said the pitiless father.

"Papa!"

Lady Potterby was at last goaded into giving the matter serious attention. "Good heavens, Darryl, are you certain? Do we speak of the same Jack Langdon? That absent-minded creature who always has his head in a book? He exerted himself to have a conversation with my grand-niece? He did not hurry off to hide in a corner with his tiresome Greeks?"

"He tried," said the Devil gravely, "but Delilah wouldn't let him."

Miss Desmond took up her teacup again with an air of resignation. For some unaccountable reason, her father was set on provoking her. Well, she would not give him the satisfaction of appearing at all vexed.

"Yes, Aunt," Delilah concurred. "I am afraid I am very forward. Just one more character flaw I shall strive to overcome, with your assistance."

"But you obtained his attention?" asked the lady eagerly.

"Fortunately, Papa has overseen my education. I took refuge in Latin epigrams, and Mr. Langdon was sufficiently dazzled to respond in kind."

"Indeed," said her ladyship thoughtfully. "Latin epigrams. My, my. That was very well done of you, I must say." She meditated.

"Shall I add water to the tea leaves, Aunt? Or is it too cold, do you think?"

"Bother the water," Lady Potterby muttered. "I am thinking." She meditated a few minutes longer, then nodded to herself. "Yes, it will do. We will have them to tea, of course. Tomorrow."

Delilah shot a suspicious glance at her father, who only smiled inscrutably. "Whom do you mean, Aunt?"

"Why Rossing, of course, and his nephew. Good heavens, why did I not think of it myself? He is perfect. The soul of rectitude—and staying right next door. Mr. Langdon is one of the few gentlemen in Society who will not automatically make assumptions about your character based on your parents' behaviour. Absent-minded he may be, but he is also fair-minded. If you can win his admiration, you will have won a staunch ally. I will look no farther than that, of course, for the time being. We must not put all our eggs in one basket, my dear."

Lady Potterby, looking altogether pleased with the eggs she had found, got up and ambled out of the drawing room mumbling to herself about orders she must give Cook for the morrow.

"So that's what you were about," Delilah accused her father when the elder woman was gone. "Why did you not simply come out and ask her to invite them?"

"Because it was more amusing to entice her into proposing the matter herself. People are always more enthusiastic about their own brilliant ideas."

"I still do not see why it was necessary to utter such fabrications about my blushes. 'Pining away,' " she said scornfully. "I thought I would be ill."

"Oh, you were not pining?" the father asked, all innocence. "How stupid of me. I thought that was why you were languishing by the window this morning as Mr. Langdon rode away."

Miss Desmond feigned a yawn. "How very amusing, Papa. But do divert yourself as you like. I shall occupy my time in praying my muddled swain remembers to bring your manuscript with him when he comes."

Mr. Langdon hastily put down his coffee cup. The hot liquid splashed over the rim and onto his fingers, but he didn't notice. He blinked at his uncle.

"Tea? With Lady Potterby?"

"Yes. She sent a message late yesterday, but I'm afraid it

slipped my mind. You're making a mess, Jack," said Lord Rossing, peering over his newspaper. "You had better not do that at Millicent's. As it is she thinks us incapable of taking care of ourselves. Always sending her jellies and bouillons and I don't know what else. The poor creature's been like that ever since Potterby passed on—what was it— five years ago? Then she was nursing her old fright of a sister. Might have expected this. She always wants someone to look after. Pity she hasn't any children. Well, we must go and meet her relatives, I suppose." He put down his paper and took up his silverware.

"Actually, Uncle, I've already met them. I thought I'd mentioned it."

"So you did, so you did." Lord Rossing stabbed his fork into a piece of ham. "So have I. Desmond, I mean. Intriguing fellow. Quite a rogue in his day. Pursued your mama for a while. Did you know that?"

"No, I did not."

"Didn't catch her, lucky fellow. But then, he did catch more than his share, I'll warrant. Rather like your swell-headed friend, Melgrave, in that way. Only Desmond had more address. Or maybe it was simply intelligence. I don't know. At any rate, he was the only one of those loose fish I ever could have a conversation with." He gazed at the forgotten fork in his hand for a moment as though wondering what it was doing waving about in the air. Then he put it into his mouth and reverted to his customary silence.

Mr. Langdon contemplated his plate. He had completely forgotten about returning Mr. Desmond's property. Not that Jack had forgotten the property itself, though. The manuscript had rarely left his hands. He'd felt guilty, at first, about continuing to read, given Miss Desmond's violent opposition to his doing so. However, she was not by to harass him, and the book was irresistible. Now his neglected conscience sprang to agitated life. What had he been thinking of, to keep the manuscript overnight? He should have returned it immediately.

The trouble was, he was extremely reluctant to confront Miss Desmond. He had managed, with the memoirs' help, to put her out of his mind during his waking hours. When he slept, though, she crept into feverish dreams—of tumbled black tresses and hot, angry eyes and silken white skin . . . of heated struggles that subsided into long and languorous joinings of another kind. He would awake perspiring, to find the bed-clothes tangled into knots and his breath coming in gasps.

Jack Langdon was accounted an eccentric and known to be shy of women. All the same, he had the normal urges of any healthy young man. He knew what desire was and how to assuage it, but he had never felt anything like desire—rather the opposite—for women of his own class. Only Catherine Pelliston had awakened in him something like passion. Certainly it had thrilled him to discover a kindred spirit in female form. Whenever he'd dared imagine an ideal mate, such was the character he'd conjured up.

Miss Desmond was no kindred spirit. She was wild, brazen, hot-tempered, and completely unpredictable. Every time she spoke to him she set his nerves jangling so he couldn't think straight. With Miss Desmond, Jack's normal discomfort in feminine company increased a hundredfold, because added to his usual consciousness of his dull inadequacy was the disconcerting awareness that he'd wanted her from the moment he'd knocked her down.

Jack forced a bit of his omelette into his mouth and, with a mighty effort, swallowed it. He must go, like it or not. He dared not entrust the ersatz book to his uncle, because the viscount was certain to open it and read it on the way, as he walked.

Jack would have to return it himself. He would have to converse with the Desmonds and hope the ugly thing consuming him was not evident in his countenance. Then he would be done with them. As to the thing itself—this unspeakable desire was nothing more than an appetite. Like others, it might be channelled into more appropriate directions, if he would but apply himself.

=6=

MR. LANGDON WAS so eager to be rid of the manuscript and thereby end all reasons for communicating with the Desmonds that he hurried his uncle out of the house well in advance of the time appointed for tea.

Lord Rossing and his nephew entered the vestibule just as Mr. Atkins was being handed his hat by a haughty Bantwell. Mr. Atkins did not appear happy. Miss Desmond, who stood beside her father, appeared even less so. Lady Potterby, who'd evidently conceived a keen dislike for Mr. Atkins, threw him a baleful glance before taking up the introductions.

"Ah, yes," said Mr. Atkins, when Lady Potterby had condescended to acknowledge his existence. "Mr. Langdon and I have briefly met, though not formally."

Jack pronounced himself pleased at the acquaintance, though he felt anything but. The sham book was under his arm, and Mr. Atkins was eying it with curiosity.

"What a handsome volume you have there, Mr. Langdon. I fancy myself rather a connoisseur, and it seems a rare specimen. Greek, is it?" he asked, oblivious to the company's blatant impatience with him to be gone.

"Yes," said Jack, looking to Mr. Desmond for guidance. That gentleman, however, had turned his attention to Lord Rossing to commence a review of their mutual acquaintance.

"It was a gift from Lord Streetham," Jack added uneasily, "and—and I brought it to show Miss Desmond."

"How thoughtful," said Lady Potterby with an indulgent smile. "A book of poetry, is it?"

"No, Aunt," Delilah said quickly. "Horticulture. Mr. Langdon has a perfect passion for horticulture, do you not sir?" She turned to Jack with a dazzling smile.

Jack nodded.

"Since we have some time before tea will be served, you may wish to examine her ladyship's garden." Delilah moved closer to take Jack firmly by the arm. "Perhaps you'll be kind enough to explain the differences between Greek techniques and modern methods of cultivation."

Mr. Langdon stiffly avowed himself delighted.

If Lady Potterby thought her grand-niece rather forward, she must have also recollected that Mr. Langdon, being an exceedingly shy gentleman, might require firm guidance. After giving the young pair permission to retire to the garden, she tried with all the frigid courtesy at her disposal to rid her hallway of the unwelcome visitor.

"What is that fellow doing here?" Jack asked, when they had turned into the path leading to the decorative herb garden. "I thought your father sent him about his business."

"Papa told you about him?" said Delilah, dismayed.

"Your father was kind enough to enlighten me concerning your difficulties—and I do wish *you* had, Miss Desmond. Had I understood the enormity of the problem, I would never have behaved so—so childishly. To me it was simply a wonderful story," he explained. "I never thought of the difficulties it presented you."

"Well, now you know. So you can guess that Mr. Atkins has come to plague my father again. Has Papa told you he was paid five hundred pounds?"

"No. I take it the money has been spent?"

She shook her head and appeared embarrassed. "We dare not spend it. It's been put aside as—as my dowry. Papa's income comes from cards," she explained quickly. "And no one in England will play him for high stakes. He must send money to my mother in Scotland as well as keep himself here, which means we have nothing to spare." Miss Desmond's smooth brow became furrowed. "Meanwhile, I must have a marriage portion. If I don't marry reasonably well, then we'll probably have to publish—some day. My parents are not getting any younger. It's most vexing, yet we seem to have no choice but to put Mr. Atkins off indefinitely."

"I see," Jack said thoughtfully.

"I know it sounds horribly mercenary—" she began.

"Miss Desmond, I have three sisters," he interrupted gently. "The youngest, Gwendolyn, has been paraded on the Marriage Mart for three Seasons now. I understand the business fully—and it is a business, a most expensive one. In the circumstances, I fully understand your father's caution."

"Still, there's no denying we've played Mr. Atkins false."

Jack smiled. "That's absurd. Murray had to wait months while Byron agonised about publishing *Childe Harold*."

They had reached the herb garden, an extensive formal planting that radiated out from a central sun-dial. Miss Desmond gazed about her unhappily.

"At any rate, even if we could repay Atkins, Papa's sure he won't take the money back—not while there's any chance of publishing and making a great fortune," she added cynically. "I fear he's right. Who'd have thought such a nervous little man could be so obstinate—or so devious? Papa says Mr. Atkins sent someone to Streetham Close to steal the manuscript. Now I'm sure he'll send someone here. We can't carry that tome about with us everywhere and we can't watch it every minute. The house is too large," she said, glancing back at the immense stone building. "She has nearly as many servants as Lord Streetham does, and I don't know a quarter of them."

Jack followed her gaze. The late Lord Potterby's ancestors, like everyone else in the shire, had competed fiercely when it came to home building. Though none could compare with Blenheim, all the great houses for miles around were enormous structures, built to awe the beholder. Rossing Hall was the sole exception, because there had been more than one reclusive Langdon in the family tree.

The second Lord Rossing had built his house in Elizabeth's time, but had not included lodgings for her majesty's household in the modest plans. The queen and her entourage were a deal too noisy for his simple tastes.

Jack knew every servant, down to the lowest pot boy. The labourers who maintained the building and grounds had been doing so for decades. Every face was familiar and trusted.

Stifling a sigh, he said, "I suppose, then, the book will be safest at Rossing Hall." Reluctantly he went on to outline the advantages of his uncle's house, the viscount's reclusive habits, and the virtual impossibility of strangers invading the premises, but Miss Desmond broke in abruptly, her grey-green eyes alight with inspiration.

"No," she said. "I have a better idea. We'll bury it."

"We'll what?" cried Jack, aghast.

"Here. In the garden." Miss Desmond abruptly released his arm and began walking quickly down the path which led to the perennial beds.

Mr. Langdon hastened after her. "Miss Desmond, you cannot dig up your aunt's flower beds. Don't you think the gardener will remark it?"

"She's made him move something. I heard her complaining about the bees. There!" she cried triumphantly as they reached a bed entirely stripped of the bergamot it had once contained. "He hasn't replanted yet."

"Of course not, in this heat. If you knew anything about gardening, Miss Desmond—"

"I don't need to know anything." She turned shining eyes upon him. "Because she knows nothing of ancient Greek horticulture. We'll tell her it's an experiment."

She dragged Jack off to the potting shed, where, after a

brief discussion with the distracted gardener, they possessed themselves of a few tools and several healthy seedlings.

After a brief argument, Jack dug the hole. Miss Desmond placed the book in its grave, waited until he had thrown some dirt upon it, then began stuffing plants into the loose soil. Jack knelt beside her.

"They'll die," he said, eying the seedlings. Some were packed into dirt so deeply that only the very tops showed. "It's too hot and I'm sure you've done it wrong."

"Then we'll blame it on the Greeks." Miss Desmond thrust a stray lock of hair back from her face.

It was very hot, indeed. The air was as thick as new-churned butter. Mr. Langdon had removed his coat, but his waistcoat was plastered to his shirt, which was stuck to his skin. He noted that Miss Desmond had rubbed a dirty smudge onto her right cheekbone. He was about to offer his handkerchief when he saw a bead of perspiration trickle down from her temples past the smudge, along her slender white neck, past her collarbone and on down until it disappeared at the edge of her bodice. The air must have grown heavier still, because Mr. Langdon suddenly found it quite impossible to breathe.

Miss Desmond looked towards him then. Her eyes widened slightly and her cheeks began to glow faintly pink. She scrambled up very quickly. Too quickly, apparently, in the heat, because he saw her hand go to her head as she began to sway.

Jack rose hastily. "Miss Desmond, are you ill?" he asked, putting out his hand to assist her.

"No," she said, backing away. "Just dizzy for a moment. I—"

She did not complete the thought because she tripped on the trowel and lost her balance.

Fortunately, she stumbled forwards instead of backwards, and Jack was able to catch her before she fell. Unfortunately, once he'd caught her, he was presented with an interesting example of the mind-body dichotomy. His mind told him to let go of her. His hands clasped her upper arms more firmly. Then his gaze locked with hers and, drawn like the tides to the moon, his head bent slowly until his lips met soft ones, tasting slightly of salt, and while his brain watched, horrified and helpless, he kissed her.

Mr. Atkins had no business in the garden. Though Desmond had put him off in his usual urbanely evasive way, Lady Potterby had made plain her disapproval of the publisher's unexpected visit. Naturally she would not approve. He carried with him that distasteful aroma of the City which only aristocrats could discern. No doubt she thought him a mushroom, presuming upon a chance acquaintance with the Desmonds in order to encroach his way into noble households.

Mr. Atkins could not afford to be thin-skinned, however. He had delayed his departure well beyond the limits of her ladyship's patience because he must leave empty-handed, which meant he would be ruined, and he was as reluctant to face ruin as any more sensitive fellow.

He had stolen into the garden because he was grasping at straws. Why had Mr. Langdon clutched that curious volume to his breast as though it were his firstborn? Why had Miss Desmond been so eager to hustle the young man out of the house?

Hoping desperately that the answers to these questions would somehow lead him to the manuscripts, Mr. Atkins trespassed quietly past the herb garden and on towards the perennial beds. There he found the puzzle solved and his hopes dashed. In short, he caught sight of the pair at the precise moment in which Mr. Langdon was confronting the mind-body dichotomy.

Mr. Atkin's head began to throb as he turned and headed back to his gig—and, he was certain, bankruptcy.

*   *   *

Miss Desmond was not altogether shocked at first. She had seen the same hot light before in other men's eyes. Though she was surprised to see it in Mr. Langdon's, she'd sensed what was coming and instinctively backed away. The trouble was, this sober young man had an uncanny knack for leading her to step wrong—today quite literally.

Once she found herself in his arms, she'd decided she might as well let him steal his kiss—only because she was curious—and thereafter reward him with severe bodily injury. These admirable intentions had been delayed of execution because the first tentative touch had softened her stony heart. He was too shy to *really* kiss her, poor man. In a moment he would jump back, embarrassed, stammering every sort of apology.

What followed in that moment could not have been more opposed to her expectations. His hands slid to her back, and in an instant, it seemed, the kiss became sure, thorough, and . . . debilitating.

Miss Desmond had rarely before suffered a kiss for more than a few seconds. She knew too well the consequences, especially for one of her dubious heritage. Now those seconds had passed, she found herself slipping into uncharted and surprisingly stormy waters.

As his mouth, tender but sure, moved over hers, she was strangely unable to do anything but respond in kind. In the next moment, without warning, the bright afternoon sun was submerged in the dark wave that engulfed her as his lips grew more demanding and his hands pressed her closer. Her mind grew dark as well.

There was far too much warmth, suddenly, and something like electricity darting through her as his arms tightened about her to crush her against his chest. Her own muscles grew weak, as though his drew their strength from them. It was, finally, the trembling of her weakened limbs that alerted her, that made her recollect to what—and whom—she was succumbing.

She jerked herself free and slapped him as hard as she

66

could. Then she only stood where she was, because though she was furious—and perhaps a tad alarmed—she was too weak-kneed to storm off as she wished to.

Had she been herself, the blow would have staggered him. As it was, he scarcely winced, only stared at her in horror. "Oh, my God," he said, as his face reddened to match the mark she'd left there.

"You—you cur!" she spat out. "How dare you? But of course you dare, you—you wolf in book-worm's clothing. You're just like all the rest."

"Miss Desmond, please. I beg your pardon. I cannot think what I—"

"I can think what you are. You can count yourself lucky I hadn't my pistol with me or you'd never think again."

"Oh, my God." He stared blindly about him, his expression that of a man who has just trodden upon a nest of angry cobras. "Am I losing my mind?" He turned to her then, and in his grey eyes she saw, outraged as she was, genuine anguish.

"As an excuse, that is hardly original—or complimentary," she said tartly.

"Miss Desmond, I cannot make any excuse. I can scarcely imagine any apology that would be remotely adequate. It is simply—" He hesitated.

"Yes, it is simply a matter of taking me for a lightskirts—which is, naturally, what everyone does, and I suppose I should be used to it by now."

"It's nothing of the sort." He ran his fingers through his hair, which she noted was already untidy.

Good grief, Delilah thought, had she made it so? She could not remember where her own hands had been a few moments before. She wanted to dash into the house and up to her room where she could hide under the bed, but she had too much pride to retreat. She stood waiting, watching, as he seemed to struggle with something. Finally, he spoke.

"Miss Desmond, I find there is—I mean, I have an

intensity of . . . feeling for you that . . . that I cannot understand—or control, apparently," he ended feebly.

"It is usually called lust, Mr. Langdon," she snapped as the recollection of his recent power over her stirred up her fury again. "Though I'm relieved to hear you don't understand it, because I certainly could not. After all, I am not paper and ink and bound in morocco. Or will you claim you were touched by the sun and took me for a volume of Ptolemy? That would be far more original than this equivalent of 'I don't know what came over me.' "

His grey eyes darkened, and his face became rigid. Even before he spoke, Delilah knew she'd gone too far.

"Whatever my tastes, madam—and I do admit I am more than average fond of reading—I am not made of paper and ink, either," he said coldly. "I am still a man. I suppose I may have moments of weakness like other men? We all of us, despite our best intentions, occasionally forget we are gentlemen. I had such a moment, and I do humbly beg your pardon. Or is there some further penance you wish to exact?"

Delilah knew what penance he referred to. She knew she had, technically, a right to claim he'd compromised her. For an instant she was even tempted to do so, because she could think of no more fitting punishment than to make him marry her, disgrace his name, outrage his family, and be miserable all the rest of his days. Pride—and perhaps a twinge of guilt—overcame anger, however. She was not so desperate for a husband. Furthermore, it was most unwise to arouse his enmity, considering all he knew about the manuscript.

"Now you are being unfair," she said. "It's the lady's prerogative to be insulted and the gentleman's to be penitent. You did far better when you were all abject apologies. You were so beautifully insincere."

"I was entirely sincere," he returned angrily.

"If you were, then why do you pick on me now? If you must be wicked enough to try to seduce me in my great-aunt's garden, you might at least allow me to be insulted and faint and scream and become hysterical. That's *supposed* to be how it's done."

He opened his mouth to retort, then shut it and looked around instead for his coat. He snatched it up from a bush and shrugged himself into it. It was a very well-made coat, Delilah noted, even as she was wondering how to mollify him. It fit him quite nicely.

"You hate me," she said.

He gazed at her in exasperation. "I was not trying to seduce you, Miss Desmond."

"Well, I most certainly was not trying to seduce *you*. Why are you so angry with me?"

"I wish," he said quietly, "you had your pistol. I wish you would just shoot me and be done with it."

Delilah sighed. "Oh, very well, have it your way," she said. "I apologise for whatever it is I've done, though I do think you are monstrous unjust and ungallant in this. Still, I can't let you go in to tea looking like an outraged Zeus or Aunt will be scolding me for hours. She'll probably send me back to Scotland," she added.

"She ought to," said Jack. "You are perfectly impossible."

"I know," she said, her face penitent.

Delilah Desmond penitent was a sight calculated to unman the most obdurate of tyrants, which Mr. Langdon certainly was not. He was, in fact, painfully aware that his behaviour had been criminal in the first place and rude and insolent in the second. Even though she had slighted his masculinity, he had no business being enraged. He'd slighted it himself often enough. All the same, he was very upset. Her sarcastic remarks still smarted, and he wanted to throttle her. He wondered fleetingly if he were possessed, because by rights he should throttle himself.

"Miss Desmond, I am not angry," he said wearily. "I am deeply ashamed of my behaviour. I promise never to repeat it. We've disposed of the book. Can we please dispose of this distressing conversation?"

"Yes," she said in an oddly subdued voice. "Do I look a fright?"

No, he thought, only more maddeningly beautiful than ever.

"Yes," he said. "You have dirt on your face and the state of your hair makes you look like Medusa. You had best go tidy up or we'll be subjected to a most intensive interrogation. No one will mind me," he added with a wry glance at his stained trousers. "It's exactly what they expect."

As an unusually docile Miss Desmond took herself away to be tidied, it may have occurred to her that, in Mr. Langdon's case, people really had better not place too much reliance upon their expectations.

Mr. Atkins returned to his latest inn, which was only slightly less uncomfortable than the first, with every intention of proceeding to Streetham Close as soon as he had revived his sagging spirits with food. His hostess was slow, however, and by the time he had finished his meal, the sky was darkening ominously.

He had just climbed into his vehicle when lightning crackled. From a distance followed the low boom of thunder. In the next moment, the heavens burst about his ears, and by the time he'd regained the shelter of the inn, he was drenched.

Nonetheless, he set out for Streetham Close the following morning, sniffling and sneezing the whole way. The earl, never eager for his company in the best of circumstances, did not trouble to disguise his disgust with the repellent spectacle before him.

Mr. Atkins refused to be cowed. Doggedly, between blowing his nose and sneezing, he reported what he'd seen. He declared that even a simple man like himself could see Lord Berne would have a very difficult time obtaining the young lady's trust when she was so busy trying to ensnare Mr. Langdon.

"I think, My Lord, we'd best increase our offer," the

publisher went on. "The alternative I shudder at—though I suppose it can be done. That is to say, the manuscript must be somewhere in the house, and I understand there are persons who may be hired to—to deliver it up to us."

Lord Streetham drew himself up. In no uncertain terms he informed the publisher that bribery and theft were not in his line. Persuasion was another matter. "As I have already pointed out to you," he said, "my son is perfectly capable of persuading the young lady."

"He hasn't done it yet," Mr. Atkins muttered, rubbing his red nose.

Of this his lordship was frustratedly aware. Aloud, however, he only cited the heir's many responsibilities, and advised Mr. Atkins to return speedily to London where Mrs. Atkins might give him proper care.

After Mr. Atkins had taken his nasal leave, Lord Streetham summoned his son.

"I see I must deal with this myself," his lordship said frigidly. "Obviously you cannot be counted upon to assume any of the responsibilities of your position. While you amuse yourself at common hostelries, Jack Langdon is seducing Miss Desmond—in her great-aunt's garden, no less."

Lord Berne was, sad to say, a very fickle young man. His interest in Miss Desmond had dwindled with every passing hour of her absence, which time he had pleasantly whiled away in a rendezvous with his father's former mistress and a lively flirtation with the fair and saucy Sarah. Along with decreasing interest in Miss Desmond had grown an increasing reluctance to antagonise her formidable parent.

Men far more reckless than himself became circumspect when dealing with Devil Desmond or anything connected to him. To deceive his daughter, especially for a useless lot of ink and paper, seemed wantonly self-destructive.

Now, however, as he left his irate father, Lord Berne was

outraged. That poky Jack Langdon should succeed with the girl so easily—in a mere day or two—when that same young woman had proved so incomprehensibly indifferent to the viscount's own irresistible charm . . . it was not to be endured.

=== 7 ===

DELILAH GAZED IN disgust at the Gordian knot of stitches that was supposed to pass for embroidery. "Isn't that typical?" she muttered. "I make a mess of everything."

Her father looked up from his sporting journal. The two were spending a few quiet hours together while Lady Potterby visited an ailing neighbour, and they were abnormally quiet. Normally, Delilah and her father could converse endlessly. Today she was unable to find any entertaining topic because yesterday's garden episode preyed on her mind.

She still could not believe that she, Delilah Desmond, had very nearly succumbed to the clumsy embrace of the provoking, stodgy Mr. Langdon. She had travelled over half the globe with her parents and encountered every sort of scoundrel. She had met with every seductive trick and heard honeyed speeches in half a dozen languages. Always she had been immune, observing her pursuers' efforts with the same cool detachment with which she studied her cards and bluffed her way to victory over the most cunning Captain Sharps.

She could not understand why her instincts had failed her yesterday—and with him, of all people, a muddled, naïve book-worm. It was too humiliating for words.

Now, as Delilah met her father's calm scrutiny, her conscience pricked her. She was not used to keeping secrets from him.

"Papa, if I tell you something," she began, "will you promise not to do anything violent?"

"If I didn't yesterday, why should I today?" was the disconcerting reply. "As you saw, Mr. Langdon left with all his limbs intact—though I cannot speak for his mind."

The daughter's eyes widened. "You saw?"

"The entire household might have seen, for all I know. The corner window of the drawing room looks out over that section of the perennial beds. Luckily, Lord Rossing and your great-aunt were dithering at each other on the opposite side of the room, so I had no need to act the role of outraged parent, thank heavens. Beastly weather, worse than the West Indies. At least last night's storm has cleared the air somewhat."

Miss Desmond's embroidery had fallen unnoticed to the carpet. "It was an accident, Papa, I assure you."

"Indeed? Which part?" he asked as he laid his journal aside. "Did you entomb my memoirs accidentally on account of sunstroke or are you referring to the subsequent performance?"

Embarrassed, Delilah took the offensive. "You were spying on me!"

"Not at all. I was looking out for Mr. Langdon. When you hauled him so hastily out of doors, I began to fear for his life. I grew increasingly alarmed when I saw that trowel in your hand. Awkward things, trowels."

Delilah glared at an insipid porcelain shepherdess standing on the small table at her elbow. "I suppose you found the entire scene immensely entertaining," she grumbled.

"More entertaining, I think, than Mr. Langdon did. When he came in to tea he looked as though he'd been fighting the Thirty Years' War single-handedly. I wish you would not plague him so, Delilah. He is supposed to be our ally."

"I—plague him! When he took advantage—"

Her father raised an eyebrow.

"I certainly did not encourage him," she said hotly.

74

The door opened and Bantwell entered to inform Mr. Desmond that Lord Wemberton had arrived.

"We'll pursue this discussion later, Delilah," said her papa as he rose from his chair. "Wemberton has very kindly offered to have a look at the grey. He has a taste for ill-behaved beasts. Takes it as a challenge, I suppose."

While her papa was occupied with Lord Wemberton, Delilah decided to work off her irritation with a walk into Rossingley. No wonder her brain was fuddled. She was not used to being so inactive. Gad, but ladies had a dull life of it.

She knew she ought to take Joan along, but the abigail always whined if she had to stir more than a few yards. Instead, Miss Desmond strapped her knife sheath to her calf and tucked her small pistol into her reticule. If she were in danger, these two would do her a deal more good than Joan would.

Delilah had walked scarcely half a mile before she met up with Lord Berne travelling in the opposite direction. As soon as he caught sight of her he brought his curricle to a halt and offered to take her up.

"I will take you out of your way," she said as she took in the dashing picture of snug blue coat, nankeen breeches, and gleaming top boots. His beaver hat, slightly tilted, gave him a rakish air which his angelic blue eyes stoutly contradicted. He was a devastating combination of dangerous masculinity and boyish innocence—and he knew it.

"That is impossible, since it was you I came to see," he answered with a winning smile.

Miss Desmond was not in a humour to be won so easily. She pointed out that she'd already outraged propriety by going out without her maid. She would not compound the error by driving with him when he was without a tiger.

"I had not thought we needed bodyguards, Miss Desmond," he said. "It is broad day, and no highwayman has been seen in these parts in over a decade."

"My reputation can bear a highwayman, My Lord. A libertine is another matter." She offered a brilliant smile and proceeded on her way.

The viscount promptly turned his carriage and came up beside her again.

"If you mean to follow me to Rossingley, I shall be cross with you," she said. "You raise a deal of dust and my frock will be spoiled."

"I can't help it. I'm curious."

She paused. "About what?"

He glanced at the cushioned seat of his equipage, then at the floor, then turned round to study the small rear seat where his tiger would normally be perched.

"About how I can possibly seduce you in the curricle without relinquishing the reins," he answered ingenuously. "With, in fact, any degree of safety and comfort."

His baffled glance met an amused one.

"Clearly, I am not as imaginative as you are, Miss Desmond. Would you be kind enough to explain how the thing is to be accomplished?" he asked.

"Certainly not." She went on walking, and the curricle went on beside her. After five minutes of silence, she swore to herself, stopped, and looked up at him.

"You are very obstinate," she said. "Do you really intend to follow me all the way into town and make a spectacle of me?"

He nodded.

She sighed. "Very well, I'll ride. But only back to Elmhurst. I don't mean to set the whole village buzzing."

As he moved to help her, she waved him back, telling him to mind the horses. "You can't be chivalrous when you've no tiger to take the reins," she said, climbing up easily.

"That's better," he said as, to the great annoyance of his cattle, he turned the curricle once more. "Now you might satisfy my curiosity more comfortably. On another topic, I mean," he added quickly as her eyes narrowed. "What is all this about your reputation? What harm is there in a short drive in broad day, even with a libertine?"

"That should be obvious."

He only looked baffled.

"My parents," she said impatiently.

"What has that to do with you? You haven't joined a theatre troupe or carried on a series of dazzling escapades and love affairs. Quite the opposite. You've been exceedingly decorous, and I can't tell you how depressing I find that." He shook his head sorrowfully. "You wouldn't even drive with me, simply because I came without my groom. I hope you won't think me vain, Miss Desmond, if I tell you no one has ever done that before."

"Well, I'm here now," she said. "Pray be as vain as you like."

"I can't. I'm consumed by guilt. I never considered the damage my coming to call might do. I've been inexcusably thoughtless."

"I would not refine upon it too much, My Lord. Lady Potterby will not allow you past the doorstep anyhow. If we manage to reach Elmhurst without being seen, then I may escape this unscathed."

She felt his gaze upon her. As she turned to meet it, she saw a flicker of something in his eyes, but it was gone in an instant, and she could not tell what it was.

"Miss Desmond, I think this is monstrous unfair," he said, sounding indignant. "People have no right to judge you by your parents, even if they were right in judging your parents so harshly—which I do not accept, either."

"In the abstract, perhaps they have no right, but this is the real world. In the real world, Lady Potterby's neighbours want nothing to do with her while Papa and I are about. I had not expected to be welcomed with open arms, but I had thought at least one or two people might give me a chance before snubbing me." She smiled cynically. "I was mistaken."

"Jealousy," he said. "Envy. That's what it is—and a deal of hypocrisy besides."

She shrugged.

They drove on in silence for a while, the viscount appearing lost in thought. Then, as they were turning into the drive leading to Elmhurst, Lord Berne spoke.

"I wonder what the world would think," he said, "if the Devil's daughter reformed the libertine."

She stared at him.

"Reflect, Miss Desmond. How would the world regard a woman who could make me mend my wicked ways?"

She considered. "I daresay she would be proposed for sainthood. The job is worth half a dozen lesser miracles, I'm sure."

"Then I recommend you be measured for a halo as soon as may be. I'm not joking, you know. The miracle can be accomplished," he promised, "because I mean to help you. Miss Desmond, I wish to be reformed."

"And I should like to be Queen of Egypt."

"I am quite serious," he insisted, with another melting smile. "You have no idea how much you've alarmed me. If you're never invited anywhere, when am I to see you again? You tell me your aunt will send me packing if I come to the house, and I cannot possibly expect to happen on you in the road every time I come to Rossingley. I must be reformed because there appears to be no alternative."

She could not help smiling in return. He was not to be trusted, but she appreciated charm, and that he had in abundance. All the same, she pointed out rather sternly that his motives did not seem remotely saintlike.

"My motives are selfish, Miss Desmond," he said softly, "and selfishness is always to be relied upon."

It must be acknowledged with regret that Mr. Langdon was not a devoted churchgoer. Since he was given to quiet pursuits, he found Sunday no longer or drearier than any other day. Normally, he was content to spend the Sabbath with an improving book.

This Sunday, however, he rose from a breakfast he must have been trying to read—for he certainly didn't eat any of it—and told his uncle he thought he might find out whether Mr. Blenkly's sermons had improved at all in the last decade. The uncle only nodded absently and returned to his dog-eared copy of Mr. Jeremy Bentham's *Introduction to Principles of Morals and Legislation*.

Oblivious to the stares and whispers about him, Mr. Langdon took his place in the family pew. He studied the stained glass which had for centuries illuminated in picture form what the uneducated faithful could not read in the Bible. He gazed up at the ceiling and admired the skill of twelfth-century craftsmen, while absently noting several stains bespeaking an urgent need for roof repairs. Then, almost but not quite as absently, his gaze drifted to the pew where the late Lord Potterby's ancestors had attended divers lessons in Christianity.

Miss Desmond wore a pale green bonnet with dark green ribbons, under which her wayward hair must have been throttled into submission, for not one disobedient strand escaped. Her high-waisted frock was the same cool colour, embroidered with sprigs which matched the ribbons on her bonnet. She was a cool bouquet of mint, and he wanted to crush her and inhale the fragrance of her . . . which was *not*, he angrily reproached himself, the sort of thought to be having at all, let alone on the Sabbath, in church.

Mr. Langdon was so busy rebuking himself and trying to tear his gaze away that he never noticed how the whispering had swelled into a communal gasp. He saw only that Miss Desmond had turned to look over her shoulder, and that for three full seconds her gaze locked with his before jerking unsteadily to the rear of the church.

He turned as well, and instantly joined in the general astonishment. Lord Berne had entered.

The viscount serenely returned the parishioners' bold survey, then catching Jack's eye, made for him.

"Couldn't keep away either, I see," Tony whispered as he slid in next to his friend.

"I only came to find out whether old Blenkly is as rambling as ever," Jack said stiffly.

"And to assure yourself she isn't a figment of your overheated imagination. I see your case is nearly as bad as my own. Gad, how cool she looks—and how I should like to warm her."

Mr. Blenkly's entrance spared Lord Berne the throttling his friend was instantly most eager to administer. Mr. Langdon was forced to make do with a murderous glance and the fervent wish that lightning would, as the congregation seemed to expect, strike the spot where the provoking viscount stood.

The service was thoroughly incomprehensible from beginning to end. Mr. Blenkly had wanted only one glimpse of the two gentlemen in a pew which had stood empty for most of the past decade before what little poise he possessed flew up to the heavens. He had planned to enlighten his parishioners regarding the Parable of the Sower. Unfortunately, the sight in the Langdon family pew—especially the taller, golden-haired spectacle—was too much for him. He became hopelessly entangled between the Parable of the Prodigal Son and vaguely related proverbs dealing with loving parents, sparing the rod, wise and foolish offspring, and some deranged reference to loaves and fishes.

Even if he had managed a more logical discourse, it would have been utterly wasted on its object. Lord Berne had long since mastered the art of appearing devotedly attentive while his mind fixed on other topics altogether. Since the minister did not expound upon the Song of Solomon, the viscount's present meditations could scarcely be deemed appropriate.

Mr. Blenkly knew nothing of this. He saw a notorious libertine gravely attending his speech and wondered if the end of the world had come. He was dumbfounded when, after the service, that same young libertine engaged him in a brief conversation, at the end of which Mr. Blenkly possessed a pledge for repairs of the church roof.

In ten minutes, all the parishioners who'd lingered to stare at Lord Berne and exchange speculative whispers were also possessed of the information. Thus the news reached Lady Potterby's ears.

She had fully intended to keep Lord Berne at a safe distance from her grand-niece, but his appearance at the service elicited certain interesting speculations of her own. His astounding act of philanthropy gave her further reason to ponder. Thus, when he approached, Lady Potterby was too curious to be as unwelcoming as she'd intended. She even went so far as to applaud his generosity.

"I wish, My Lady, I could say I fully deserved your kind words, but the credit does not belong to me. I only acted upon inspiration—and it was your young relative who inspired me."

The young relative looked blank.

"Delilah told you the roof leaked?" Lady Potterby asked, her dignified countenance belying certain agreeable surmises within. "But she has not been in the church before today."

Mr. Langdon, who had lingered in the cool, dark church after everyone else had exited, joined the small group as Lord Berne was answering.

"Miss Desmond awakened in me yesterday a lively concern for the state of my immortal soul," said the viscount, bestowing an adoring glance upon that fair evangelist. "Accordingly, I came to church, and as I gazed heavenward, hoping my prayers for forgiveness would be heard, I noticed the stains on the ceiling. As I looked downward to confirm my suspicions, my eyes lit upon Miss Desmond's bonnet. If it rained—as it has almost incessantly—and the roof leaked, her bonnet would be ruined. The thought was insupportable."

Miss Desmond glanced away to hide the smile she could not suppress . . . and met Mr. Langdon's sober grey scrutiny. Her smile vanished, though her colour increased.

"You would have done better, My Lord," said Lady Potterby as severely as she could, considering the hopes blossoming within her breast, "to have reflected upon your soul—not young ladies' bonnets."

"One should never underestimate the power of a bonnet," his lordship returned. "It is the ladies who teach us to be good—but first they must obtain our attention."

"It is certainly not good of you to insult their intelligence," Mr. Langdon put in. "You speak as though Miss Desmond would stand there witlessly, allowing the roof to leak upon her."

The image conjured up was evidently more than Miss Desmond's composure could withstand, because she giggled.

Lord Berne was good-natured enough to chuckle and Lady Potterby permitted herself to smile. "Indeed, I hope my grand-niece has better sense," said she.

"My Lady, your grand-niece is the most level-headed young lady I have ever met," said Lord Berne. "A great many others would do well to emulate her—though that would be difficult," he added solemnly. "They have the advantages neither of your kinship nor your wise guidance."

"Yet you believed I had so little sense I would stand under a dripping roof," said Delilah. "You contradict yourself, My Lord."

"His lordship is confused," said Jack. "Clearly, the experience of hearing a sermon was too great a shock to his senses. It has addled his wits."

"Mr. Blenkly was addled enough himself," Lady Potterby calmly intervened before Lord Berne could retort upon his friend. "I could not make heads or tales of his homily. Yet I still retain sufficient perception to note that the sky darkens. Dear me, and the day had begun so bright. We had better go home, Delilah."

"I do not know whether this is very good or very bad," said Lady Potterby when they were safely within the carriage. "To attend services here instead of at home . . . to travel at least twenty-five miles in each direction . . . and after the same journey yesterday . . . and to behave so respectfully towards you. That is most puzzling."

"I may take it then, that unlike his friend, Mr. Langdon regularly attends services?" Delilah asked.

"Dear me, no. Only a marriage or a baptism might lure him here. Still, there is no predicting what that young man will do. He may have come to admire the architecture—or a young lady," she added slyly.

The grand-niece frowned.

"You needn't look so grim," said Lady Potterby. "I admit he's not dashing, but he's perfectly eligible. He has twenty thousand a year of his own. When he comes into the title the figure will increase considerably. You could do worse."

"I will, of course, do as you tell me, Aunt, but I hope you will not let Papa's ill-considered remarks influence you. I'm sure the only reason Mr. Langdon tolerates me is out of respect for your long-standing friendship with his uncle. Whenever Mr. Langdon looks at me he makes me feel there's dirt on my nose—or that I've got my bonnet on backwards."

"That is merely his way," Lady Potterby said dismissively. "At least you have nothing to fear from him. On the other hand, Lord Berne is a sorry rascal. Still, a new roof does give one pause. The expense is not inconsiderable."

So Lord Streetham pointed out to his son some hours later when that young man described his recent activities. Nor was the earl in any way appeased when Lord Berne embarked upon an impassioned soliloquy regarding the young lady's numerous perfections, among which her intriguing hard-headedness figured most prominently.

He had no business being intrigued, his father retorted. Mindless infatuation had no place in business matters. All Tony had accomplished was to degenerate into a moonstruck schoolboy, while both the young lady and the memoirs remained as unapproachable as ever.

Lord Streetham coldly observed that he'd erred gravely in entrusting so sensitive an enterprise to his fribble of an heir. Accordingly, he ordered his son off to Brighton, where the fresh salt air might clear his fevered brain.

Lord Berne hastened to defend himself. He'd made an excellent start, he insisted. Even the formidable aunt had behaved almost amiably. "In another two days they'll be convinced I mean to offer for the girl. What better way than that to obtain Miss Desmond's confidence and trust?"

"What better way for them to trap you is more like it," Lord Streetham returned.

"So you'll keep me in leading strings to protect me from an inexperienced miss? And while I'm safely in Brighton, Langdon will seduce her."

"Inexperienced—hah! That embrace Atkins reported was the chit's doing, rely upon it. Jack has never seduced anyone in his whole life. She was trying to ensnare him— as she will you. You are too much taken with her. You are sure to forget yourself, and her family will be quick to cry Dishonour if you so much as kiss her hand. Remember, Desmond is not like the other fathers you've outraged. He will not be quieted with a bribe—not when he can make that black-haired wench of his a countess."

"But surely your influence—"

"One has no influence over knaves who leap out of alleys in the dead of night. You forget of whom we speak. Besides, if he has made a laughingstock of me in his curst story, I will have as much influence in the world as the coal scuttle. As usual, the Devil holds all the winning cards. You will go to Brighton or I shall cut off your allowance."

=8=

WHILE LORD BERNE was quarrelling with his father, Delilah was confiding in hers. Until the viscount had appeared at church, she had not permitted herself to consider his scheme seriously. Now she was forced to consider it, but she wished to have her father's perspective as well.

When she was done, Mr. Desmond leaned back comfortably in his chair and acknowledged that Lord Berne's was an interesting approach to the problem.

"It is brilliant, Papa," she answered. "I only wish you could have seen the parishioners today. They were positively agog. Even Aunt Millicent was impressed. Lord Berne's reputation must be far worse than I thought, if one appearance at church could cause such a stir. Still, I cannot help but question his motives. Though it seems a deal of trouble to go to, I do wonder if he only wants to win my trust so he can seduce me."

"That's simple enough," said her father. "Don't get seduced."

She did not appear to hear him. Her brow was furrowed.

"I find your expression ominous, Delilah," said Mr. Desmond. "You are hatching something, and I am certain it is mischief."

She was staring at the carpet, and when she spoke, it was as though she were simply thinking aloud.

"Not being seduced is simple," she said. "What is difficult is maintaining his interest. He is reputed very fickle." Absently she rose from her chair and began pacing the room. "If it could be done, he might be brought round—eventually. But is there time—and is he worth the effort, I wonder? Still, he will be Earl of Streetham one day and—" She glanced at her father, who was watching her with every evidence of amusement.

"He is very beautiful, Papa. That we must admit."

"I am sure there is not a prettier fellow in the kingdom."

"He is exceedingly conceited," she went on, "yet he is amusing. He is rather wild—"

"Very wild."

She bit her lip. "Well, I'd rather not marry some dull, conventional fellow if I can help it. I should be bored to death and driven to some atrocity sooner or later, I know it. At any rate, Lord Berne is at hand and wishes to pursue me. I think I may let him do so . . . until I catch him," she finished with a faint smile.

"And if you do not?" her papa enquired.

She shrugged. "Then I'm no worse off than before. I'll go to London with my aunt as planned and try to catch someone else."

Mr. Desmond gave a theatrical shudder. "Such a cold-blooded creature you are, my dear. Whenever you begin making wedding plans I feel I have entered a damp, chilly dungeon. No more, I beg you."

He rose from his chair and crossed the room to her. "Your aunt is napping," he said. "If I swear the servants to secrecy, will you indulge your aged parent in a game of billiards?"

Her smile broadened into a mischievous grin. "I promise to trounce you soundly."

"I shall see that you don't. You know, while we are on the tiresome subject, I ought to remind you of *his* parents. Your behaviour must be most circumspect if you wish to enslave them as well. I'm afraid that will tax your patience."

"I will do my part not to make a scandal, Papa," she said with some indignation. "I only wish you would do yours. Something must be done about that odious Mr. Atkins."

"Leave him to me. If worse comes to worse, and he proves recalcitrant, we shall simply burn the manuscript."

"Actually, I begin to think we should do so immediately."

"So confident of your viscount, eh?" Mr. Desmond offered his daughter his arm.

As she took it she said, "It would be one less worry."

"My dear, a single young lady has only one true worry, which is not getting seduced. All you need do is not believe anything an idle young man says until he says it before the parson and witnesses, pursuant to placing a ring upon your finger."

She squeezed his arm affectionately. "I will remember, Papa," she promised. "Now—to battle."

Lord Berne spent his first day in Brighton dutifully inhaling the salt air during a restless walk upon the Steyne. In the usual way of things, he would have promptly banished Miss Desmond's image by fixing on one closer to hand. The circumstances were not usual. He had not wandered away on his own caprice, but had been sent away against his will, like a naughty child ordered to bed without his supper. Now, precisely like a spoiled child, Lord Berne wanted no other treat but the one denied him.

Consequently, he persuaded himself there was no other female upon the earth as desirable as Delilah Desmond; that, furthermore, he had never loved before, all the rest being puerile infatuations.

That her image haunted him (at least twice a day) proved beyond doubt he'd come upon the grand passion of a lifetime. Yet what had he done? He'd scurried off to Brighton because his father threatened to stop his allowance. An idle threat. Lord Streetham had too much pride to allow his son to wander about the kingdom on foot, in rags, like a beggar.

Meanwhile Lord Berne's beloved would have concluded

he'd abandoned her—that he was a worthless, unreliable knave. She must not.

Lord Berne hastened back to his lodgings and penned a very long letter full of bad grammar and execrable verse, in the course of which he claimed to be called away to sit by the sickbed of a friend. Then he ordered his curricle and posted off to Rye.

In the country, one day can be so tediously like all the rest that the smallest piece of news becomes a nine-days' wonder. All the same, few of Lady Potterby's neighbours could work up much excitement about Squire Pegham's sow's difficulties in labour and the consequent suffocation of three of her numerous offspring. This local sensation was cast entirely in the shade by the bizarre behaviour of Lord Berne.

Streetham Close might be twenty-five miles away, but Lord Berne's periodic sorties into the Rossingley environs and the feminine devastation he left in his wake had made him a common foe. The local gentry were therefore mightily curious about the young lady who had (if reports were to be believed) so far subjugated this enemy as to lure him to church, where—and this was utterly confounding—he had not nodded off once. He had capped this miracle by pledging a large sum of money for repairs to a church not even in his own parish, thus sparing the Rossingley parishioners the disagreeable necessity of reaching into their own pockets.

All this he had done, it was said, in an effort to overcome Miss Desmond's prejudices against him. Miss Twiggenham herself had heard him say as much, having on Sunday been placed by an accidental though fortunate conjunction of circumstances close enough to overhear his lordship's remarks. Miss Twiggenham's evidence was strengthened by Mrs. Blenkly's avowal that Lord Berne had said practically the same thing to the minister.

In short, as Lord Berne had predicted, and more speedily than even he could have guessed, Rossingley developed a lively interest in Miss Delilah Desmond. Lady Potterby was besieged daily by callers, all of whom had hitherto been studiously unaware of the Desmonds' entry into the neighbourhood.

They came primarily out of curiosity and went away still curious. Admittedly Miss Desmond was handsome. All the same, Lord Berne had his pick of not only rustic beauties, but Society's most dazzling Incomparables. There must be something more than her looks.

Unfortunately, no one could ascertain what the "more" was, exactly. Miss Desmond's manners were unexceptionable, and her conversation was very properly limited to deference to the opinions of her elders. She seemed very much like any other gently-bred young miss. Only when people recollected she was Devil Desmond's daughter did this conclusion appear at all remarkable. Thus she became a mystery all Rossingley was in a fever to solve.

Miss Desmond might have enjoyed her triumph wholeheartedly had she not been so acutely aware that Rossingley's interest in her would fade as abruptly as it had blossomed if the reason for its interest vanished. The reason—Lord Berne—showed every evidence of doing so.

When he had not called by Friday, Miss Desmond's spirits—already sorely tried by the necessity of behaving circumspectly before an endless stream of company—sank into the Slough of Despond.

Lord Berne was obviously as fickle, selfish, and thoughtless as everyone said. She must have been totty-headed to have taken him seriously even for an instant, especially on such light evidence as one whimsical promise. She had not been her usual hard-headed self, that was certain, Delilah reflected as she wandered unhappily out to the garden.

The sun shone, but today its beams were gentle, and a cool breeze drove away all traces of the unusual humidity which had oppressed the countryside. The milder weather had not, she soon discovered, been of much use to her horticultural experiment. Two more seedlings had succumbed. As she gazed sorrowfully upon their withered remains, she made a mental note to speak to Jenkins, the gardener. Until she thought of a better hiding place, there must be no more planting here. Mr. Langdon had not dug a very deep hole. He'd been too busy demonstrating his prowess in other ways. Well, he'd discovered his mistake soon enough and had slunk off to hide among his dusty volumes.

By now he must have persuaded himself the embrace had been all her doing, because she was a wanton adventuress, bent on entrapping him. *Was there some further penance she wished to exact*, he'd said, in those cold, patronising tones. The nerve of the man! He was despicable.

She stomped down the path until she came to a wrought iron bench placed conveniently in a shady corner. Muttering imprecations upon Mr. Langdon and occasionally— when she remembered—Lord Berne, Delilah flung herself onto the seat and fell into a sulk.

She had been thus amusing herself for about ten minutes when her maid appeared bearing a letter, as well as a lengthy recitation of her trials and tribulations, the letter being the most recent affront to Joan's dignity. She did not see why a lady's maid must act as messenger when there were plenty of footmen lazing about the house, gaping and gawking the livelong day for want of anything to do. Her ill-tempered mistress only added to these injuries by curtly dismissing her.

While Joan marched back to the house in high dudgeon, Miss Desmond was eagerly tearing open the letter. She quickly scanned the bold, black lines, then, with her first genuine smile in at least three days, sat back to read again more slowly.

When she had finished savouring Lord Berne's lyric prose for the tenth time, Delilah made for the house, to acquaint her father with this latest, most promising development on the rut-ridden road to matrimony.

She found him in the late Lord Potterby's study, perusing an epistle of his own and grinning. "Ah, there you are," said he. "I was intending to come out to share this with you, but you've spared my aged body that labour. What do you think, Delilah? We have yet another publisher who wishes to become my bosom-bow—and at twice the price."

He handed the letter to his daughter, whose joyous countenance reverted to its previous gloom while she read.

"This is dreadful, Papa," she said when she was done. "I thought Mr. Atkins assured us of secrecy. How on earth did this man learn of your memoirs?"

"Easy enough," said the parent with a shrug. "I daresay one of Atkins's clerks has a passion for listening at keyholes and a loose tongue. An unfortunate combination, but one prevalent, I fear, in every class of society."

"Indeed. I expect all of London knows by now."

"If that were the case, I should receive a great many more offers than this. Rest easy, my dear. Businessmen are always spying upon one another and they are not above paying their rivals' employees for useful tidbits."

Delilah could not rest easy. She began pacing frantically, her skirts whirling about her in a manner which would have sent her great-aunt into paroxysms. Fortunately, the only observer at the moment was her papa.

"Yes, my love," he said. "I am certain you have inherited your legs from your mama, but I hope you will be cautious about revealing that circumstance beyond our small family circle."

Miss Desmond dutifully threw herself into a chair. "Thank you for the reminder, Papa. Aunt Millicent has told me a hundred times to move with more decorum. But it will scarcely matter whether I lift my skirts and run howling through the village if we do not silence this horrid man."

"Silence him? But my dear, he offers double what Atkins did. If I accept, I might repay our nervous friend and commence a less tiresome relationship with his colleague.

Although I must say," he added, "Atkins has astonished me by keeping away this whole week. I wonder if he's returned to London?"

Delilah had no time for wonderings. The crisis at the moment was this letter. It must be dealt with. If her papa accepted the offer, she might as well go back to Scotland to her mama. She could not endure any more anxiety.

"What on earth is there to be anxious about?" her father asked mildly. "My memoirs are safely entombed. Another few weeks of rain and they will have rotted away. Or is it your elusive golden prince who troubles you? You should not be cast down, my dear. Reformation is a most wearisome enterprise, particularly for fickle young libertines. You cannot be surprised that after an eternity of five whole days he has altogether forgotten your existence."

"Oh, has he?" was the arch response. "Then I wonder why he writes so desolately of missing me." Delilah bounced up from her chair to wave Lord Berne's letter triumphantly in her father's face.

Mr. Desmond smiled. "Has he, indeed?" He took the letter and skimmed it. "Defy his parents . . . his life heretofore a shallow mockery . . . nothing but this pernicious accident could have kept him away. Good heavens," he said, looking up. "His courage and resolution take my breath away."

Whether he was breathless or not, Delilah told her parent, he must wrench his mind from Lord Berne for the moment and fix it on this new publisher, who must, she averred, be answered immediately.

"You must tell him he is mistaken, Papa. Tell him the memoirs do not exist. If you do not, the rumours will be all over London in another week and I will not dare show my face there until I am as old as Aunt Millicent."

Her papa sighed and declared his only wish, of course, was to cater to her every whim, regardless how silly. He obediently took up his pen and wrote as his adamant child dictated. When the letter was sealed up, the two departed for Rossingley. Nothing would do, certainly, but to post it themselves, forthwith.

Lord Streetham had reached an unhappy conclusion. Desmond's daughter was far more wily than the earl had imagined. Whatever favours Tony might eventually obtain from her, the manuscript was not one of them. Having admitted his error—a painful enough exercise—the earl must now face an even more disagreeable fact. There were only two ways left to get the manuscript away from Desmond. One was to steal it, which was now not only impossibly difficult but exceedingly risky. The other was to buy it, which was demeaning and expensive. On the whole, Lord Streetham thought he'd rather swallow his pride than risk swallowing a much harder object—like the end of Desmond's sword.

No man had ever run afoul of the Devil and emerged from the experience intact. Lord Gartwaite's jaw had been so severely dislocated that he'd been subsisting for the past twenty years on gruel. Billings was mouldering in the family crypt because he'd made an ill-chosen remark about the former Angelica Ornesby. Even the Devil's own brother had walked with a limp ever since attempting to cheat the Devil of the few trinkets left in their father's will to the younger son.

These represented the smallest fraction of gentlemen who had at one time or another taxed Devil Desmond's patience too far. The curst fellow always found out somehow what was said or attempted behind his back.

Lord Streetham gave a superstitious shudder as he turned his carriage through the gates of Elmhurst, then shrugged off the sensation. Desmond could not have known his belongings had been searched at Streetham Close, or he'd have given his host a most unpleasant time of it. The man did not have eyes in the back of his head, regardless what others believed.

*   *   *

Having steeled himself for a humiliating interview, Lord Streetham was both relieved and frustrated to learn, shortly after he met his hostess, that Mr. Desmond and his daughter had driven into Rossingley. The earl was relieved enough to wish to return home immediately, his purse and dignity still intact, but that would only mean he must repeat the same unpleasant journey Lady Potterby was at the moment commiserating with him about.

"Such unusual heat we have had, My Lord," she said as she led him into the drawing room. "So oppressive. We are sadly behind in our baking because the dough will not rise properly. Even when it does, who is to do anything with it, with the kitchen hot enough to bake bricks and the staff collapsing into the soup kettle?"

Lord Streetham agreed that the weather had been most un-English of late. Even the rain was far more like that of India in the monsoon season.

"Whatever it is, it cannot be like Greece," said Lady Potterby. "Those seedlings my grand-niece and Mr. Langdon planted are half of them dead already. Indeed, I do wonder they made such an experiment. Surely Mr. Langdon knows ours is not a Mediterranean climate. Jenkins is most distressed," she added, shaking her head. "But what could he do? They were so eager to test one of the theories in that lovely volume you so generously gave Mr. Langdon."

Lord Streetham had prepared himself to endure Lady Potterby's endless prosing for hours, if necessary, and had assumed the same state of half-attention he usually accorded his wife. He could not help wondering, however, why two young persons of the upper class (Miss Desmond was at least technically a member) should be labouring over seedlings. Why hadn't they left it to the gardening staff, who were paid to make themselves hot and dirty? Or was Miss Desmond's planting merely some needlessly laborious pretext for taking advantage of a naïve young man?

"I'm afraid I am not familiar with the book's contents—

which does not surprise me," said the earl. "My collection is so extensive and the demands on my time so great. Yet I supposed Mr. Langdon's interest was purely academic. After all, did not the ancients place great reliance upon conjunctions of certain planets and sacrifices to their pagan deities? Hardly the sort of theories to put to scientific experiment, I should think."

Though he spoke casually, Lord Streetham's mind was working at full speed. The massive tome Jack had clutched . . . the panicked look he'd darted at Desmond. The pages themselves . . . something odd . . . not thick and rough-edged—because, perhaps, they had never required to be cut?

Lady Potterby sighed. "I do not know what Mr. Langdon was thinking—who ever does? But he was a perfect sight when he came in to tea. Lord Rossing said he put him in mind of the grave-diggers in *Hamlet*, and asked whether they'd unearthed poor Yorick's skull." She did not notice the earl's slight start. "Delilah's maid declares she will never be able to remove the stains from that frock. How odd," Lady Potterby added, glancing toward the corner windows, her brow knit. "Now I think of it, I do not recall seeing the book again. Dear me, I hope Mr. Langdon did not leave it in the garden. He is dreadfully absent-minded, you know."

Lord Streetham too looked towards the window, though what he perceived was in his mind's eye—the stunning reality of what had occurred.

It had been Desmond's book contained in that elaborate binding, and the earl himself had given it to Jack. Then Jack, so easily manipulated, had done the Devil's bidding and buried it—there, just a few steps away, in the garden.

Not the slightest flicker of excitement was visible in his lordship's countenance, however, as he turned back to his hostess to agree in a good-natured, avuncular way that Jack was indeed absent-minded.

"We are still collecting articles he left behind, poor

fellow," he said with a small smile. "When his valet is not with him, one can only pray he will not present himself at dinner in his night-shirt. Very likely he did forget the book, and one day he will appear upon your doorstep, flustered and embarrassed, looking for it."

"One day!" cried Lady Potterby. "In the middle of February, no doubt. Good heavens, that fine volume might be lying in the dirt yet—and we have had two storms since Friday. I had better send one of the servants to look."

Lord Streetham rose. "No need for that. You've made me most curious about his experiment. If you don't mind, I'd like to have a look myself."

They went out to the garden, where they found the plants, as Lady Potterby had predicted, in various stages of decline. The book, however, was nowhere to be seen.

Lord Streetham stared hard at the woebegone flower bed. "You know," he said thoughtfully, "I wouldn't put it past the lad to have inadvertently buried the book in the process of turning the soil."

"Buried it! Good heavens, he could not be so muddled as that—and with Delilah by. Surely she would have noticed."

"If Jack was declaiming on Greek wisdom, she very likely had given all her concentration to following his discourse," said the earl smoothly. "I think I had better find a spade."

Less than an hour later, Lord Streetham was once more upon the road. A thick tome, its cover damp and dirty, lay at his feet. One quick glance at the contents had been sufficient to assure him of what he'd found.

Obtaining possession of the volume had been simple enough. He'd insisted upon doing the digging himself, because it would never do for the gardening staff to know of Mr. Langdon's folly. Then the earl had only to express the charitable wish to have the book repaired secretly, to spare Jack embarrassment. Lord Streetham had solemnly assured Lady Potterby the restored volume would be discreetly returned to the young man. All they had to do was keep the matter to themselves. After all, Jack was a very good fellow, and absent-mindedness was a trivial flaw in the great scheme of things, was it not?

Lady Potterby, properly impressed by this show of magnanimity, had yielded up the book without argument.

While his father was returning home with his ill-gotten goods, Lord Berne was gazing discontentedly in the general direction of France. To soothe his troubled soul, he compared his beloved's hair to a waterfall of black pearls, her ears to shells, her lips to pink oysters, and her eyes to the rolling ocean. He made a mental note to jot down these revelations for future use as soon as he returned to his lodgings.

He gazed with lackluster eyes upon a fancy bit of muslin who smiled encouragingly as she passed. He looked away towards the ocean once more and sighed heavily. These activities being not quite so productive as when performed for an audience, he resolved to leave for home first thing tomorrow.

Lord Streetham closed the cover of the book and smiled at the soiled binding.

The references to himself were so easily amended that it was foolish to destroy the manuscript, as he had in certain panicked moments thought of doing. The book would take England by storm, just as Atkins had insisted. The lively adventures, the impudent, witty style, together with the occasional scandalous revelation, guaranteed tremendous popular success. There might be lawsuits, but the profits could easily absorb the legal costs—and since Desmond had taken care to show Prinny and his siblings in a favourable, indulgently humourous light, there was small likelihood of sedition charges from that quarter.

At any rate, being the largest shareholder of the firm, Lord Streetham had a right to make the occasional correction. Even Desmond must admit as much—if, that is, he ever got wind of the matter.

Lord Streetham opened the book, carefully removed the pages from the false binding, and carried them to his writing desk.

Half an hour later he sat, pen poised mid-air, exactly as though some evil spirit whispering in his ear had distracted him.

Here was a remarkably tactful though highly entertaining account of Lord Gaines's drunken interview with a notorious bawd of the day.

Lord Streetham recalled the episode, having formed one of the small party of revellers, and wondered now why Desmond had been so discreet. He'd left out altogether the best part: the bawd's loud expressions of pity for poor Lord Gaines. His lordship had tried every one of her girls with so little success that she'd recommended he avail himself of Dr. James Graham's Celestial Bed as the only certain cure for impotence.

Lord Gaines had recently subjected one of Lord Streetham's propsoals to a scathing satire in the House of Lords, resulting in a most humiliating defeat. It would serve the foul-mouthed rascal right, said the fiend at the earl's ear, to have his personal inadequacies exposed to John Bull's mockery.

And what of Corbell and Marchingham? These thorns in Lord Streetham's side had once been numbered among Desmond's cronies. What amusing tales could be told of those two! With a judicious phrase inserted here, a short passage there, an occasional substitution of one word for another, these recollections would do a great deal more than make a fortune.

Lord Streetham smiled and set to work.

=9=

"To DINNER?" JACK echoed hollowly. "Here?"

Lord Rossing removed his spectacles and placed them on his writing desk. "That's what I said. There's no need to make a Greek tragic chorus, Jack. I've asked the Wembertons, which means, it turns out, we must expect Lord and Lady Gathers and their daughter as well, because they're visiting. Also, Streetham and his countess—though I never dreamed they'd accept, considering the distance."

"Good God," Jack muttered.

"I believed I ought at least offer to repay their hospitality to you—though one dinner can hardly repay a lifetime of it. They propose to stay with the Wembertons as well, and I daresay they'll all be quite cozy." Lord Rossing sniffed in disdain, then went on. "Also, Blenkly and his wife, and Lady Potterby and her guests. I've already sent out the other invitations, but Lady Potterby's ought to be delivered personally. Just run across, will you, Jack?" said the viscount as he handed his dismayed nephew the invitation. "I'd go myself, but last night's storm has stirred up my rheumaticks again."

Jack looked down at the folded sheet in his hand and sighed. "I wish you had war—mentioned this to me sooner. I was planning to return to London."

"Your valet has just come up from Town. Why did you make him take the journey if you only meant to go back again? Really, Jack, I begin to wonder at you. I would assume you had a touch of the sun, but you haven't been out of the house in nearly a week—and all you do in it is take out books and leave them strewn about while you gape out the windows. You're not ailing, are you, boy?"

"No, Uncle."

"Well, you'd better not. Let Fellows attend to you before you go. If you appear at Millicent's with that woebegone expression and your hair all up on end—stop that!" Lord Rossing commanded, as Jack's fingers began raking his hair. "One look at you and she'll start dosing you with brimstone and treacle and heaven knows what other foul concoctions."

Jack's hand dropped to his side and he walked slowly from the room.

Only when the door had closed behind him did his uncle give vent to a low snort of laughter.

"Mr. Langdon," said the valet reproachfully.

"Yes, yes, I know. My uncle just told me. I suppose I'd better comb my hair," said Jack, moving to the dresser. "He wants me to deliver an invitation to Lady Potterby. To dinner. Can you believe it?" He stared at his reflection in the glass. "I've been coming here since I was in skirts and not once do I recall my uncle entertaining. Not once."

"If you mean to go out, sir, you had better change. With the Hessians it must be the green coat and buff pantaloons," said the valet. He collected these objects and laid them out.

"I'm only running next door, Fellows."

"Indeed, sir, but you are not departing in that costume, unless you plan to muck out Lady Potterby's stables. As it is you will astonish the horses."

Plainly, Mr. Langdon's valet was not of the stoically all-enduring, self-effacing variety. Mr. Fellows had tried that technique early in his employment and found it unproductive. He had learned that if his master was not to disgrace him in public, the servant must speak his mind and maintain a tight rein.

Mr. Fellows was well aware that his employer, having

recently suffered a setback in an affair of the heart, required a suitable period of mourning. That is why Mr. Langdon had been indulged a solo trip to his uncle's. However, in Mr. Fellows's considered opinion, a week or so was quite sufficient period of lamentation for a healthy young man. It was now time for Mr. Langdon to be marched back—properly attired—to the world of the living. Besides, there was a young lady next door whose abigail's acquaintance Mr. Fellows had made this morning and wished to pursue. If the lady thought Mr. Langdon's appearance shabby, her maid would entertain similar conclusions about the gentleman's gentleman.

Immaculately groomed but heavy-hearted, Mr. Langdon walked slowly along the path which intersected the graceful line of tall elms forming the boundary between the two estates. Ahead the way cut through a rolling expanse of lawn dotted with oaks and more elms. In the shade of one venerable oak a herd of sheep languidly grazed.

All about him was the familiar tranquillity Jack had left London for. He'd come here hoping the serenity and isolation of Rossing Hall would soothe away all memories of his failure with the one young lady who might have made him happy. True enough, the disappointment and shame had subsided—but only because they'd been so violently uprooted and hurled aside by a tempest in the form of Delilah Desmond.

Jack knew he was infatuated with her. He had sense enough remaining to recognise that. But for the life of him he could not understand why. Always before his senses had responded in accord with his character and tastes. Even the impures he'd occasionally taken up with had been the quieter, more genteel of their breed. He loathed noise, confrontation, violence, and argument, yet he was obsessed with a Fury in human form. Well, not exactly a Fury, he amended, but she was at least as capricious and temperamental as any of the ancient female deities.

She screamed at him and struck him and humiliated him and scorned him, and through all the turbulence that seemed to whirl constantly about her—even on those rare occasions when she was relatively subdued—he wanted her. That was all, and that was everything.

This morning, after another tormented, sleepless night, he'd reviewed his situation and concluded he must either return to London and trust time and absence to cure him, or offer for her and let *her* cure him—or kill him. The last, he thought, was a deal more likely.

Though she despised him, she might consent. Given Society's prejudices, she may not have another suitable offer. He felt, as he always did when he considered her situation, a surge of compassion for her and anger at his fellows.

That was almost the worst of it. If the world had not persisted in visiting the sins of the parents upon the offspring, Miss Desmond might never have crossed his path. She might have been shackled as soon as she emerged from the schoolroom, and he would not be in so pathetic a case as to contemplate wedding a woman so admirably designed to make him wretched.

Besides, he chided himself as he took a shortcut through Lady Potterby's garden, marrying Miss Desmond was too extreme a remedy, even if she were desperate enough to consent. It was like cutting off one's head to cure a toothache. He would return to London directly after this curst dinner party.

As he approached the terrace, he came upon Miss Desmond, who, head bent and skirts whirling, was agitatedly pacing. Mr. Langdon had but a fleeting glimpse—though one sufficient to make him groan inwardly—of a pair of exceptionally fine ankles before she became aware of his presence and abruptly halted.

Then she did the strangest thing. She smiled, and the upward curve of her sensuous mouth sent every thought of London flying from Mr. Langdon's head.

As she stepped forward to greet him, he apologised for interrupting her meditations.

"You're a very welcome interruption, Mr. Langdon," said she, to his inutterable amazement. "We've been plagued with company all day. I only came out to talk to myself, since that was the only party with whom I could have a natural conversation. Decorum is heavy work," she explained.

"Then I fear you'll recall the welcome when you learn my errand, because I'm sent to bring you more of the same." He held up the invitation. "My uncle desires the pleasure of your company—and that of your father and Lady Potterby as well—at dinner Wednesday evening. I hope this is not excessively short notice. You might have wished more time to plan an escape to Mongolia perhaps."

Another smile. Mr. Langdon grew dizzy.

"You know there's no escape for me, Mr. Langdon. Anyhow, I did have notice. Lord Rossing was by earlier in the week to ask my aunt whether the date was convenient. Your errand only formalises the plans."

Mr. Langdon was too stunned by his remarkable fortune in finding Miss Desmond in gentle humour to think of questioning why his uncle had withheld this information.

"As long as my errand is not urgent, perhaps we might delay the formalities," he said, moved to unheard-of boldness by her amiability. "May I pace the terrace with you awhile and eavesdrop upon your 'natural conversation' with yourself?"

A faint colour tinged her cheeks as she shook her head. Several pins dropped to paving stones, loosening the long black curls they'd held. Jack looked at the pins and at the hair, and he was done for.

"Pacing is forbidden before company," she answered. "In fact, I'm supposed to restrain myself even in private so as not to feed a bad habit." She sighed. "The trouble is, I'm so full of bad habits that when I leave them off there's hardly anything left of me."

"Only a beautiful shell? Well, I shall have to make do," said Mr. Langdon. "Since you're so dangerously inclined to pace, perhaps we'd better avail ourselves of that genteel-looking bench behind you."

When they were seated, Miss Desmond told him of her trials and tribulations with all the callers who came expecting a "common little baggage," as she put it, and must be conquered by her unspeakable propriety. "It is perfectly excruciating," she complained. "After an hour I want to scream. After two hours I want to commit murder."

"You remind me of my friend Max," said Jack, smiling. "He's always complaining that propriety wrings all the spirit out of a chap and Convention is just another word for Strangulation."

"A man after my own heart," said Delilah. "You've mentioned him before, I think? Is this not the same fellow who claims that if something is pleasant, it cannot be correct?"

Mr. Langdon must have appeared very surprised because she laughed and said, "You needn't look so stunned. Sometimes I do listen, you know—and when I do, I usually remember. I have an excellent memory—comes of all those card games, I suppose."

"Then I'll be sure not to play you for high stakes, Miss Desmond. And I'll certainly be careful what remarks of Lord Rand's I share with you. Some of his pearls of wisdom are not fit for feminine ears."

"Yet you seem to admire him—or like him at least."

"He's one of the finest fellows I know," said Jack, neglecting to add that this noble fellow had stolen away the love of his life. "An old and trusted friend."

"Lord Berne is another such, I take it? He told me you've been friends since you were babies. I find that intriguing. You're a most puzzling man," she said. "From what you repeat of Lord Rand's wisdom and what I've seen of Lord Berne, they seem not at all the sort of friends I'd expect you to have."

"Because I'm so dull and conventional, you mean?" he asked. "Because I always have my nose in a book?"

"You mustn't imagine insults where none are intended. Besides, you know perfectly well that if I meant to insult you I'd do so without roundaboutation," she rebuked.

"Then what is so puzzling about my choice of friends?"

"I only meant that you're contemplative and serious," she answered, looking down at her hands. "Lord Berne has probably never had a serious thought in his entire life. I cannot understand what would make his company rewarding for you."

Jack smiled ruefully. "I can't expect all my friends to be Aristotles. I'd probably be bored to death if they were. Maybe I cling to these fellows because they make a change from the monotony of my own company. Is that so odd? Would you wish all your bosom-bows to be exactly like yourself?"

"Egad, no," she answered with a show of horrour. "I should throttle them all in five minutes. Only I haven't any bosom-bows. Nor will I get any," she added, glancing towards the house, "if anyone learns I've been entertaining you all this time unchaperoned."

She rose and Jack was obliged to follow, though it was not at all what he would have preferred. For nearly an hour they'd talked and she hadn't berated him or hit him once. He hadn't felt so serene in weeks.

Perhaps it was simply the vehemence of her behaviour—the flurry and collision and high emotion—which triggered so much emotion in himself. Maybe now that she had settled somewhat into her new life, she would not agitate him quite so much.

The end of this tranquil interlude, could Jack but have known it, appeared early Wednesday afternoon in the form of a cloud of dust. This gradually resolved itself into a pair of sweating horses pulling a dashing black curricle upon whose seat Lord Berne was perched. He'd decided that while rivals were all very well in the case of puerile infatuations, they would not do at all when it came to a Grand Passion. The enemy must be routed. There would be no more clandestine embraces in gardens or anywhere else, save where Lord Berne played the male lead.

The viscount did not customarily abuse his cattle, and would have arrived with a deal less lather if he hadn't needed a potent excuse for stopping at Rossing Hall. Jack's uncle might have easily enough walked over or around Lord Berne had that young man been lying mortally wounded in his path, but for dumb animals Lord Rossing had compassion.

For the weary horses' sake, then, he grumblingly allowed Lord Berne entrance. This did not mean the reluctant host wished to talk to his guest, however. He promptly abandoned Lord Berne at the library door and headed in the opposite direction.

Wasting no time, Tony launched his offensive as soon as he entered the library. Citing Atkins's report of what had transpired in the garden, the viscount demanded to know Jack's intentions toward Miss Desmond.

Being not only greatly taken aback by this unlooked-for assault but altogether unable to satisfy himself upon this very subject, Mr. Langdon was utterly incapable of responding.

Since Lord Berne had no intention of heeding any reply in the first place, Jack's stammering bewilderment spared his having to feign attention. The viscount mounted his attack.

"You cannot toy with her affections, Jack. I know what her father is and what he's done, and I know what people say of her mother, but that is no reason to take advantage of an innocent girl."

"Take advantage?" Jack repeated, dazed. "What are you saying?"

"You know very well what I mean. You think—" Lord Berne stopped short to stare at his friend in consternation.

"Oh, Lord, what *am* I saying? Forgive me, Jack. I must be mad." He began pacing, speaking rapidly as he did so. "I don't know what's happened to me. I tried to stay away, truly I did. But she draws me. No woman has ever—no, you will not believe it. You'll laugh—no, your heart is too generous for that. Oh, Jack, your friend is brought low, indeed." Lord Berne threw himself into a chair.

"Good God, Tony, what on earth is the matter?"

"The matter," the viscount repeated bitterly. "Everything is the matter. I can't eat, can't sleep, can't think. Oh, Jack, I love her. Can you believe it?"

"Well, yes, actually, I can. You're always in love with somebody," said Jack rather unsympathetically.

"Never like this. When before could I find no comfort elsewhere? But how can I think of my comfort, knowing the undeserved burdens that innocent angel must bear? An ill-fame, not of her making, blights her youth even before it blossoms. How can I find happiness anywhere, knowing the world is determined to destroy any chance of hers?"

His stunned foe sank into a chair.

Lord Berne got up from his to recommence his agitated march upon the carpet. "She wishes nothing to do with me, and I cannot blame her. Yet how can I keep away when there remains any hope I might be able to help her? Perhaps that would make her think a little more kindly of me. Only a little, Jack. I know I can't expect her to care—and I'm sure she deserves a worthier fellow. Yet if she'd but smile kindly upon me once, I think I could live on that, and die, if not happy, then a better man for it."

Any expression of selflessness was so utterly foreign to Lord Berne's character that Mr. Langdon might be excused for blinking once or twice to assure himself he was not dreaming. This could not be Tony Melgrave who strode back and forth before him declaiming upon his unworthiness of the seraphic being known as Miss Delilah Desmond. Tony deserving of her—of any woman's—scorn? Impossible, Jack told himself.

Aloud he said, "I see what the matter is, Tony. She's the first woman in your experience who did not collapse helpless into your arms the instant you smiled upon her. The novelty of the experience has obviously been too much for you. You're merely frustrated, and having never been so before you confuse the emotion with love."

"Why should you believe me?" Lord Berne ceased his pacing to take up a tragic pose at the mantel. "You know what a paltry, insensible beast I am. No one would believe me, and there's no one to blame but myself. Perhaps my family has indulged me overmuch, but I cannot blame them. A man makes his own character. Only I bear the guilt, and only I can make amends." He turned upon his friend a gaze so desolate that Jack experienced a profound twinge of guilt.

"No more," said Jack hastily. "You're making yourself overwrought, which always makes you behave recklessly. I'll ring for wine and you must try to collect yourself."

"I'm perfectly collected. You needn't fear I'll do myself— or your neighbours—as injury. I've thought the matter over long and hard, and I cannot bring myself to believe the situation is hopeless."

Lord Berne moved from the fireplace to perch on a chair opposite his friend. "You've seen her recently?"

Jack admitted he had.

"Did she speak of me? Did she mention what I said to her when we last spoke?"

"You were mentioned only in passing."

The viscount nodded sadly. "She suspected I wasn't in earnest, and my going away only confirmed her suspicions. But enough self-pity. I'd better tell you what I proposed." He proceeded to repeat the scheme he had suggested to Miss Desmond.

"So that explains the business at church," said Jack. "No wonder she was complaining of the visitors and calling herself a curiosity piece."

"Then they've begun to relent?" the viscount asked eagerly. "They've welcomed her?"

Jack admitted that such appeared to be the case.

"Then there's hope!" Lord Berne exclaimed. "That's all I wanted. My way is clear now. I will not rest until she's securely established, until no one will dare breathe a word against her."

The wine was duly provided, but it refreshed neither party. Lord Berne was too busy talking to remember to drink his, and Jack was too busy with his troubled thoughts to taste what he drank.

Mr. Langdon examined his own feelings and found them base. He was tormented only by lust, which had certainly not inspired him with any true compassion for its object or any heroic plans for her future happiness. He'd thought only of his own needs and railed inwardly against her for arousing them. There was nothing of finer sentiments in this, nothing remotely worthy of the name Love. Being a just man, he felt he must ease his friend's mind regarding the "intentions" referred to earlier.

"I hope, Tony, you won't give the business in the garden another thought," he said, feeling very awkward. "You see, she tripped and stumbled into my arms and . . . and I lost my head. I got soundly slapped for my impertinence. I was also told in no uncertain terms that my attentions were profoundly unwelcome. That was and is the end of it, I promise you."

After a moment's reflection, Lord Berne responded magnanimously that he had been over-hasty in seeing evil where it was not, and pronounced himself satisfied.

Not to be outdone in generosity, Mr. Langdon revealed that the subject of their discussion would be dining at Rossing Hall this very evening. He said he'd be most pleased if Tony would make one of the party, and later avail himself of a guest chamber.

"I'll make it all right with my uncle," Jack added with a weak smile. "Now you're here, he'll think the damage done.

Besides, if he can tolerate Blenkly, he can endure your company as well, I expect."

Having transformed himself into a model of unselfishness, Lord Berne offered to absent himself from the house for a while—after, that is, he had washed and changed—to spare Lord Rossing unnecessary irritation. There was no need to explain that his chosen place of exile would be the house next door. Jack was intelligent enough to recognise the impossibility of his friend's doing anything else.

Lord Berne was just turning into the front walkway of Elmhurst when he came upon Mr. Atkins, who'd recently been turned out.

Mr. Atkins's lot was not a happy one. Following his last interview with Lord Streetham, the publisher had returned to London to nurse his cold and contemplate ruin. No sooner had he arrived than he'd had the idea of appealing to Desmond's greed by forging a letter offering more money for the manuscript. The reply had been most disheartening. Today he'd come hinting at legal action, only to meet a stone wall of injured innocence.

Desmond had claimed to be the victim of scoundrels. His manuscript had disappeared, he'd insisted. After observing that one couldn't get blood from a stone, and assuring the publisher something would turn up, and vowing an unspeakable vengeance upon those who had stripped him of the fruits of his labours, the Devil had politely eased Mr. Atkins out the door.

Now the publisher was faced with the unenviable task of discovering whether it was his business partner or his author who was playing him false, and the hopeless task of wrenching the manuscript from either of these fellows' grips.

Mr. Atkins cast an unfriendly eye upon Lord Berne. Had the earl not placed so much confidence in this young coxcomb, the matter might have been handled in a properly businesslike way from the start.

Lord Berne immediately took umbrage at being glowered at by this low, sweating tradesman.

"Still nosing about, Atkins?" said he. "Looking for more scurrilous tales to carry to my father? You'd better take care. Neither Mr. Desmond nor Lady Potterby will be best pleased to hear how you lurk about the property spying upon the family."

Mr. Atkins answered that he had not been spying on anyone. A man was entitled to professional interest in the products of his trade, he hoped. "I only wanted—"

"My good man, what you want can be of no possible interest to me, I am sure," said Lord Berne in perfect imitation of his father at his supercilious best. "I hope you will not tax my credulity too far by attempting to persuade me Lady Potterby now cultivates literature in her garden. She's growing a library there, perhaps, and you were curious about her choice of fertilizer? Or did you suspect your publications were the manure used to enrich her soil? Indeed, that would explain your obsessive interest. Good day, sir," his lordship concluded, rudely brushing past him.

Mr. Atkins stood a moment staring after the viscount in mute indignation. "Insolent, sarcastic puppy," he muttered to himself. "You feign to misunderstand me, do you, and insult my trade—as though it did not pay for your coats from Mr. Weston and your starched cravats and all the rest. Manure, indeed. *My* work enriching the soil and—"

And then Mr. Atkins had a vision—of a spade handle standing a foot or so from an embracing couple. He saw as well Mr. Langdon coatless and spattered with dirt. Mr. Atkins asked himself, much as Lord Streetham had a few days earlier, why two members of the idle upper class should take to agriculture on such a punishingly hot day.

Lord Berne discovered to his regret that he'd been overtaken by Time's winged chariot, for he was shown into the house just as the two ladies were about to go upstairs to prepare for the dinner party. He therefore had the honour of a mere ten minutes' visit, during which he found no opportunity to speak privately with Miss Desmond.

Still, he made the most of the precious minutes. He appeared as subdued, chastened, and decorous a visitor as any fastidious duenna could wish. His speech had just the right air of mournfulness to persuade any onlooker he was the hapless victim of a merciless conqueror. The sad, furtive way in which his gaze helplessly sought Miss Desmond's left no doubt as to whom this tyrant could be.

"Plague take the fellow," the Devil muttered under his breath, when the viscount had taken his dejected leave. "Kemble is a clownish amateur compared to him."

The fair despot might have been touched by the moving sight of a young lord in the last stages of romantic decline had she been able to spare him her attention. This was impossible, because Delilah's mind was taken up entirely by Mr. Atkins. His reappearance had been most disquieting, and she had not been at all appeased by her father's entertaining reenactment of his performance.

If they had not been engaged for the evening, Delilah would very likely have dashed out to the garden, dug up the manuscript—had it been there to be disinterred—and either burned it or thrown it into the duckpond. Unfortunately, they were engaged, and she must bathe and dress and then sit still for an eternity while Joan battled with her mistress's unruly hair.

= 10 =

THE DINNER PARTY turned out to be a foreshadowing of the reception Delilah might expect in London. Even the tentative acceptance she'd recently achieved in Rossingley was not reflected in the manner of Lord Rossing's more prominent guests.

Lord and Lady Streetham were more patronising than ever, while their Gathers counterparts simply pretended Miss Desmond was an uninteresting piece of furniture. Since the former were now, like the latter, houseguests of the Wembertons, even that heretofore kindly group appeared stiffly ill at ease.

Delilah's situation was not at all improved by Lord Berne, who hovered about her constantly, despite his mama's apparently inexhaustible supply of stratagems to call him back to Lady Jane's side. Though Delilah wished he would consider her predicament and not make such a cake of himself, she was not entirely displeased with his behaviour.

Lady Jane was all sharp angles. Her chin was small and pointed. Her nose was narrow and pointed. Her eyes were very black and very sharp, and her voice, in perfect keeping with all this staccato, was high and clipped. She had curtly acknowledged their introduction with a snap of her chin, as though she were a pair of scissors and would like to snip Miss Desmond out of the scene altogether. Lord Berne's devotion was some recompense to Delilah for this rudeness.

Still, it was a relief to be seated by Mr. Langdon at

dinner, with Lady Jane and Lord Berne the length of the table away. As usual, Mr. Langdon was the soul of courtesy. He did not gaze upon Delilah with moonstruck eyes, nor heap fulsome compliments upon her aching head.

After dinner, though, he had to remain with the gentlemen, while the ladies retired to await them in the drawing room.

There Lady Potterby was drawn into conversation with Mrs. Blenkly, while Delilah, pointedly ignored by Lady Jane's allies, struggled to keep up something like a conversation with an excessively nervous Miss Wemberton. The latter was too tender-hearted to snub Miss Desmond, yet too aware of the ill-feeling towards her to converse enthusiastically. She kept glancing uneasily across the room at her mother, who was deeply engrossed with her houseguests.

"Is it wise, do you think, Eliza," Lady Gathers was saying, "to allow Mary to sit with her?"

Though Lady Wemberton was torn between loyalties, Lady Gathers's hint that Mary might be easily led astray was not at all acceptable.

"A few minutes' conversation will hardly corrupt my daughter," said Lady Wemberton, drawing herself up. "Besides, Millicent is a dear friend. One cannot choose one's relations, you know."

"One can decide whether or not to acknowledge them," Lady Gathers retorted. "But I daresay she grows senile and you tolerate her frailties for old times' sake."

"I can hardly cut the grand-niece without cutting the great-aunt," said Lady Wemberton.

"Yes, I suppose that is also Lord Berne's problem," snapped Lady Jane.

"The young men must sow their wild oats, my dear," said Lady Streetham, hastening to her darling's defence. "If he had any respect for that creature, he would not subject her to such unseemly ogling."

"Indeed, you know you would blush, Jane, to be regarded so," Lady Gathers concurred.

All the same, the ladies must have agreed it was more unseemly that Lady Jane not be regarded at all, for they soon united to place that paragon center stage.

The men had scarcely appeared when the ladies began hinting for music. Naturally, Lady Jane must perform first, since she had precedence over the other maidens.

"I knew it," Lord Rossing muttered to his nephew. "Sooner or later we must be treated to a lot of amateurish caterwauling and applaud it as musical accomplishment." More audibly he pronounced himself enchanted with the prospect, and begged Lady Jane to offer the company her Euterpean tribute.

When all the ladies except Miss Desmond looked blank at this, Jack seconded his uncle with the more lucid request that Lady Jane accommodate them with a song.

Lady Jane made a proper show of modest hesitation, then took her place at the pianoforte and trilled out a sharp staccato version of "Barbara Allen." Perhaps she ought to have sung "Greensleeves" instead, but Lady Jane had too much dignity to sing of being cast off discourteously. Nevertheless, her voice did grow a tad more shrill as Lord Berne crossed the room to stand near Miss Desmond and drop several sad, tender glances upon her.

He proved equally deaf to Miss Wemberton's melodic offering, though her tones were sweeter and softer than Lady Jane's. By the time Miss Desmond's turn came, there were several pairs of hostile eyes fixed on her.

Colouring somewhat, she demurred.

"Come now, Miss Desmond," said Lady Streetham with excessive condescension. "You needn't be shy. There are no harsh critics in this informal group."

Miss Desmond flushed more deeply then, though she dutifully moved to the pianoforte. With a brief glance about her she removed her gloves. Then she sat down and struck the first notes of an unfamiliar melody.

It was nothing like the old ballads typically heard at such small gatherings in the country. The song was Italian, and

Jack noted with dismay that the lyrics were not precisely proper for polite company. He glanced about him nervously, but all he saw was wonder in most of the faces about him as Miss Desmond's mezzo-soprano easily conveyed every throbbing nuance of the passionate song. Evidently few of her listeners were well-versed in Italian. He breathed a small sigh of relief as he turned his gaze to her.

When she'd seemed so reluctant to begin, Mr. Langdon's heart had pounded in sympathy for her apparent stage fright. Now, as he listened to her rich, beckoning voice, his heart beat with pride . . . and a longing that made him ache.

He glanced at Lord Berne and saw the same feelings openly displayed upon his friend's handsome countenance. Of course Tony loved her. He couldn't help it, any more than he could help showing it. Still, he might have been a tad more discreet. Miss Desmond would surely be the one to suffer for his lapse, as the expression on Lady Jane's face clearly augured. Her eyes were narrowed to two black points like stilettoes aimed at her rival's heart.

When the applause had died away—Lord Berne contributing a solo tattoo for a few seconds after the others had stopped—Lady Gathers smiled, showing all her teeth and most of the gums as well.

"Very pretty, Miss Desmond," said she with excessive condescension—and loud enough to drown out the other compliments. "You are generous indeed to treat so small a group to a display of your considerable gifts—though one trusts you plan to share that gift with a wider audience in time. No doubt you have thought of going upon the stage, as your mama did. I never had the pleasure of seeing her perform, but I daresay you have inherited her talents."

Jack heard more than one gasp, but his eyes were on Miss Desmond's father. The Devil said nothing, only gazed about him with a cynical smile before turning back to his daughter. Though she was rather pale as she rose from the piano seat, the face which met her father's glance was inscrutable. She turned towards Lady Gathers and smiled.

"You are too kind, My Lady," she said.

"Not at all," said Lady Jane, taking up the gauntlet. "Mama is quite right. Talent such as yours ought not be hoarded for small private gatherings, when it might delight the public."

"Ah, you believe one's skill should be used to the common good."

"Indeed it must. That is virtually an obligation."

"Then I wonder, Lady Jane, why you have not offered the public the benefits of your exquisite taste and elegance by becoming a couturière," said Miss Desmond sweetly.

Before Lady Jane had time to counterattack, Jack leapt into the fray.

"Really, it is most gratifying to hear the ladies speak so knowledgeably of Benthamite philosophy," he said hurriedly. "In order to be good, according to them, the object examined must be useful. The object, of course, refers to the matter under discussion, whether it be an abstract quality or a physical fact."

Apparently oblivious to the bafflement of most of his audience, Jack soared into the empyrean realms of the most abstruse philosophy, citing Plato, Aristotle, St. Augustine and others with no regard whatsoever to relevance or coherence, and with a great deal of Greek and Latin thrown in for good measure. He continued in this vein for at least a quarter hour, at the end of which time most of the company had withdrawn from the battlefield to less mystifying conversations. At last, when even his uncle had apparently dozed off, and Tony had retreated to the window—where he stood looking bored and cross—only Miss Desmond of Jack's listeners remained.

As he paused to look about him and draw his breath, Jack found Miss Desmond's eyes upon him. She smiled, and in that smile was so much gratitude that he could not resist drawing closer to bask in its warmth. He drew near enough to join her at the pianoforte, where she still stood.

"You are a 'verray, parfit, gentil knight,' " she said softly. "Thank you for coming to my rescue. I'm afraid I nearly provoked a scene."

"It was *she* provoked it," said Jack heatedly. "The effrontery of the woman, to speak to you as though you were a damned organ grinder's monkey. And her ill-bred daughter to take it up—pure, malicious ignorance. But that is what you get, Miss Desmond, for casting your pearls before swine. You sang like an angel, and made me wish I could banish this common herd from the paradise you created."

He had not meant to say so much, and for an instant wished he could recall the words. But only for an instant, until his gaze was drawn once more to hers and he discovered a soft light shining in her grey-green eyes.

"How beautifully you smooth my ruffled feathers," she said. "As beautifully as you routed my enemies. You have depths, sir, I had not imagined."

As a man accustomed to consider himself the most uninteresting, prosy fellow who ever existed, Mr. Langdon could not help but be agreeably surprised. Her words set chords vibrating within him, and this inner music crept to his tongue. "I wish," he began—then a shadow fell upon him. He looked around to meet his erstwhile friend's frown.

"Really, Jack, I do think you've edified the company sufficiently for one evening," said Lord Berne. "Have some consideration for our fair songbird. You give her not a moment to catch her breath." He bent a killing glance upon Miss Desmond.

She appeared not to notice, but another young lady must have because the latter was, as Jack noted, making her way towards them with all deliberate speed.

"I am hardier than you think, My Lord," said the songbird. "One tune is not so great an exertion as to require extended convalescence."

"But perhaps you want a change of scenery," he hinted.

"Now that is what I should like," said Lady Jane as she nipped out a position for herself between Lord Berne and Miss Desmond. "We spend every summer in the country, though I beg Papa to take us to Brighton instead. Everyone is there now, it seems. Is that not so, Tony? Aunt Lilith wrote that you were upon the Steyne every day. I wonder you did not remain longer. I daresay Brighton was as lively as London in the Season."

Lord Berne looked abashed, and to Jack's surprise, allowed his chattering companion to lead him away.

As Jack turned back to Miss Desmond, he experienced a disagreeably familiar sensation of something throbbing in the air about him, like the first ominous rumblings of a volcano.

"I wonder," she said in suppressed tones, "what invalid makes his sickbed upon the Steyne."

Mr. Langdon looked baffled.

"He wrote me, you know," she explained, her eyes very bright. "He was called away to some bosom-bow's bed of pain. In Rye. Really, what a full evening this has been. Most enlightening. I have learned precisely in what estimation I am held by the lords and ladies. She sings and remains a lady. I sing and immediately descend to the ranks of ballet dancers—only a bit higher on the social scale than the village idiot *he* appears to take me for."

Her low tones were crisp enough, but the glitter of her eyes and the slight trembling of her lower lip betrayed her. With a sinking feeling Jack perceived it was this last— Tony's falsehood—which had made the deepest cut.

"Miss Desmond, the ladies had to strike at the only place where they thought they could wound you, because you wounded their pride," Jack said quietly. "You know how matters stand with Lady Jane. Surely you're aware of her— and his—parents' plans."

"Indeed, I am sorry their plans do not proceed apace," Miss Desmond answered, lifting her chin. "Yet that is certainly not my doing. It's all his, but he lets them make a scapegoat of me—after he's made a fool of me."

Mr. Langdon underwent a short, fierce struggle with his conscience. Though he didn't want to defend Tony, the impassioned speech of this afternoon had left its mark.

"I know that can't be, Miss Desmond," he said finally, unhappily. "He should not have lied about where and why he'd gone. I suppose it was improper of him to write at all—yet I'm sure he did so because he feared you'd despise him otherwise. His father sent him away, you know," Jack added, growing uneasy under her searching scrutiny, "and his father controls the purse strings. It was only Tony's pride prevented his confiding this to you. That he's returned, in defiance of his parents' express command, speaks volumes, I think, of his regard for you."

Unable to meet her gaze with equanimity, Jack had dropped his own. It fell upon one white hand whose fingers nervously traced a corner of the pianoforte. Though her hands were graceful, they were not small and delicate. They were strong and expressive, with long, slim fingers that could play a deadly tune upon a pistol as easily as they could a passionate one upon the pianoforte. He thought sadly, that she might play any tune upon him she liked. He longed, even as he defended his friend, to feel those fingers in his hair.

He could not know that Miss Desmond, at this precise moment, had any thoughts of obliging him. She had struggled with her rage and hurt while he spoke. She had struggled, too, with embarrassment at what those feelings had caused her tongue to reveal. She would not for worlds have anyone know just how deeply she had been hurt, repeatedly, this evening. She too had her pride.

But pride, hurt, and rage had gotten all mixed up somehow with another sort of agitation she could not or would not define. She saw her companion's clear, compassionate grey eyes cloud over with some inner sorrow, and she wanted to comfort him as he'd tried to comfort her.

She wanted, at least, to push back the errant lock of hair that had fallen onto his forehead, as though by smoothing out his hair she might somehow smooth away his trouble as well.

Lord, what was she thinking of? She was not the maternal type. Delilah glanced towards the window where Lord Berne stood, entirely self-assured, his arrogant self again as he talked with Lady Jane. He certainly wanted no mothering, any more than Papa did. She looked away from Lord Berne and sighed.

While Lord Rossing's guests were either enjoying or making themselves miserable according to individual inclination, Lady Potterby's servants were engaged in the usual modest dissipations attendant upon their mistress's being out for the evening. The human denizens of the stables had settled down in their quarters to cards and drink, while the household staff had retired either to the housekeeper's room or the servants' hall, according to rank, to partake of punch and gossip about their betters. In their innocent enjoyment of an evening's freedom, not one loyal retainer suspected that a serpent lurked in their beloved mistress's garden.

If there was nothing sleek and sinuous about him, if his form was more porcine than reptilian, and if he was insufficiently cold-blooded for his task and trembled with terror every step of the way, Mr. Atkins could lurk as well as the next man, and lurk he did. He crept into the garden as the sky began to darken and slunk uneasily, starting at every imagined sound, to the bed where the ill-fated seedlings had been planted.

He would have felt a bit less terrified—but only a bit—if this had been an utterly black, moonless night. In such a case, however, his task would have been more difficult than it was already. He dared not carry a light and, not being as familiar with the site as he could wish, must find the spot before the descending sun made its departure from the heavens altogether.

What with starting and hesitating and imagining foot-steps where there were none and turning back half a dozen times for every dozen he went forward, he discovered the one barren square of soil just as darkness truly fell. Still, having come so far, he could not—would not, for fear and greed drove him on—go back and wait for a better oppor-tunity. He drew out his few hand tools (he had not dared bring anything so loudly incriminating as a shovel) from the pockets of his overcoat and began to dig.

He dug a hole, not so deep as a well nor so wide as a church door but, as Mercutio had once observed, it would serve. The excavations Mr. Atkins effected might have served, in fact, to bury a host of volumes and one or two owners besides. These efforts, to his unspeakable despair, did not serve sufficiently to produce what he sought.

Hours after he'd begun, as a few bold stars twinkled defiantly through the heavy overcast of late-night sky, Mr. Atkins sank down on his knees, defeated and near tears with frustration. It must be here. There was no other explanation. Yet there must be some other, because it was not.

He sat and mourned and raged by turns and rubbed his dirty, blistered hands against his forehead and got dirt into his eyes, which made them water, and up his nose, which made him sneeze. A slug began oozing over his fingers towards his shirt cuff. Shuddering, the publisher struck at it with the trowel, but only succeeded in gashing his wrist. While the slug crawled away unharmed, Mr. Atkins, eyes smarting, nose running, muscles aching, and wrist throb-bing in excruciating counterpart to his head, collected his tools, rose, and trudged out of the garden.

=== 11 ===

THOUGH HE'D EXPERIENCED some confusion the night before, an untroubled night's sleep was sufficient to revive Lord Berne's customary aplomb. He appeared at Elmhurst the morning after the dinner party, fully prepared to recover whatever credit he had lost. When the butler informed him that Miss Desmond was not in, Lord Berne was not too shy to ask where she had gone.

Bantwell certainly had no business telling him. Unfortunately, the butler was suffering the aftereffects of dissipation and, due to what seemed like a hundred nails driving themselves into his skull, was not thinking clearly.

Thus Lord Berne learned Miss Desmond had gone riding. He had only to bribe a groom to obtain a mount. Finding the young lady was not difficult, either. Forbidden any pace speedier than a trot and not allowed beyond the park boundaries, she could not go very far.

He found her decorously following the bridle path which circuited the park, her groom trotting at a discreet distance behind her. Peters, the groom, looked even more ill than the butler had. He was, in fact, rather green about the gills.

Lord Berne smiled. The gods were with him this morning. He erased the smile as soon as he was alongside his beloved, whose expression was not at all welcoming. Without further ado, Lord Berne threw himself at her mercy. He was despicable, he declared. He wished he might be flogged—no, a rack would be better—for the falsehood he had, in a moment of utter despair, committed to paper.

He was informed in flinty tones that his wishes could be of no possible interest to her.

Miss Desmond's icy hauteur immediately aroused Lord Berne as no coquetry could have done. Perhaps this was because, as Jack had supposed, such treatment was a novelty. Lord Berne had encountered feigned indifference before, but this Arctic fury was another species altogether, and held all the exotic thrill of travel in uncharted lands.

"It's as I feared, as I knew it would be, then," he said. "You will not forgive me, and it were futile to explain, to exonerate myself."

"I wish, sir, you would divest yourself of the delusion that anything you do or say could be of any possible concern to myself."

"Is it a delusion, Miss Desmond? Would you be so angry—would you hate me so if what I had done were a matter of indifference to you?"

Her eyes flashed, telling him he had scored his point.

"Spoken with all the conceited arrogance of a true coxcomb," she retorted hotly. "But what do you care how you insult me? I only wonder you take the trouble with one so utterly beneath your notice."

No woman in his whole life had ever spoken to him so, and no one could look so ravishingly enraged while she did. Lord Berne grew giddy with desire.

"Despise me, then," he said. "Loathe me. Tell me I disgust you. At least there's feeling in that. At least I inspire you with some sort of passion." He saw her raise her riding crop. "Will you strike me? Do it," he urged. "I cannot tell you the relief it would bring me."

"How dare you!" she gasped, goaded nearly to tears. "But of course you dare. You think you can say any filth to me you like. And like a fool I remain passively enduring it. Well, I've amused you long enough." She spurred her horse and dashed ahead.

Being by no means taken unawares, Lord Berne set off in pursuit, as did the less prepared groom. Unfortunately,

Peters's physiology was in no state amenable to a gallop. In less than a minute he was forced to halt, so that he could dismount and vomit into the bushes. By the time he could look up again, Miss Desmond and her pursuer were out of sight.

"Atkins, I admire persistence. A man gets nowhere in this wicked world without it. But I must tell you frankly, sir, that your case now passes the bounds of British tenacity and hovers on the brink of obsession. I told you I haven't got it. You may offer a million pounds, and the Crown of England in the bargain, and I still won't have it. The manuscript is no longer in my possession."

Mr. Desmond's smile was regretful, even pitying, yet something in his eyes caused Mr. Atkins to step back a pace.

Desmond, even at his amiable best—which he was not this morning—was a formidable figure. All the same, Mr. Atkins was desperate. If he was obsessed, he was entitled to be, when his entire future was at stake, when ruin and desolation stared grinning into his face.

"Are you quite sure, Mr. Desmond," he asked poignantly, "you have no idea who *has* got it? No suspicions?"

"If I had suspicions," the Devil answered, "I would act upon them, don't you think? If I suspected, for instance, that you would not accept the word of a gentleman, don't you think I might be a little affronted?" He went on, still smiling, but with a warning in his voice that matched the warning in his glittering green eyes, "Yet as you see, I am perfectly at ease. I imagine no such slight to my honour. You are only concerned I may have experienced a momentary absence of mind—a failing, like physical enfeeblement, regrettably common among men of my advanced age."

As he spoke, Mr. Desmond advanced upon his guest, who found himself backing towards the door.

"I appreciate your concern," the Devil added, as Mr.

Atkins collided with the door handle, "but I do hate to be fussed over, you know. Ungrateful creature that I am, it makes me irritable. I had much rather, Mr. Atkins, you ceased fussing."

Mr. Atkins's courage—no reliable quality in him anyhow—deserted him entirely as the towering dark figure closed in on him.

"In—indeed, sir, I understand per—perfectly," he stammered. "Most annoying, I'm sure. Very sorry to have troubled you. Good day, sir." He grasped the door handle, wrenched the door open, and stumbled into the hall and against a very large potted palm. The tree tottered and Mr. Atkins made a grab for it, dropping his hat in the process. The tree swayed back into place, its fronds quivering. Trembling likewise, Mr. Atkins turned to retrieve his hat and found Mr. Langdon standing in the way, frowning at him.

Mr. Langdon's frown was attributable to the fact that his life had become a burden to him. From the moment last night when he'd caught Miss Desmond's furtive glance at Lord Berne and heard the ensuing sigh, Mr. Langdon had seen the light. Or perhaps the darkness was more apt a metaphor, because what he saw threw gloom upon every facet of his existence.

It was Tony she sighed for, Tony she longed for, which ought to be perfectly agreeable, since Tony was sighing and longing for her and they were well matched in every way, from their physical beauty to their restless, passionate natures. Yet try as he might, Mr. Langdon could find no joy in contemplating this pair formed by nature for each other. He found so little joy in it that he wished he were dead.

Still, whatever he felt, he knew he had no business behaving so rudely to Mr. Atkins. Though he would like to knock the fellow down for continuing to plague the family, Jack had no right to do so. No one had appointed him guardian of the Desmonds' peace.

Accordingly, he schooled his features into a thin semblance of politeness and—perhaps to make up for this poor show—retrieved the publisher's hat and returned it to him with something like a pleasant greeting.

"Th—thank you, sir. Kind of you, I'm sure," Mr. Atkins mumbled, turning the hat round and round in his hands. "So clumsy of me. Business, you know. So pressing." He darted a frightened look at the study door, then, with a stammered "Good day," scurried away.

Mr. Langdon scarcely heard the farewell, being preoccupied once more with the matter of hands. How curious that so well-fed and well-groomed a City-bred fellow should have such ill-cared-for hands. Mr. Atkins's fingernails had been ragged and grimy, the digits themselves red and blistered. This was odd in a man whose primary labour was the shifting about of pieces of paper and the consumption of vast quantities of ink.

The butler appeared, breaking in upon Mr. Langdon's reflections.

"Her ladyship has just come in from the garden," said Bantwell. "She says that if you will be so kind as to excuse her appearance, she will be pleased to meet with you in the drawing room."

Mr. Langdon was duly led in and announced in unsteady tones by the red-eyed, but otherwise pale, butler.

Lady Potterby looked rather peevish and ill as well, an appearance she explained was the result of unwelcome news from her gardener. "He insists we are overrun with moles, Mr. Langdon, which is most distressing."

"Moles?" Jack echoed blankly.

She nodded. "Jenkins tells me there are holes everywhere. He's beside himself. The lavender half uprooted and the lilies a shambles and I don't know what else. At least the worst of the damage was—" She caught herself up short as Mr. Langdon's eyes widened. "Well, it is most tiresome, and I shall spare you the details."

Mr. Langdon, upon whom an awful suspicion had just

dawned, hurriedly dispatched his errand by returning Lady Potterby's fan to her. He then asked after Miss Desmond.

Upon learning the young lady was sufficiently recovered from last night's jollities to go riding, he expressed his satisfaction and made a hasty departure.

He had just broken into a run, preparatory to a mad dash back to the Rossing stables for his horse, when, turning the corner of the hedge, he narrowly missed colliding with Mr. Desmond.

"All this dashing about in the height of summer—it is a wonder you young people have not succumbed to heat prostration," said the Devil. "Well, you *are* young."

Mr. Langdon rather incoherently concurred with this observation.

"Since you are thirty years at least younger than myself, Mr. Langdon, I wish you would get my horse back for me, and save me some exertion."

"I beg your pardon?" said Jack distractedly.

"That knave—Berne, I mean—has borrowed Apollyon and gone gallivanting with Delilah. I particularly wanted to ride today and I particularly want my own horse," said Mr. Desmond in aggrieved tones. "Apollyon and I are accustomed to each other. We are quite intimate. I got him from Wemberton two days ago in trade for an ill-natured grey."

"Indeed, sir," said Jack, practically hopping with impatience.

"So will you not borrow a mount and get my horse back for me? Her ladyship's stable is nearer to hand," the Devil added, "and I am in rather a hurry."

No horse can sustain a gallop forever, regardless how inconsiderate its rider. Miss Desmond was boiling mad, but she was not inconsiderate. Out of compassion for dumb beasts she was eventually compelled to slow her mount.

She glared at Lord Berne when he rode up alongside her once more.

"Go away," she said, panting. "Go to the devil."

"I come to his daughter instead. Gad, but you ride well," he said admiringly. "We must hunt together one day."

"Are you deaf? You are not wanted. Go away."

"You know I can't. You are the woman I've been searching for my entire life." His voice dropped to low, thrilling tones of urgency. "You must let me speak."

"To insult me further?"

"There was no insult in what I said. Only you made it so. Still, it served my purpose."

"Your *what*?"

"I wanted to be rid of the groom, which you did for me by becoming enraged and galloping away. Were you not aware he was too ill to follow?"

Miss Desmond glanced behind her and knew an instant of alarm. She was alone and unprotected in the company of a libertine who had deliberately manipulated her into this predicament. Nonetheless, she reminded herself, this was her great-aunt's property. He would not dare misbehave. She willed herself to be calm as she turned to meet his gaze, and was taken aback by the piteous longing in his countenance.

"It was only because I could not speak what was in my heart while others were by," he said tenderly. "I must speak because, despite your mistrust—oh, I admit you have reason—but despite that, despite my parents' warnings, Hope persists. How can I help it, worshipping you as I do? I must hope . . . or die."

In her short life, Delilah had heard enough sweet talk to fill all seven volumes of *Clarissa*. Since she had never, however, heard Lord Berne at his heart-stirring best, she might as well have spent her twenty years in a convent. His voice easily drowned out the one in the back of her head which was shrilly recommending she return to the house immediately.

He raised every objection she could have to him just as though he had direct access to her brain, then answered each objection as brilliantly as if he had been on trial for his life. It was not so much his rhetoric that held her, however, as the boyish innocence of his handsome face and the sincerity of his tones as he gave her to understand she was the most beautiful, brilliant, altogether admirable woman who had ever existed.

Upon Delilah, who had endured virtually unceasing disapproval in recent days, his idolatry fell like rain upon an arid field. Even had she been less vulnerable, she would have been hard put to resist the kind of heartfelt declarations which had so effectively crushed a considerably more objective Mr. Langdon only the day before. When it came to the game of love, Lord Berne was a tactical genius. Had Napoleon been a woman—though every bit as brilliant a commander—the viscount might have dispatched him in a week.

It was not so surprising, then, that even Miss Desmond's skeptical heart was touched. Though she said little, her countenance must have spoken for her, because Lord Berne's tones changed subtly from pleading to coaxing. In a remarkably short time he had persuaded her to dismount and walk with him, so that he might pick a nosegay of wildflowers for her.

They walked, and he picked the flowers, and looked so much like a schoolboy experiencing his first calf love that he made her laugh, which undermined her defences even more effectively than the rest.

"You don't laugh nearly enough," he said tenderly as he presented the posies to her. "If you were mine—"

He did not complete the sentence because, evidently, his heart was too full. Or perhaps his arms were too full, since they'd already encircled her. In the next instant, the bouquet fell neglected to the ground as he kissed her.

It began with a mere touch of his lips upon hers, light and teasing—but clearly skilled, because in seconds and virtually without her realising, the kiss grew deeper and more fervent, just as the light circle of his arms strengthened into a crushing embrace. He worked so subtly and quickly, in fact, that Delilah felt like one caught in a treacherous undertow which was tugging her gently but inexorably towards the open sea of destruction.

Just as it was dawning on her to disentangle herself, Lord Berne drew away and apologised. Then he promptly embraced her again, declaring himself helpless, lost, confused, bewitched, overcome.

He did not, however, declare himself in the more formal, accepted manner. That is to say, no hint was given concerning rings or parsons or a company of witnesses, and Delilah, though rather giddy, only teetered on the brink of being swept off her feet. Then she regained her balance and pushed him away.

His eyes glistening with tears, he begged her to take pity on him. He worshipped her. Just one more chaste kiss— that was all he wanted. He took both her hands and kissed the fingers, then the palms. Then he fell to his knees, still firmly clasping her hands, and—apparently too distracted to realise what he was doing—began pulling her down to him.

Though Delilah was not a fragile young miss, she was hardly a match for a six foot, twelve stone male in excellent physical condition. She tried to pull free, but his grip was relentless. He was deaf to her protests, being utterly absorbed in his all-consuming passion for her, and she had neither dagger nor pistol with which to restore him to full consciousness.

She would have to kick him in the usual place, she concluded—though, despite her apprehension, she rather wished she didn't have to. Still, Papa had ordered her not to be seduced, and she most certainly had no intention of being ravished in a field, like some unfortunate dairy maid. She closed her eyes, steeled herself, and was just raising her foot from the ground when she heard what sounded like thunder.

She opened her eyes again and looked towards the sound. Lord Berne, surprised, looked too, and released her hands abruptly when he saw what it was.

Though his was not a violent nature, the spectacle which met his eyes as he rode across the meadow threw Mr. Langdon into a towering rage, and an impulse seized him to trample his childhood friend into a bloody pulp.

Fortunately, Jack's better nature reasserted itself. Masking his fury, he coldly informed Lord Berne that Mr. Desmond's horse was wanted.

"You'd better go at once," said Jack, "because you're wanted at Wemberton as well. A message came from your mother not an hour ago," he lied, "and I've been looking everywhere for you."

Though Lord Berne's mother was forever summoning him and he saw no greater urgency in this latest demand, he did suspect that withholding the Devil's horse while simultaneously attempting to ravish his daughter was a tad excessive. Besides, with Jack by, there was nothing more to be accomplished with Miss Desmond at present. Quelling his frustration, Lord Berne consoled himself with one languishing glance at his beloved before taking his leave.

Jack now turned his own gaze to that dazzling object. "Where's your groom?" he demanded.

"I haven't the least idea," Delilah answered with great nonchalance. "Probably several miles back, casting up his accounts. Not that it is any concern of yours, sir," she added haughtily, though two spots of colour blazed in her cheeks.

"If you ride with Tony unescorted the matter will be everyone's concern, Miss Desmond."

"I am still unescorted, as you put it," she returned. "If you have so much regard for petty gossip, you would be better employed finding Peters." She marched towards her horse, which was tethered to a nearby bush.

Jack quickly dismounted and followed.

"Since I am obviously not a lady, I can mount without assistance," she told him as he came up beside her.

Mr. Langdon lost his temper. "Damn it all!" he snapped. "I'm very sorry I interrupted your *tête-à-tête*, Miss Desmond, but I wish you'd save your righteous indignation for later. I only came because we have a problem. That is, *you* have a problem. Really, I don't know why I've been galloping about Rossingley like a lunatic and telling lies to my friends when you're so splendidly capable of managing your affairs." So saying, and oblivious to her sputter of outrage, he flung her none too gently into her saddle.

A stunned Delilah gazed for a moment speechlessly down upon the unkempt brown head of this unexpectedly masterful Mr. Langdon.

"What problem?" she finally managed to gasp out.

"I saw Atkins just now," said Jack, glaring at her right boot. "His hands were all blistered and dirty. Then your great-aunt told me some nonsense about moles invading her garden. I think Atkins has got hold of the memoirs. I thought you'd wish to know. I should have told your father instead," he grumbled. "He at least doesn't use me as a whipping boy."

He stomped back to his own beast and mounted.

Delilah drew up beside him. "Are you sure?" she asked, alarm quickly superseding all other emotions. "How could he possibly have found out? And why would he be at the house again if he's already got them?"

"I don't know. I know only what I saw and heard," was the grudging response.

"Oh, please, don't be angry with me now," she begged. "I'm sorry I was nasty, but I was—" She hesitated.

"Was what?" he asked testily.

She bit her lip and dropped her eyes. "I was embarrassed."

Her frankness was disarming and Jack was, in spite of himself, disarmed. She had only to appear the slightest bit repentant or troubled and his heart went out to her, in spite of his brain's warnings that she was a consummate actress. Really, it was no good his brain telling him anything, because he just wouldn't listen.

Suppressing a sigh, he told her he was not angry, only anxious. They had better hurry back to find out if they could whether his suspicions were founded in fact.

With a nod, Miss Desmond urged her horse on, and the two hastened back to the house.

"Oh, Lord," Delilah cried as they arrived, panting, at the book's grave-site. The flower bed looked as though it had been bombarded with cannon.

"If he did find it," said Jack, "it was obviously not on the first attempt. And one cannot tell from this whether he did dig in the right place."

"Well, I'm going to find out," said Delilah. She started moving down the path towards the potting shed, but Jack stopped her.

The gardener, he told her, was already beside himself. Jenkins would not remain quietly elsewhere if anyone set foot in his domain with a spade in hand. Furthermore, he'd be sure to inform Lady Potterby, and how did Miss Desmond propose to explain further outrages to the garden?

"I'll make some excuse," she answered impatiently.

"You have no more excuses. There's no sign of the seedlings. They're obviously destroyed."

"So I'm to stand idly by, not knowing whether the manuscript is already on its way to print?" she cried.

"I wish you'd keep your voice down," Jack warned. "Do strive for a little patience, Miss Desmond. I'll come tonight and search. Tomorrow morning first thing I'll report to you."

"No, you will not. I can search tonight myself—"

"You most certainly cannot. A young woman—at night—all alone—digging in the garden? Are you mad? If Atkins failed last night he may try again—or he may send someone better adapted to such labour. You don't know who you may run up against."

Delilah glared at him. "What does that matter? I'll bring my pistol."

"This is no enterprise for a lady."

"Since I'm obviously not—"

"Miss Desmond, I just told you I'd see to it—and I'll see to it *my* way. If you even think of leaving the house tonight I shall—" He paused briefly, then in steely tones went on, "I shall *spank* you."

Delilah stared at him. As usual, his hair was untidy and his clothes had subsided into their customary matching state. At the moment, however, his face was that of a stranger. It was positively feudal. The eyes gazing down his long, aristocratic nose at her were as steely as his voice, and the set of his jaw was the very model of dictatorial obstinacy.

She was not in the least impressed by this display of masculine arrogance, she told herself, though her heart proceeded to raise a fuss all the same.

"How dare you?" she said, rather breathlessly. "I am perfectly capable of digging a hole." She lifted her chin and turned to leave.

He seized her wrist. "What *you* are capable of is beside the point. I'll do what needs to be done, and that doesn't include spending the night worrying about the safety of a rash female."

Worrying? Was he truly anxious about her safety? Really, that was rather . . . quaint of him, she told herself, while her heart drummed against her ribs. Then she became acutely aware of the hand closed about her wrist and a most puzzling sensation of weakness in her limbs. Baffled, she stared hard at his hand. He quickly released her.

"Excuse me," he said. "I did not mean to manhandle you."

"No, I suppose not," she answered, feeling dreadfully confused. "Not unless I'm disobedient, I gather."

He gave her a faint smile. "But you won't be, will you, Miss Desmond? You won't try my patience, I hope?"

Miss Desmond sighed and promised to do as he bid.

= 12 =

As he learned a while later, Mr. Langdon had not told falsehoods after all. There had indeed been a summons for Lord Berne, who had already left to accompany his parents back to Streetham Close by the time Jack returned to Rossing Hall.

Relieved that he would not have to endure his friend's quizzing, Jack quickly set about preparing for his evening's skullduggery. The first order of business was to get rid of his valet, who was given the night off. Though Mr. Fellows lingered in the house until after dinner—to make certain his master donned proper attire—he did leave at last, and Jack could ransack his own wardrobe free of prying eyes and ironic comments.

Eventually he found an old set of clothing suitable to his purposes. After donning these, he sat down with a volume of Andrew Marvell's poetry to wait.

Delilah had intended, as soon as she returned to the house, to inform her father of Atkins's apparent treachery. She could not. Mr. Desmond had gone out and did not plan to return until very late that evening, Lady Potterby disapprovingly informed her grand-niece.

"Some card game or cock fight, I suppose," Lady Potterby muttered. "But that is to be expected. I only wonder he has remained so quietly at home all this time."

As predicted, he did not return for dinner and when, several hours later, he had not yet put in an appearance,

Delilah decided this was just as well. She really ought not say anything to him until she was certain the memoirs were gone. Otherwise he might go after Mr. Atkins and get himself taken up for assault on an innocent man.

Since no festivities were scheduled for tonight, the household made an early bedtime. By ten o'clock, having dismissed her maid, Delilah was curled up in the window seat of her bedchamber, gazing out at the darkened expanse of park towards Rossing Hall.

She would have preferred a view of the garden, but her room was on the wrong side of the house. As it was, she doubted she'd be able to see anything, even if Mr. Langdon did come that way, and she had no way of knowing whether he would.

Still, she waited and watched as the old clock in the hall downstairs tolled eleven o'clock, then midnight. The clock had scarcely left off chiming when she discerned a faint light moving between the row of elms. Immediately her heart began pounding.

Lud, wasn't that just like him—to bring a lantern. What if one of the grooms was up and about in his quarters by the stable and spied the light?

Jack darkened his lantern and placed it on the ground. Having decided that, if caught, he would simply confess all, he had brought along a spade, which he now plunged into the earth. He had just emptied his third shovelful when he heard a faint creak, then rustling. There was a light patter of footsteps, and Jack looked up to see a dark figure approaching. It was not a tall, dark figure. He uttered a sigh.

"I told you to keep away," he whispered as the figure drew near. "Must you be so pigheaded?"

The object of his rebuke hesitated but a moment before stepping closer. In the moonlight Mr. Langdon was able to ascertain that Miss Desmond had thrown on a coat obviously not her own. The coat, which dragged on the ground, would have comfortably covered two or three Miss Desmonds. Though she clutched her large wrapping tightly about her, a peep of white at the neck and another near the toes sufficiently indicated what was beneath.

Drat the woman! She'd come out in her night-rail, for heaven's sake. How in blazes would he explain *that* if they were caught?

"Go back in the house this instant," he whispered harshly.

This Miss Desmond firmly refused to do. Since arguing with her was bound to prove only an exasperating waste of time, Jack decided to ignore her and go on digging.

Because he had not dug a very deep hole originally, not many shovelfuls were required to confirm their fears: The false book and its contents were gone.

Miss Desmond stared for a long while at the empty hole. Then her head bent and her shoulders began to shake, and in another moment Jack heard the unmistakable sounds of weeping.

He thrust his spade securely into the dirt and stepped back to take her in his arms. Accepting the offer of comfort without protest, Miss Desmond pressed her face against his chest and sobbed like a child while he patted her back and muttered every sort of consolation he could think of.

Even if Atkins had the memoirs now, there was no reason her father could not get them back again, Jack told her. Was her papa not a brilliant man? Besides, Atkins was terrified of him. One confrontation and the nervous little fellow would give up his purloined goods. He must. Since he hadn't yet paid in full for them, he didn't legally own them.

Under this calming influence, Miss Desmond's weeping gradually abated. Regrettably, Mr. Langdon did not have the same tranquilizing effect upon himself. At the moment, the young lady was a somewhat awkward bundle, but it was *she*, all the same. The feel of her face pressed against his coat was very pleasant. The proximity of her person, even with all that coarse wrapping, was agreeably warm. His comforting pats gradually became gentle stroking, and very soon, Jack was in agonies.

He wanted to bury his face in her hair. His fingers itched to caress her neck, her shoulders, to fling away the dratted coat and . . .

She raised her head just as his right hand was about to plunge into her tangled hair. The hand paused mid-air.

"Oh, Jack," she said softly. "You're always so sensible."

Jack? "Jack?" he echoed stupidly, stunned by the beckoning sound of his own dull name. His hand dropped to her shoulder. His face was beginning to lower to hers when another word intruded upon his consciousness: *sensible?*

As she saw him withdraw, Delilah immediately set about persuading her crestfallen self she was vastly relieved. She had sensed a kiss coming, and certainly he had no business . . . but that was no good, she realised with dismay as she drew away from the comfortingly strong arms. She'd wanted him to kiss her. Good heavens—she'd even called him by his Christian name!

"Excuse me, Mr. Langdon," she said, backing away and nervously rubbing her nose on her coat-sleeve. "I should not have been so familiar. I was—distraught. Thank you so much. You have been very—very—kind. I—I had better go in now, I think. And you had better go home. The night air, you know. Most insalubrious, my aunt says," she babbled. Then she turned and fled.

She sped up the backstairs, pausing only to return Bantwell's overcoat to its peg, and on to her room.

She threw herself down at the dressing table and began savagely brushing her hair. Two minutes later she put down the brush and went again to the window. By now he was gone, and what possible consolation watching the faint light move through the park could have been to her, she could not imagine.

Delilah leaned her head against the glass. How very

comfortable and safe she had felt, held securely against his hard chest. Well, that was nothing. Jack Langdon was as safe as houses, quiet and diffident and scholarly and serious.

She blinked. Not when he kissed her, though. Not when he lost his temper and *threw* her onto her horse. That had left her dumbfounded. She hadn't realised he was so strong. After all, hadn't they been well matched during their tussle at the inn? Or had that been more of his chivalry? Very likely. He'd held himself back because a gentleman could not hurt a woman, murderess or not. Damn his gallantry. Why must he be so honourable, always, and make her feel more ill-bred than ever?

Her eyes itched, threatening tears. Angrily she rubbed them away, telling herself it would serve him right if she used that honour to manipulate him into marrying her. Certainly that would solve her problems very easily. She'd never need have a moment's anxiety about her parents' future. After all, Papa was not getting any younger. He could not go on living by his wits forever.

Mr. Langdon would take care of her parents. She needn't fear they'd be tossed into debtors' prison or be left to languish in a workhouse or spend their declining years in sordid lodgings, waiting to die. At the same time, their daughter would be spared the mortification of striving to be accepted by a Great World which didn't want her.

Given the way Lord Berne's family and friends had reacted, gaining acceptance was going to be a more formidable battle than Delilah had imagined—even if her own heedless behaviour did not continue to trip her up. Now, with the memoirs gone, it seemed she was to be defeated before she'd even begun.

All the same, she chided herself, Delilah Desmond was no coward. Here was a man who, while perhaps physically attracted—which was nothing, since every male seemed to be—could barely tolerate her, and who only irritated her and made her behave badly. A choice between entrapping him and tackling Society was no choice at all. She left the window, kicked off her damp slippers, and crawled into bed.

Directly after breakfast the following morning, Delilah asked her father to ride with her. As soon as they'd left the stables, she informed him of all—or nearly all—that had transpired the previous day. She thought it wisest not to mention her struggle with the love-crazed viscount.

Though mildly amused at Mr. Atkins's intrepidity and unable to suppress a chuckle when he learned of Mr. Langdon's midnight assault upon the unfortunate flower bed, Mr. Desmond endeavoured to show a proper sympathy for his daughter's distress.

"In truth, my dear, I do curse the day I ever began the dratted thing," he said. "I never dreamed my paltry tale would arouse so much powerful emotion in so many breasts. Chicanery, collusion, deceit on every side. Conspiracy in the dead of night. Where it will all end, I shudder to guess. No doubt we can expect rioting in the streets of London. Wellington will have to be recalled to restore the peace. Prinny will be most cross with me. I will probably be imprisoned for sedition."

Delilah gasped. "You're teasing, I hope, Papa."

Her father smiled. "Exaggerating, perhaps. Yet he was not happy with the Hunts. They were sentenced to two years in prison for the unflattering portrait of him they printed in the *Examiner*."

"Surely far worse insult than what you wrote appears in the print-shop windows daily."

"Florizel is capricious, and at present we have insufficient funds for lawyers."

"Good grief," she said, dismayed. "And all I worried about was scandal."

"You worry far too much, my dear. I do not understand why you cannot be like your peers and leave worrying to the lower orders."

Mr. Desmond appeared to study his daughter with profound curiosity. Then he shrugged and said, "All the same, I suppose I had better attend to Mr. Atkins forthwith. I shall depart for London tomorrow."

"*We* shall depart," Delilah corrected.

The parent raised an eyebrow, but the stubborn set of his daughter's mouth boding a tiresome argument, he resignedly agreed she might as well see a bit of London before the Ton descended in force.

The matter settled between them, it remained only to be settled with Lady Potterby, who at first, as was expected, made every objection. She was no match, however, for two persuasive Desmonds. By mid-afternoon, her ladyship was driving herself and her servants distracted with a frenzy of packing.

So great was the uproar within Elmhurst that time for only the barest exchange of civilities could be spared the two visitors who simultaneously appeared upon the doorstep. Lord Berne and Mr. Langdon were hustled in and out of the house so speedily that their heads were spinning as dizzily as those of the servants.

Dear Mr. Langdon,

I hope you will excuse the family's rather cold reception today, and in particular my own inability to express my gratitude for your exceedingly kind assistance. Papa has asked me to convey his thanks as well as his apologies for the great inconvenience we have caused you.

We were unable to thank you properly because we have been all about the ears, trying to do a week's worth of packing in twenty-four hours. As you may expect, we leave immediately for London, in pursuit of The Odious Mr. Atkins (though, naturally, my aunt believes it is on other business).

I suppose it is improper of me to write you, but Papa could not, being occupied with supervis-

143

ing arrangements. I thought it the lesser impropriety to write than to leave without a word. You will pardon me, I know. You are too chivalrous to do otherwise.

Please believe me your most grateful,
Delilah Desmond

Of course she'd go, Jack told himself as he stared numbly at the paper in his hand. He'd known that even before he'd entered the frenzied household next door. Her father would be off in pursuit of Atkins, and the daughter must go with him because she refused to believe men were capable of managing their own affairs.

All the same, if the Devil was so clever, why did he not pack his daughter back to Scotland at least, out of harm's way, while he handled matters himself? In London she was bound to get herself into some sort of trouble or other. Town held too many temptations, too many ways of going wrong, and being Delilah Desmond, she was sure to plunge headlong into all of them.

Slowly Jack traced the handwriting with his finger. He'd never seen her writing before, yet that too was what he would have expected. It was strong and bold, nothing delicate or ladylike about it. But it was a woman's hand nonetheless, just as hers was a woman's body, supple and curving . . . and he had just better not think about *that*.

The trouble was, as it had been from the start, he could not stop thinking about her. He had not known a minute's genuine peace since he'd met her. Now at last he would be rid of her maddening presence. Rossingley would be tranquil again, and he might read his beloved books in untroubled solitude.

He gazed about him at the rows of volumes which filled his uncle's library and grew unbearably weary.

"Don't," he murmured to himself. "Don't be stupid."

He got up and took a turn about the room, stopping once at a window to gaze disconsolately at the row of elms that blocked his view of the house nearby. Then he left the library, walked upstairs to his room, and summoned his valet.

"I'm leaving for London," said Jack. "Tonight. You may follow tomorrow or the next day—whatever is most convenient. I shall want you to bring all my things."

Mr. Fellows might have raised a protest had he not previously learned that a young person named Joan was to be hauled to London much against her will the next day. Therefore he merely nodded and immediately set about packing his master's belongings.

While the Desmonds, accompanied by a greatly baffled Lady Potterby, were completing the first stage of their journey to Town, Lord Berne was having another row with his father. This was not surprising, for the viscount was very much out of sorts.

He had been on the brink of achieving his heart's desire with Miss Desmond when Jack Langdon had rudely interrupted. Now the dazzling enslaver was on her way to London, where private audiences would be a deal harder to come by. Nonetheless, Lord Berne was not daunted by the challenge, nor by his sire's thundering and threatening when informed of the son's intentions to depart for Town.

Lord Streetham might as well rail at Fate or the weather. He could not disown his heir, whatever he threatened, and the bills would come regardless of the stoppage of allowances. The earl elected another tack.

"I appreciate your conscientiousness, Tony, but it is quite absurd to keep after the chit. I have no use for her now. The memoirs are safe in hand. I was able to deal with Desmond myself," the father mendaciously added.

Lord Berne returned that he didn't give a bloody damn about any stupid book. Some matters had a greater claim on a man than tiresome business dealings. Furthermore, he was not to be imprisoned in the country with a lot of razor-tongued, narrow-minded, sharp-faced females while the grandest girl in the world languished neglected nearly two hundred miles away.

He did not add that what he truly feared was not Miss Desmond's languishing neglected, but quite the opposite. One more peril of Town was the abundance of idle young gentlemen like himself. Instead, the viscount made his papa a curt bow and stalked majestically from the room.

Mr. Atkins entered not long after. Having given the matter long and painful thought, he'd decided to advise his partner to give up the memoirs as a lost cause. He also gallantly recommended that Lord Streetham dispose of his shares in the firm while there was still time to salvage something from the wreckage.

Lord Streetham smiled as he stepped away to his writing desk briefly. He returned with a handful of pages which he gave to the baffled publisher.

"The memoirs," said the earl—unnecessarily, for Mr. Atkins had already begun reading.

A moment later, Mr. Atkins looked up. The glow of his face was almost beatific. "My Lord, this is extraordinary. How did you do it?"

"Let us simply say I left no stone unturned. Desmond is deep, devilish deep, but even he can be excavated, if one is diligent."

"Devilish indeed," said Mr. Atkins, too filled with wonder to appreciate the earl's puns, though these amused the noble gentleman immensely. "This bit about Corbell—I had not remembered it being quite so revealing."

"Yes, it is a great piece of wickedness, but that is what the hypocritical public demands. I will want a few weeks to complete my review—it goes slowly because Desmond's hand is virtually illegible. Then you may be sure I will personally deliver the work to you. Meanwhile, I suggest you take a well-deserved vacation, Atkins. I would recommend a location some distance from London."

Small drops of moisture appeared upon the publisher's brow. "I b—beg your pardon, My Lord?"

"Desmond is not to be relied upon, as you have already learned to your cost. I am concerned he will once again experience a change of heart and demand his work back. If you are not at hand, however, he cannot trouble you. I am forced to go to London on pressing family matters, but you may rest easy on that score. The work can be stored with my solicitor, and I shall take only parts of it to Melgrave House as I need them."

The handkerchief came out and was applied to Mr. Atkins's brow.

"Do not make yourself anxious, Atkins," said the earl with a thin, cold smile. "But do set out at once, and be sure to keep me apprised of your direction so that I may contact you when the time is right."

= 13 =

WITH THE RISING of Parliament and the coincidental rising of the stench of the Thames, London becomes a vast wasteland. Though the City itself may appear to be teeming with life, the West End acquires a funereal air, for the majority of the upper classes have departed. Some go to their country estates and others to any of several resorts, of which the Prince Regent's architectural whims have made Brighton the most fashionable.

Mr. Beldon, to his unspeakable frustration, was not a participant in this exodus. He was temporarily confined to London due to a misunderstanding with his tailor, vintner, boot-maker, and landlady which could not be resolved until he first came to an amicable arrangement with a money-lender. This, to Mr. Beldon's great astonishment, had proved exceedingly difficult.

As he wandered listlessly up and down Bond Street, Mr. Beldon was weighing a future in King's Bench Prison against exile to whatever godforsaken spot of the continent was not in the greedy grasp of the Corsican monster. These meditations came to an abrupt halt, as Mr. Beldon did, when a far more animate and spellbinding vision appeared before him. He blinked, rubbed his eyes, blinked again, and pinched himself. Then, being a true patriot, he hastened to alert the kingdom.

Within hours, the few benighted souls remaining in London were apprised of the startling circumstance that Devil Desmond was in Town, and with him a black-haired beauty who must be Cleopatra or Helen of Troy reincarnated.

By the time the news reached Brighton, it was enhanced by more intriguing information: The beauty was none other than the Devil's own daughter, an even more exotically gorgeous creature than her infamous mother. Upon seeing her, it was said, Lord Argoyne had driven his phaeton into a hackney. Sir Matthew Melbrook had tripped over his own walking stick and fallen face down into a puddle. In short, every time London's gentlemen spotted Miss Desmond in public, they fell to pieces.

Fortunately, these occasions were exceedingly rare, because Lady Potterby, for some reason—possibly to whet appetites—seemed determined to keep the girl under wraps.

Mr. Langdon was surprised by neither the stir the Desmonds' arrival caused in London nor the rapid influx of previously rusticating members of the Beau Monde. In fact, he might have predicted with precision which gentlemen would be camped upon the doorstep of Potterby House—if, that is, Lady Potterby had permitted such an outrage. She did not. Neither she nor her grand-niece was at home to any of the gentlemen, which was only to be expected.

It would do Miss Desmond's reputation no good to be receiving a lot of idle rogues when none of the ladies wished to have anything to do with her. As Jack learned from the gossips, not one of Lady Potterby's numerous feminine acquaintance had deigned to call.

Though he, like all the rest, had been denied every time he had called, Jack persisted. Finally, after he'd been in London nearly a fortnight, he had the luck to meet up with Mr. Desmond in St. James's, and that gentleman was gracious enough to escort Jack to Potterby House himself.

The visit was a distressing one. Miss Desmond strove

mightily to appear untroubled, but anxiety was writ plain in her shadowed eyes.

As he was leaving, Jack could not help taking Mr. Desmond aside to express his concern.

"Yes, I know she looks ill," said the parent. "She worries too much. I have not been able to locate Atkins, though I've had both his house and his office watched day and night. Then, of course, there's the Great World. They don't want her, it seems."

"Would it not be best," Jack suggested hesitantly, "if she were to return to Scotland—temporarily at least?"

"It would be best, but she's stubborn, and I'm afraid her great-aunt abets her in this. Neither will admit defeat. I tell you, I'm greatly tempted to tell her ladyship the truth about the book. I have threatened to do so, to make Delilah go back to her mama, but my heart is not made of stone, Mr. Langdon. How am I to resist my daughter's tear-filled entreaties? Really, sometimes I think we have all lost our minds. Perhaps I should have shackled her to the blacksmith after all."

"Of all the unjust, narrow-minded, un-Christian, hypocritical, perfectly beastly—why this is infamous!" Lady Rand cried. "There, Max, did I not tell you it must be so? When every time I asked what ill they knew of Miss Desmond, those nasty creatures would only tell me tales of her mama and papa. Where should I be, I ask you, if the world judged me by my papa?" She jumped up from her chair. "Oh, I have been much amiss. I *knew* I ought to do something—but I let a lot of horrid prigs intimidate me. Where is my bonnet?"

"Settle down, Cat," said the lady's husband. "You can't go off slaying dragons at this hour. Besides, if you go rushing to Potterby House looking all wild-eyed, they'll pack you off to Bedlam."

"Certainly the matter will keep until tomorrow," said

Jack, taken aback by his hostess's sudden tempest. "I only wanted to make sure—"

"Of course you did," Lady Rand interrupted, rushing back to him to take his hand in a firm clasp. "You were quite right to tell us. Only I do wish you had done so sooner. That poor girl—to endure such humiliation—and how poor Lady Potterby can bear it—to see her so-called friends all turn their backs on her. Really, it makes me so angry I can hardly see straight."

Mr. Langdon was not sure at present whether *he* could see straight. He had not remembered Catherine's being so volatile. Sympathy for Miss Desmond's plight he'd expected, for Lady Rand had a powerful sense of justice. He had not, however, expected an explosion of outrage, and certainly not that the viscountess would contemplate dashing into the streets to right Society's wrongs on the spot.

The Catherine Pelliston he had known had always been coolly intellectual and quiet-mannered. Except once, he recalled, when a villain had attempted to wrong *her*. He and Max had posted off to her rescue only to find that the small, fragile-looking creature had rescued herself by dint of crippling her adversary.

"Of course you're angry, sweetheart," said Lord Rand. "But if you can't see straight, you dashed well won't think straight. Can't be going off into fits. Also, I wish you'd leave off clasping Jack's hand to your bosom," he complained. "It's starting to make me see red—or maybe that's only the colour his face is turning. Have a heart, will you, Cat, and leave the poor chap alone. Ain't he got enough on his mind without you trying to seduce him in front of your husband?"

Mr. Langdon's hand was abruptly dropped as the lady rounded on her lord.

"You," she said, "are a low-minded wretch. Here we are talking about an innocent female driven from pillar to post and you—"

"My apologies, madam. You were only trying to comfort

him, I suppose. Still, you must remember we were rivals once."

"And you are monstrous tactless to say so." Lady Rand reverted to Jack, her face reddening now as well. "Really, I wonder you continue friends with such a clodpole. Please forgive us both."

"Actually," said Jack, "I'm flattered that such a dashing fellow still considers me a rival. I suppose," he added, glancing down at his cravat, "it is this handsome waterfall arrangement of Fellows's."

Thus the awkward moment passed. In fact, as he left his friends some time later, Jack was surprised at how very un-awkward their reunion had been. Though he liked Catherine no whit less than he'd always done, he had felt no stir of envy or regret for what might have been.

Until he'd met her, he had never been able to carry on an easy conversation with a woman of his own class. But she'd understood him from the first, had never been puzzled or irritated by his bookish ways. She had taken him just as he was, and in her company he had discovered the delights of feminine conversation. Those glimpses into a woman's mind, so different in such surprising ways from a man's, had been glimpses into a new and fascinating world. He had been sorry to lose that.

Now he perceived he'd been unforgivably foolish to believe either Catherine or Max would drop him simply because they married. They were so far from doing so that they'd leapt at the opportunity to do the favour he asked.

The following day, Lady Potterby was stunned by Bant-well's announcement that Lady Rand was at the door.

"Good heavens, show her in!" she cried. "What are you waiting for?" As Bantwell was exiting, she turned to her grand-niece. "The Demowerys, my dear. Excellent family. Lord Rand is brother to Lady Andover, a great hostess, and their papa is the Earl of St. Denys—and even his Royal Highness is afraid of *him*. Oh, I wish you had taken more

152

trouble with your hair. It is such a jumble I don't know what Lady Rand will think."

Delilah bit back the automatic retort that she didn't care two straws what Lady Rand thought. She did care, very much.

This was the first female visitor they'd had since they'd arrived, and Delilah's heart fluttered with anxiety as she pushed hairpins back into place. If Lady Rand didn't like what she saw, Miss Desmond was doomed.

That she was to be spared social destruction for the time being was evident within five minutes of the viscountess's entrance. Lady Rand began by apologising to Lady Potterby for presuming upon a very distant—perhaps forgotten—acquaintance, but she understood that Lady Potterby had known her mama.

"Of course I have not forgotten your lovely mother," said Lady Potterby. "Indeed, to see you is to see her again, as she was in her first Season."

Lady Rand gave her a gratified smile. "Yes, I believe she and your mama," she said, turning to Delilah, "came out in the same Season. I am very sorry your mother has not come to Town with you," she went on, as Lady Potterby's eyes opened wide in consternation. "I should have so liked to meet her. I am sure she is one of the most courageous women I have ever heard of."

"She believed her presence would reflect badly on me," said Delilah, determined not to skirt the issue, despite her aunt's warning frown. "Men are forgiven everything and women nothing. Courage, you see, is not the quality usually attributed to her."

Lady Rand made an impatient gesture of dismissal. "The world is too often unjust and utterly blind. 'Convention is the ruler of all'—and no one understands that some souls are strangled by convention."

Miss Desmond's rather defensive mien softened. "Yet we cannot each make our own rules or we should have chaos," said she. "So our elders tell us, anyhow. Mama broke the rules. Don't you think that in admiring her you countenance the overthrow of civilisation?"

"Delilah, pray do not be impertinent," Lady Potterby warned.

"*Are* you impertinent, Miss Desmond?" Lady Rand asked ingenuously. "I thought we'd embarked upon a philosophical debate, and I was just beginning to enjoy myself." She turned her enormous hazel eyes full upon Lady Potterby. "Pray let us continue. I was about to quote Ovid."

"Ovid?" Miss Desmond repeated, wracking her brains for the apt quotation, while her great-aunt appeared ready to faint from shock.

"I was about to remind you 'the gods have their own rules.' "

"And Mama is now raised up to Olympus. How immensely gratified she will be to hear of it!"

The exchange following was so rapid, so filled with Greek, Latin, and French, that Lady Potterby threw up her hands in defeat. Still, unbecomingly intellectual as the debate might be, it was a conversation, and both young women seemed happy. The mention of Mrs. Desmond had given Lady Potterby a turn, for she'd instantly expected more unpleasant reminders of the family disgrace, like those they had endured at Rossingley Hall.

Lady Rand was evidently not of the Gathers's ilk, however. Even if she had odd notions, she was one of the few permitted them. An eccentric Lady Rand was still a Demowery, a member of one of Society's first families. If she liked Delilah—and it appeared she did—the rest of the Beau Monde must learn to like her as well.

The Beau Monde received its first lesson the following afternoon, when Lady Rand took Miss Desmond driving in Hyde Park and made short work of any persons who dared show her companion anything less than deferential courtesy.

The second lesson was provided on the evening of the following day, when Lady Andover's dinner guests found the Devil's daughter in their midst.

By the third day, the invitations began trickling in to Potterby House. It had been discovered in the interim that Lady Rand and Miss Desmond were bosom-bows, not to be parted. More important, it had also been learned that Miss Desmond had taken tea with Lady Rand's mother-in-law, the Countess of St. Denys.

If this was rather hard on the ladies, it was doubly so on the gentlemen, many of whom had cherished hopes of making Miss Desmond's acquaintance without the usual restrictions.

"Still, she's bound to go wrong, sooner or later," Mr. Beldon assured his friend, Sir Matthew Melbrook, as they entered Lord Fevis's house together. "It's in the blood. Then they'll drop her like hot coals, mark my words."

Mr. Beldon's opinion represented one faction of Miss Desmond's male admirers. This group was convinced it was only a matter of time before she showed her true colours, committed some social outrage like those her parents repeatedly had, and was ostracised. In that case, she would need a protector. How long until this occurred and the person to whom she would turn in her hour of need were the subjects of intensive wagering.

The other, smaller, camp was more philosophical. These gentlemen secretly hoped Miss Desmond would not fail any of Society's tests or stumble into its many traps. She was a great beauty. Her conversation was lively, which made her company most agreeable. A lifetime of such companionship seemed equally agreeable, especially to those gentlemen sufficiently wealthy and securely positioned to marry where their fancy took them.

Lord Berne found neither camp to his liking, though the latter troubled him a great deal more. He knew that in his case marriage was out of the question. In any case, the notion of Delilah Desmond in another man's arms was insupportable to the point of madness.

He was, in short, boiling with frustration. When he'd finally been allowed into Potterby House, he had confronted a score of rivals, not to mention their frantic female counterparts. The women, except for those of the Demowery family, had no love for their dazzling rival. Still, wherever she was, they had to be as well—otherwise they were in danger of being ignored altogether. Besides, there were advantages to flocking about Miss Desmond: This formed a virtually impenetrable barrier between herself and the gentlemen.

As if there were not barriers enough, Lord Berne sulked as he restlessly prowled Lady Fevis's ballroom. One must be content with a single dance and then subside to the sidelines or else fight the crowd to snatch twenty seconds' meaningless conversation with her.

It was all Langdon's doing, the viscount was certain. There he was, the dratted meddler, politely elbowing Argoyne aside so he could bore Miss Desmond to death with his endless intellectualizing. Which of course the poor girl was forced to endure out of gratitude.

The viscount had no way of knowing it was Mr. Langdon's endurance being tested at the moment. He had just learned that Miss Desmond had promised a waltz after supper to Lord Berne.

"Are you mad?" Jack demanded. "Where the devil was your aunt when you consented? Has she not explained that you can't waltz without permission from one of Almack's patronesses?"

"One, yes," Delilah snapped. "Two, reminiscing with Lady Marchingham. Three, yes, but I forgot."

"Of all things to forget—"

"Because it isn't important," she interrupted. "As you know perfectly well, even Lady Rand cannot get me admitted to Almack's—and if the patronesses will not have me, I do not see why I must abide by their idiotic rules."

"This is the first ball you've attended. You don't even give them an opportunity."

"For what? To judge whether the daughter of an actress is fit for civilised company?"

Miss Desmond might have spared her breath, for Mr. Langdon had stalked off.

Damn her for the pigheaded creature she was, he raged silently as he tripped over the cane of some decrepit roué. As he was apologising, Jack spied Lady Cowper in conversation with Lady Andover. He made for the patroness and, his face crimson, choked out his request.

Emily Cowper was the least forbidding of the Almack's patronesses whom Jack had once incautiously labelled Gorgons. Naturally, the epithet had reached their ears, and they'd never let him forget it—though they'd not gone so far as to ban him from Almack's. This was not simply because he was too valuable a piece of merchandise in the Marriage Mart, but because most of these ladies found it more amusing to get their own back by tormenting the easily flustered book-worm at every opportunity.

Though she was better natured than the others, even Lady Cowper could not forbear teasing him unmercifully for several minutes, before Lady Andover intervened, asking her friend to take pity on the poor wretch. The patroness considered for another agonising moment before consenting. Then she crossed the room and presented Mr. Langdon to Miss Desmond just as the first notes of the waltz were struck.

Instantly, nearly every eye in the room was upon the couple. Behind their fans, disapproving matrons and disappointed debutantes—all of whom knew of Langdon's feud with the patronesses—clucked and whispered. Half a dozen young ladies who had sighed after Mr. Langdon all last Season in vain gazed with ill-concealed hostility at the black-haired newcomer with her strange, most un-British, tip-tilted eyes. Well, she would disgrace herself sooner or later. It was in the blood, was it not?

The newcomer was oblivious to the enmity she'd aroused. As one gloved hand lightly clasped her waist and the other her hand, her temperature shot up ten degrees. As if that were not bad enough, her heart must also take leave of reason and commence beating erratically. Delilah looked up at her partner in amazement.

"Are you sorry?" she heard him ask through the thundering in her ears.

"Yes," she gasped. "I think I am." She dropped her gaze to his neck-cloth and stared blindly at his diamond stickpin, which seemed to wink evilly at her.

"They'll stop staring in a moment, Miss Desmond. Only think what it would have been like had you done this without proper permission."

"It isn't them—" She caught herself as she realised what was on the tip of her tongue.

"What is it, then?" he asked, concerned. "What has discomposed you?"

"Nothing. I thought I'd missed a step."

"Impossible. You are the most graceful woman in this room. I'm sure every man here wishes I would be struck by lightning. Tony is glowering, for I have prevented his being first to waltz with you publicly."

True, Lord Berne was staring in a most threatening manner at his friend, but Miss Desmond could not spare any thoughts for him.

At present, she felt rather as though *she* had been struck by lightning. She was monstrous uncomfortable, despite her partner's assured grace. Her limbs felt awkward and stiff, and her heart was rattling along like a poorly sprung carriage. What the devil was wrong with her?

"I—I'm sorry," she stammered. "I seem forever to be causing you trouble."

"It's no trouble, Miss Desmond."

"You cannot deny I was most provoking."

"I should not have been provoked."

She glanced up at him in disbelief, and he smiled.

"I'm glad you wanted rescuing," he said, his eyes unusually dark. "I only wish I could claim every other waltz as well."

His hand pressed her waist more firmly, drawing her closer.

"Mr. Langdon," she feebly protested.

"Trust me, Miss Desmond. I am an accurate judge of distance." He spun her into a turn that brought her, for a moment, against his chest. But in the next they were the requisite twelve inches apart.

"You're very daring," she observed breathlessly.

"No," he said. "It only wants practice, and a naturally graceful partner. To be able to skirt the bounds of propriety, I mean."

"Only just, I think." Her eyes were once more upon the stick-pin.

"A few minutes ago you were prepared to flout convention altogether," he reminded with a smile.

"Are you trying to teach me a lesson, sir?"

"Oh, no. That is a prodigious waste of time. You will not be led, except in dancing. But we men are determined to lead in something, and I could not resist exploiting the rare opportunity."

It was the dance, she told herself. Waltzing was too much like embracing to music. It was too giddy-making, all this whirling about with everyone else whirling round you as well, in every colour of the rainbow—though yellow seemed glaringly predominant—and all that glitter of precious jewels. The room was too hot and too bright because there were too many candles and too many people.

Also, Mr. Langdon was much too close, or she would not have been so conscious of a crisp herbal scent, so light, yet decidedly *male*. Still, to increase the distance between them was to appear missish, which Miss Desmond most certainly was not. She only wished her brain would settle down so she could think.

Her brain refused to settle down, however, even after he

returned her to Lady Potterby, who promptly commenced the lecture Delilah knew she deserved. Being genuinely sorry, she tried to attend and make properly penitent answers, but her mind was elsewhere.

Repeatedly, Delilah's attention was drawn to one masculine figure. Her gaze followed Mr. Langdon as he made his way with easy grace through the crowd, pausing now and again to chat—usually with the gentlemen.

As she watched, she gradually became aware that she was not the only one. Countless young ladies were surreptitiously following his movements. Several even attempted to engage him in conversation.

Good heavens, they batted their eyelashes and fluttered their fans just as though he were . . . well, Lord Berne, for instance. And who was that brazen, carrot-haired baggage who dared to touch Mr. Langdon's coat-sleeve and treat him to that simpering smirk? As she watched him smile in that absent way of his and drift away from the coquette, Delilah drew a sigh of relief. Then, vexed with herself, she fanned her hot face furiously.

She was not left long to agitate herself, for her partners did not allow her to catch her breath again until supper was served. Then Miss Desmond had all she could do to keep from swatting her supper partner with her fan. Lord Argoyne was so dull, prosing on endlessly about his tiresome crops. Luckily, Lady Rand came to her rescue and very neatly rechannelled his grace's discourse in Lord Rand's direction, while the two ladies took up their previous discussion of Madame Germaine's prejudices against French silks.

The conversation grew more one-sided when they reentered the ballroom, for Delilah immediately began seeking Mr. Langdon's figure in the crowd once more.

"Miss Desmond?" said a familiar masculine voice. "I believe you had promised me the honour."

Delilah wrenched her mind and gaze back to meet Lord Berne's winning smile.

The smile was the product only of years of practice, for he was at the moment thoroughly enraged. He had not at all appreciated Miss Desmond's pink confusion as she danced with Langdon—or Langdon's smirking satisfaction. Why the devil couldn't the fellow leave well enough alone? Bad enough he'd got the Demowerys to countenance her, but he must bring Emily Cowper in as well. Next you knew, Miss Desmond would be tripping about the hallowed halls of Almack's, and so filled with gratitude to Jack that she'd fall into his arms—where she'd already seemed a deal too comfortable by half.

Her eyes had been too much upon Jack all night, the viscount reflected in vexation. Even now, as she apologised for woolgathering, her smile was annoyingly preoccupied.

"Only woolgathering?" he asked, leading her out. "That's a relief. I'd feared you and Lady Rand had been debating the Greeks, and that I'd interrupted your philosophical meditations."

"Not at all, My Lord. We were talking of French silks."

"Whatever you speak of, you make a lovely picture with your two heads bent close, one like amber and the other like jet. What makes the sight more agreeable still is the evidence of genuine friendship. That is rare between ladies."

Delilah rose to the defence of her sex. "We can be as staunch friends as the gentlemen, sir."

"Do you think so? I wonder. Look at the lady's husband. But a few months ago he and Langdon were rivals for her hand. Yet there is no enmity between them. Jack was his groomsman, in fact, and the two remain as intimate as ever. How many feminine relationships could withstand such a test, Miss Desmond?"

She looked up at her partner with clouded eyes. "You have me there, My Lord," she answered in a subdued voice. "Still, love is reputed to be a woman's whole life, while it forms only a fraction of a man's. Perhaps we're less forgiving in such cases because they are of more significance to us."

Lord Berne registered her dismayed surprise with satisfaction, though he took care to appear hurt. "You underestimate the strength of a man's affections," he reproved. "For some fortunate men there does come a love that consumes all else. Some of us give our hearts completely—and only once, for all eternity."

=14=

IF MISS DESMOND had begun to suspect what her trouble was with Mr. Langdon, Lord Berne's enlightening comments put an abrupt end to this species of self-examination. Delilah had not required the viscount's additional heavy-handed hints to grasp the facts of the case: Mr. Langdon had been and evidently still was in love with Lady Rand. That was unfortunate, considering the lady had given her own heart and hand elsewhere and seemed ecstatically happy with her choice.

Still, that was Mr. Langdon's problem. Human beings had been disappointed in love since the beginning of time, yet the human race continued. She need not go into mourning seclusion just because *he* was unhappy.

All the same, in the following days, her social life seemed to lose its sparkle. Potterby House was crammed with callers and the same glittering group of Fashionables surrounded her at every affair. They only made her weary.

She felt she never would fit in this world and began to understand why her parents had been as pleased to shun Society as it was to shun them. With the rare exception, such as Lady Rand, everything seemed so false about these people. Their excessive politeness barely masked a great deal of bored discontent, ill nature, and varying degrees of treachery to relatives and friends alike.

Caroline Lamb was only the most glaring example of the immorality that was all too commonplace, and she was castigated mainly because she had been indiscreet. Not that

Delilah wished particularly to contemplate Lady Caroline or the lady's abused husband. Miss Desmond saw too many similarities to her own temperament and wondered if she, like poor William Lamb's temperamental wife, must be one day goaded by boredom, frustration, and hunger for sensation to cast discretion to the winds.

Certainly the world seemed to expect it. Delilah could not shake off the feeling that the Beau Monde was waiting for her to fail . . . and fall.

There was as well her own mounting anxiety about the manuscript. Papa had been unable to locate either it or Mr. Atkins. Until that business was settled once and for all, how could she possibly feel at ease among the victims of her papa's pen? Even if the matter were settled at last, how long before she could settle her own business and get a husband? It seemed she would have to be a paragon of rectitude for ages before anyone would be sufficiently convinced of her virtue to marry her—and by then she would be too old. She'd never dreamed she'd be tested so. This might have been expected, since it was the way of the world, but she could not help feeling profoundly discouraged all the same.

Nonetheless, Delilah was not sufficiently weary of life to reject Mr. Langdon's invitation to drive with him, a few days after Lady Fevis's ball. His proposing an unfashionably early hour only added to his offer's appeal.

At least, she thought as he guided the horses into Hyde Park, the entire Beau Monde would not be there to gawk at her. For all that she was tired of being ogled, she had spent two hours fretting about what to wear. She was still fretting. She knew her green frock became her very well and her new capote was entirely *à la mode*, yet her companion appeared utterly oblivious. Or perhaps, being too honest to lie and too tactful to tell her she looked a fright, he had simply decided to hold his tongue altogether.

That he was the epitome of sartorial elegance—his linen crisply immaculate against the form-fitting brown coat—

only irritated her. Perhaps this was why she did not behave, as she'd intended, entirely carefree and delighted with her recent popularity. Surely this must be why, instead, all— or nearly all—her pent-up frustrations came spilling out of her, and she found herself confiding in Mr. Langdon more freely than she had even her father.

Papa was never home, she complained, and for all his investigations, day and night, could obtain no word of his manuscript. Aunt Millicent still scolded at least a dozen times a day, until the grand-niece despaired of ever pleasing her. Not a single occupation in which Delilah was truly skilled was she permitted. If she played cards, it must be for chicken stakes—and with idiots. She couldn't go anywhere without a chaperone. She could not go to gaming hells, Manton's, or Tattersall's at all. She was, in short, bored to tears.

"At least you have your routs and balls," said Mr. Langdon, after sympathising with these trials. "And, of course, all your beaux. That must be some compensation."

"I didn't come to London just to dance and flirt," she said crossly. "I came for a husband. I'm denied everything that might be pleasure and then I can't even get my business done."

He threw her an odd glance. "That is plain speaking."

She sighed. "Mr. Langdon, if I cannot be frank with you, then there's no one. Except for Lady Rand, the ladies do not invite confidences. If I were frank with most of the gentlemen, they'd get an earful, I promise you. But I must be unspeakably proper and pretend they're properly respectful, even when they stare at me in that disgusting way."

"They're bound to stare, Miss Desmond. But disgusting?"

"They *leer*, and I assure you it is not at all agreeable."

"I'd have thought you'd be accustomed to attracting attention," he said philosophically. "If the men do leer sometimes, you must understand that they may be unable to help themselves."

"They ought to help it. They could if they wished to. They don't treat other young women so. Imagine any of them *daring* to ogle Miss Melbrook."

"Miss Melbrook is not as beautiful as you are."

"She's accounted a diamond of the first water—and I am not begging for compliments, Mr. Langdon," she added, though to her distress she did feel unspeakably gratified. "They look at me the way they do because they're all waiting for my wicked character to reveal itself."

"That is a grave error on their part," he said. "You're not at all wicked. What you are is dangerous. I only wonder you haven't shot anyone so far, if you're so displeased."

She could not help smiling. "I cannot shoot them, since I cannot carry my pistol about with me," she said. "Evening dress is a tad too revealing, and a weapon does weigh down one's reticule."

"Still, if this behaviour distresses you so, we must put a stop to it. I could, I suppose, call the fellows out—but there seem to be a great many of them, which means a lot of rising at dawn and spoiling my boots in some muddy field. "No," he said gravely, "Mr. Fellows would never countenance that."

"I suppose he would not," she sadly agreed.

"You'll have to fight the duel yourself," he said as they approached the Serpentine. "But instead of swords or pistols, you must use a more formidable weapon—your eyes."

He drew the carriage to a halt.

"Now," he went on, "look at me—not at my cravat, Miss Desmond, though I admit it is an astounding sight. Full into my face."

Puzzled, she obeyed, though the instant she met his gaze she felt so uneasy that it took all her concentration not to look away. She'd never noticed before how thick and dark his lashes were or the faint beginnings of laugh lines at the corners of his eyes.

She grew more uncomfortable still when the dreamy grey eyes abruptly became those of a stranger. An exceedingly wicked stranger, moreover, whose bold survey began at her bonnet and continued appraisingly down to her neckline, at which point she felt she might as well not be wearing anything at all. He had not touched her—had not moved a fraction closer, yet it seemed as though his mouth and hands had been everywhere his glance had been.

An eternity later, it seemed—though it had been but a moment—the feral expression vanished.

"Was that the way of it?" he asked, quite as though he had merely recited a verse from the *Iliad*, instead of practically *ravishing* her with his gaze.

"Y—yes."

"I thought so. You nearly turned purple, Miss Desmond." Heedless of her sputter of indignation, he continued, "What you must do is immediately fix your mind elsewhere and stare right through the fellow."

"Elsewhere? How in blazes am I to do that with you— you leering so?"

"If you concentrate on what he's doing to you, you're bound to blush and appear discomfited, which will please the chap no end. If, however, you appear coldly indifferent, both to the stare and to him, you'll discomfit and confuse *him*. It does work, I assure you," he added. "I've seen Gwendolyn do it countless times, on far less provocation."

Whatever Gwendolyn could do, Miss Desmond must obviously be twice as capable of doing, she adjured herself as her companion once again commenced his visual assault. Though her pulse rate had apparently quadrupled and her entire body seemed to be burning up under his impudent appraisal, Delilah did as he ordered.

She stiffened her spine, adopted an expression of ineffable ennui, and let her own gaze flicker coldly over his face, as though instead of beholding a disturbingly handsome countenance, she were regarding a slug.

Since they were only playacting, it was with some surprise that she observed his colour deepening. A muscle twitched under his left cheekbone.

"Well done, Miss Desmond," he said rather stiffly. "Not that I'm surprised. I've been subjected to that withering expression before."

"That's impossible. You've just instructed me."

"Actually, it was more in the nature of a reminder. The skill you already possessed. You simply didn't realise it would be as effective on these occasions as on others."

"So long as it does work," she said, "I don't care whether I just learned it or knew it all along."

"I assure you it works admirably," he answered as he gave the horses leave to start. "That particular brand of aristocratic disdain cannot be learned. One is born with it. Keep that in mind the next time anyone tries to make you feel like—" he hesitated.

"A trollop, I think you mean."

He uttered an exaggerated sigh. "Madam," he said sorrowfully, "have you never heard of euphemism?"

Delilah was able to put her lesson to practical use that evening at a ball given by Lady Rand. The technique was unfailingly effective, giving Miss Desmond the satisfying assurance that without uttering a syllable she could make a rogue just as uncomfortable as he made her. This made the affair more enjoyable than any she'd attended previously. The ball was sheer pleasure from start to near-daybreak finish, and not a little of her joy, she admitted ruefully, was attributable to Mr. Langdon's lingering nearby for a sizable portion of the evening.

He must like me, she thought later, as she sat at her dressing table, making a vague pretence of brushing her hair. He wasn't a saint. He would not be so kind and . . . protective . . . if he truly despised her. Certainly he would not have encouraged his friends to rally round her if he did. That she knew he had done for her—had perhaps known it in her heart even before Aunt Millicent had pointed it out during a lecture about ingratitude.

There was something else in her heart, Delilah was forced to acknowledge as she put down the hair-brush. When he'd eyed her in that insolent way this afternoon, he'd shocked her to the core. Yet at the same time, his look had conjured up other confrontations—one kiss in particular. And within she'd felt . . .

She shook her head and rose to remove her dressing gown, but as the silk slipped from her shoulders and fell, unheeded, to the carpet, the feeling came to her again. It had been, she realised with dismay, *anticipation*.

Mr. Langdon did not rise until early afternoon. He had not expected to rise at all.

He'd always prided himself on his cool detachment. He'd even managed in the past few weeks to keep his head— more or less—during the hundred mutinies his baser instincts had attempted against his reason. Yet this same philosophical Jack Langdon had fled Lady Rand's ball shortly after midnight in a state bordering on insanity. He'd been seized with a fit of possessiveness so fierce that he must leave the place or commit mayhem.

The fit had come upon him the instant Delilah Desmond had entered. From that point on, it was all he could do to keep from swooping down on her and dragging her away. As it was, he'd planted himself at her side for at least half the evening while he scoured every masculine countenance for a hint of insult towards her. When he discovered what he sought, he could only seethe with impotent fury because he had no right to do anything about it. That she'd defended herself well, just as he'd known she would, had not improved his state of mind—or mindlessness was more like it—one iota.

He did not want them looking at her in any way, let alone talking or dancing with her. She was *his*.

Instead of pretending to be a civilised gentleman of the modern world, he should have been attired in filthy animal skins, grunting as he dragged his knuckles along the ground. That was what he'd felt when he'd danced with her the first time. She had remarked his sleek black coat and told him, in her light, practised way, that he looked rather dashing—and he had practically growled in answer.

When he'd felt his last vestiges of self-restraint deserting him, he'd made his exit. After attempting to relieve his feelings by kicking an unoffending lamppost, he had marched off to White's, to gamble away all his money and drink himself to death.

That he'd failed in the latter was evident when his eyelids scraped open and searing pain pierced the tender organs beneath. He shut them and struggled up very slowly to a sitting position. When he opened his eyes again, he saw Mr. Fellows, tray in hand, gazing down upon him.

"Good grief," Jack groaned. "No breakfast, I beg of you."

"Breakfast today comes from the chemist's shop, sir," said the valet as he placed the tray on his master's lap. "You had better drink it before you try the coffee."

Jack eyed the tray with revulsion. "What is that?" he asked, nodding painfully at the rolled-up newspaper lying next to the coffee cup. "Where is the *Times*?"

"I think, sir, you will find this particular organ of communication more enlightening today."

Less than an hour later Jack was at Potterby House, a torn sheet of newspaper crushed in his hand as he stammered a reply to Mr. Desmond's greeting.

The Devil glanced down at the crumpled paper. "Ah, you have seen it, Mr. Langdon. It seems I was mistaken in my surmises."

He took the paper from Jack and read aloud in mincing

tones, " 'Rumours are afloat that Society will be set rocking one month from today, when the first installment of the long-awaited, much-feared Reminiscences of Mr. Darryl "Devil" Desmond are scheduled to appear.' Lurid, don't you think?" said the Devil, with a cynical smile. "Buonaparte earns from the British public little more than a disdainful sniff—while my paltry tale is to trigger an earthquake. Really, one does wonder whether these journalist fellows would not be more profitably employed by the Minerva Press."

"Of course you don't mean to let them get away with this," said Jack. "We'll go to Atkins now. I'm sure we can stop him."

"My dear young man, what is the point of that? The damage is done, don't you see? You and I are not the only persons in London who read the newspapers—if one can dignify this tattle-rag with such a title."

He studied his guest's face for a moment. "Come, sir. You look to me a man in need of the hair of the dog." He steered Mr. Langdon into the late Lord Potterby's luxurious study and sent a servant in search of proper refreshment.

The servant had just appeared with the tray when Miss Desmond burst in and pushed him back out.

"Oh, Papa," she cried, running towards him.

Jack considerately closed the door.

What followed was not altogether coherent, though the language with which Miss Desmond denounced Mr. Atkins was plain enough, being composed of nearly every oath Jack had ever heard, in more than one language. She was, he was surprised to discover, more angry than alarmed. The only alarm she expressed regarded her father's safety.

"The hypocrites would say nothing to my face," she raged. "They only pretended they could not see me. But Joan heard plenty as we shopped, from the servants—and Papa, it's just as you said. The members of Parliament are already talking of sedition. It appears," she said scornfully, "your revelations will stir the masses to revolution."

"That's absurd," said Jack. As he caught her startled look, he realised—not with any great surprise—that she'd been unaware of his presence. Stifling a sigh, he continued, "The worst we can expect to happen is that a few noble wives will be angry with their spouses. A very few," he added. "Only those who take any notice of their husbands' existence. Good grief—it's all ancient history."

Mr. Desmond raised an eyebrow.

"I beg your pardon," said Jack. "I did not mean to imply—"

"But I *am* ancient, Mr. Langdon. I will be sixty years old in November. And while I have been irresponsibly racketing about these last thirty or forty years, Marchingham and Corbell have risen to unspeakable heights of political consequence. They and my other old friends are doubtless terrified my book will make fools of them. Your upper classes, sir, have but two fears in this world: appearing foolish and being murdered by a revolutionary mob. Naturally they believe it is all one thing. It is very difficult for the British gentleman to develop and retain more than one idea in his lifetime."

"In other words, your powerful friends mean to work up some trumpery charges to throw you into prison and suppress the book," said Delilah. "Though how they are to stop odious Mr. Atkins when you have been unable, I cannot think. Not that I mean us to remain and see how they'll manage it. We must return to Scotland."

"I had rather go to prison, I believe," said Mr. Desmond unperturbedly. "One meets all one's old chums there—those at least who are not currently running the nation. Scotland is needlessly cold and damp," he complained. "Besides, I can never make heads or tails of what those fellows are saying—"

"Papa!"

"My dear, I know your mama is there, and I do miss her

grievously—but she would be appalled if I came slinking back with my tail between my legs. I could never look her in the eye again. Such fine eyes she has," he added dreamily. "You know, Mr. Langdon, I never grow tired of gazing into them, though we have been married nearly five and twenty years."

In vain did Miss Desmond try to awaken her father to a sense of his peril. Reason, threats, rage, and tears were all futile. The Devil had never been a coward, and he did not propose to begin now. His daughter may return to Scotland if she liked. He certainly would prefer that, as he was sure Lady Potterby would. He, however, would remain. Besides, he had an engagement this evening.

"Speak to him, Mr. Langdon," she entreated. "You're always so sensible. Make him understand that a man of sixty cannot long survive imprisonment, and Mama and I will not wish to survive if anything happens to him."

Mr. Langdon dutifully did his best, though he found it monstrous difficult to concentrate. Not once, he thought— not one word about *her* hopes, of the destruction of her plans. Not a hint of alarm at the formidable displeasure she must confront if she remained. It was all her parents.

Was it all? Was that why she was here—for her parents' sake? Had she not told him once that her father's skill at cards was their only source of income? What had she said? Something about her parents not getting any younger. Was her cold-blooded resolve to marry well solely determination to provide for them?

That his arguments were disappointingly weak soon became apparent.

"For heaven's sake, Mr. Langdon, you do sound as if you take his side," she exclaimed in exasperation. "Must you men always stick together, ranting about honour?"

"Miss Desmond, I can't believe your father is in genuine danger," Jack answered mollifyingly. "The work will not be made public for a month. He cannot be imprisoned on mere rumours. Actually," he went on, "it's you who can most expect to suffer in the immediate future. Mere rumour is enough to make a social outcast of you. Your father is quite right in his advice. You ought to return to Scotland."

"Yes, my dear. I fear the news will frighten all your beaux away—which, may I remind you, was the reason in the first place we decided against publishing."

"Then who wants such paltry fellows?" she retorted. "I shall certainly not run away on their account—or on account of a lot of hypocritical females, either. I have some pride too, Papa. You did not bring up your daughter to be a coward. I shall never desert you," she concluded rather melodramatically.

Melodrama or no, she had looked very fine, Jack reflected as he left the house some time later. Proud, noble—and obstinately wrong-headed, of course—but that was why he loved her.

Mr. Langdon paused, thunderstruck, as he reached the corner of the square. Then he turned to stare at the house he had just left. *Loved her?*

" 'How sweet, how passing sweet, is solitude,' " quoted Mr. Stoneham. "But—to make a proper shambles of Cowper—do you mind a friend in your retreat?"

Jack shook himself out of his unhappy reveries to welcome the scholar. Stoneham, at least, would not weary him with the current scandal.

"It seems you've found the only quiet corner of White's," said the gentleman. "Perhaps the only quiet corner of the kingdom. All London is buzzing over this impending publication of Desmond's memoirs. What is your opinion? Will the tales of Society's excesses stir the mob to revolution?"

"It's all idle gossip," said Jack, for what must have been the hundredth time this afternoon. "Desmond's appearance in Town is a nine-days' wonder, and everyone is convinced he's come with a purpose other than the entertainment of a marriageable daughter. Naturally some fool has decided it must be a book of reminiscences and that fool tells another and soon the newspapers print it as solemn truth."

"So I had thought," was the complacent answer. "Now we've had our obligatory discussion of Mr. Desmond, I am eager to pursue the matter we were debating the other day."

Jack smiled. "We've said all there is to be said, I think. You may argue until you are blue in the face, Stoneham, but you will never convince me any mortal is capable of 'improving' the Bard."

Mr. Stoneham promptly asserted that the issue was not improvement. "Is it not better that young ladies read the work in diluted form than never read it at all for fear of being put to the blush?" he asked, warming to the debate.

"Young ladies read whatever they please, in spite of their mamas and teachers. To trick them with a work of art mutilated beyond recognition is criminal."

"Bowdler doesn't mean to mutilate, I am sure. A passage here, a change of phrase there. The meaning would remain, but in more palatable form for the innocent."

"Dr. Bowdler is a meddling, officious old busybody who, if he had a grain of wit, would write his own work instead of attempting to rewrite—" Mr. Langdon stopped to gaze blankly at his companion.

"Emendations merely," Mr. Stoneham insisted.

"Emendations."

"Nothing more—and all to a very good end, I must in— Langdon? Where are you going?" the scholar asked in some bewilderment, for his adversary had bolted up from his chair, a wild look in his eyes.

"So sorry. A thousand apologies," Jack muttered. "Just recollected an appointment."

With that, he was gone, leaving a rather affronted Mr. Stoneham to stare after him.

=== 15 ===

HAD HE BEEN a less selfish young man, Lord Berne would have been deeply distressed by the chilly reception Miss Desmond received that evening at Miss Melbrook's birthday gala. Since, however, this only cleared the field of all other rivals, Lord Berne was most selfishly ecstatic.

Still, he made a creditable show of gentle attentiveness as he hovered by her, making conversation and helping her pretend the rest of the company was not keeping its distance. If he expected this thoughtfulness to soften her hard heart, he learned he was much mistaken. Miss Desmond held her head high, and though her smile was brilliant, it was unpleasantly cold.

He bided his time until they danced. Since her card was as yet nearly empty, he'd had no difficulty in obtaining a waltz. Not until they danced did he allow himself to touch upon her difficulties, express indignation with all of Society, and beg her to make use of him.

"The services of a libertine are scarcely what I require," was the unpromising answer. "Besides, they are all afraid of a little book, nothing more. It's not my trouble, but theirs."

Inwardly excusing her unflattering language as emotional distraction, Lord Berne answered gently, "You are a convenient scapegoat. I cannot tell you how my heart aches to see this injustice to one so innocent. You are a national treasure, a splendid jewel in the crown of English womanhood."

"My Lord, I am not in a poetical humour this evening. You would be better served, I think, in returning me to Lady Potterby and addressing your pretty metaphors to some other lady. I am bound to put you out of temper."

"You are distraught," he said, "though no one else would know it, you disguise your feelings so well. Only because your smallest gesture speaks volumes to me do I discern your distress. Miss Desmond, may I speak frankly?"

She shrugged, inadvertently calling his attention to the smoothness of her neck. One part of his mind speculated upon the silken attractions closely connected to that neck, while the other framed his speech.

"I confess I was rather surprised when I first heard of this memoirs matter," he said cautiously. "Your father is a man of vast experience, Miss Desmond. Naturally I was puzzled why he should wish to publish his recollections at this time, when you've so recently entered Society. Was he not aware of the repercussions that would follow? Or was the reason so pressing—"

"Good grief, can you believe my father has had anything to do with this provoking situation?" she asked incredulously.

"Then he hasn't written the story after all?" was the innocent response.

"Yes, he wrote the curst thing—ages ago, when he was ill, and concerned lest Mama and I be left destitute if he died. Since he survived the illness, there was no longer any urgent necessity to publish."

"Yet he did not destroy it."

With some impatience, Miss Desmond explained why not. Not until she was concluding did she reflect that perhaps she was unwise to tell Lord Berne so much. Aunt Millicent had insisted on denial. They must all maintain that the memoirs did not exist and the rumours were unfounded. Still, Delilah thought wearily, what was the use? In another month or so the world would only add the epithet "liars" to all the rest.

"Miss Desmond, are you telling me this work is being published without your father's permission?" He was genuinely surprised. Hadn't his father told him he'd gotten the memoirs from Desmond himself? Why, then, had the earl not destroyed them?

"Without his permission, against his wishes—and no one can find Mr. Atkins or the manuscript to make him give it up."

"No one *else*," Lord Berne corrected. "I will get the memoirs back for you, if that is what you wish."

The music had stopped, but Delilah scarcely noticed. She was not certain whether to laugh at him or hit him, so exasperatingly confident he looked.

"You make promises too easily, sir," she reproached. "I do not care to be sported with in this way."

"You've never believed my concern for your well-being is genuine, Miss Desmond. I cannot blame you. Nor will I bore you with protestations and promises. My actions must speak for me in future," he said, his blue eyes ablaze with fervent sincerity.

Mr. Langdon was rather late in arriving, having spent some hours in conference with Mr. Desmond, then a few more in consultation with his friends. All had agreed that, whatever the upshot of his current plans, the rumours must be squelched in the meantime. Accordingly, members of the Demowery family immediately set about laughing the story off. Their dismissal of the scandal sheet was sufficiently scornful to raise doubts in the minds of many of their acquaintance, some of whom—though naturally they could not admit it—were made to feel ridiculous indeed.

Thus the mood of the crowd at Miss Melbrook's party gradually softened, and soon Delilah had most, if not all, her partners back.

Though she remarked this change, she assumed Lord Berne's dancing with her had somehow brought it about. Consequently, she felt obliged to think more kindly of him.

Whatever foolish promises he might make and break, he had done her a service. That was why, when he returned a while later to beg for a second dance, she acquiesced, though she had made it a rule never to dance with any known rake more than once in an evening.

Mr. Langdon, who had kept count, was instantly outraged when he saw Lord Berne claim her a second time. Had she taken leave of her wits? All the guests were sure to remark this aberration and speculate upon it—as if they did not already have more than enough to say about Miss Desmond.

Accordingly, Jack took up a martial stance by Lady Potterby. When Delilah returned to her chaperone and her next partner appeared, Mr. Langdon curtly informed the bewildered major that he had made a mistake.

The soldier wisely retreated before Mr. Langdon's baleful glare, and an irate Delilah found herself being hauled to the dance floor.

"What do you think you're doing?" she fumed.

"Confounding the enemy," he said. "And if you have any *nous* at all, you'll endeavour to appear as imbecilely fascinated with all the rest of your partners as you did with Lord Berne."

"Imbecile? How dare you?"

"You were hanging on his every word," her partner answered.

"Because he was talking sense."

"Tony has never talked sense in his entire life."

The dance separated them briefly, but when she returned to face her partner, Miss Desmond's eyes were blazing.

"Evidently," she snapped, "Lord Berne has been saving up all his sense for when it was most wanted. He has a plan to get Papa's memoirs back," she went on, her voice taunting. "A *plan*, Mr. Langdon. Not just pretending nothing's happened and keeping a stiff upper lip."

Mr. Langdon's upper lip, along with the rest of his

countenance, did stiffen at this. He'd altogether forgotten Tony's aspirations. Naturally he'd want to dash to her rescue—and he had the necessary resources. His father had tremendous influence, and being a book collector, was sure to have useful connexions—which Miss Desmond was pointing out when the dance required they separate once more.

Abruptly Mr. Langdon's own plans seemed pathetically inept. When they came together again he felt honour bound to agree with her.

"I'm sure Tony has an excellent plan," said Jack, "as well as the means to carry it out, as you said. I do beg your pardon. My remarks were most unjust. I ought to beg his pardon as well. If he's promised to help you, he will. He would not—no gentleman of honour would—make a promise he wasn't sure he could keep."

Since the day he'd made his dramatic exit from his father's study, Lord Berne had really not given the memoirs any thought. The manuscript was his father's problem. The son's was Miss Desmond, and she had become even more of an obsession with him than the memoirs seemed to be with everyone else.

Nothing would move her. She was indifferent to the viscount's beauty and unresponsive to his irresistible charm. He'd pursued her for more than a month and was no nearer to achieving his aims than he'd been at the start. Nonetheless, he refused to believe the situation was hopeless. She was only more difficult and demanding than other women. Looks, charm, and speeches were not enough for her. At the gala he'd discovered loyalty wasn't enough, either. He would have to be heroic as well.

In the heat of the moment, heroics had seemed reasonable enough, but by the following morning, Lord Berne found himself reflecting unhappily upon the reckless promise he'd made.

He'd assumed his father had destroyed the manuscript

as soon as he got it. Now the viscount had no idea what his parent was about, nor did he wish to know. Whatever Lord Streetham's intentions, they were bound to be at odds with his son's.

Instead, therefore, of beginning with his father, Lord Berne began with Mr. Atkins. Or tried to. Mr. Atkins, as Miss Desmond had told the viscount, was not to be found.

At the publisher's office, Lord Berne heard only complaints from the assistant left in charge.

"My Lord, I must tell you I begin to doubt there is such a book," said Mr. Black in aggrieved tones. "Mr. Atkins has written to me, telling me only to have the printer prepared to start on a work at a moment's notice, and to have the first installment complete in a matter of weeks. You should hear what the printer has to say about *that*. Yet my master never says what the work is, so I cannot tell you whether it is Mr. Desmond's memoirs or Dr. Cablebottom's anatomy manual. It is most vexing. I am daily plagued with enquiries—not to mention a lot of threatening letters—and we have lost three of our best people—and Mr. Atkins will not stay in one place that one might write to him."

Lord Berne did not wait for more, but hastened instead to the printer's. That interview proved equally unprofitable. At the mention of Atkins, Mr. Gillstone only looked hostile and muttered about overdue bills and wondered how an honest businessman could be expected to survive in a world filled with cheats, liars, and frauds.

Over the next few days, Lord Berne spoke to virtually every human being connected with the business, down to clerks, errand boys—even the charwoman. He learned nothing, though he spent a lot of money doing so. A visit with Mrs. Atkins produced two fits and a flood of weeping.

In short, all the viscount could discover was that half the world was trying to find Mr. Atkins, with the same result.

A week after he'd made his foolish promise, Lord Berne had no more information than he'd had at the start. This left his father, and the young man was more loath than ever to even hint what he wanted from the earl. So much secrecy, the disappearance of Mr. Atkins—well, it looked ominous. Whenever Lord Streetham became deep and secretive, it was best to keep out of his way.

Still, the prospect of his father's rage was not nearly so daunting as that of Miss Desmond's. Tony had made too many easy promises, as she'd reminded him. If he failed in this—abandoned her in her hour of greatest need—she'd never forgive him. She'd turn elsewhere for comfort. To Jack most likely—and the viscount had rather be flogged publicly than endure the humiliation of losing her to a poky book-worm.

Accordingly, as soon as his father had left Melgrave House, Lord Berne commenced a desperate search of the premises, which yielded, as he might have expected, nothing. All the earl's important papers were kept locked in his writing desk, and the viscount knew nothing whatsoever about locks.

He sat in his father's chair a long while and stared at the keyhole in frustration. He would have to break it, and this obviously was not the time. It must be done at night and blamed on intruders.

Since it was scarcely noon, Lord Berne decided he might as well make some use of the eternity stretching before him. He had not been to Atkins's shop in three days. He might as well go again. Perhaps there was some word.

There was more than word. The viscount found Mr. Atkins himself, crouched over his cluttered desk, tearing at his hair.

Lord Berne's face immediately became a mask of sympathy as he apologised for intruding. "I heard you were back," he said. "Being in the neighbourhood, I thought to stop and congratulate you. It appears you have achieved quite a coup with Desmond's—"

"My Lord, I beg you will not speak that name," the

publisher cried. "It is cursed, and everything it touches is cursed."

"Surely not," said Lord Berne. "By now I daresay you are inundated with advance orders. This book will be the making of you, sir. Murray and Lackington—not to mention all your other competitors—will be grinding their teeth in envy. I applaud your perspicacity. Indeed, I cannot but regret my ill-chosen words at our last meeting."

"You were right," was the doleful reply. "It ought to have been buried, deep, deep beneath the earth. Where I might as well be. No wonder he has not troubled himself to come and kill me. He has no need. I am ruined. He's poisoned everything."

The publisher lifted a stack of letters and flung it to the floor. "Warnings, threats, all of them. The House of Lords wants me hanged. And that is not the half of it," he went on querulously. "My colleagues, my employees all run from me as if I had the plague. Black has given notice of quitting. Gillstone will not take it—he claims his presses are too busy. Nobody else will take it. Nobody will do business with me. I cannot even buy paper."

"Because of the threats?" Lord Berne asked, barely controlling his eagerness.

"Because the Devil has set rumours abroad that I am bankrupt. The fact is, I am short of cash at the moment—but I am not bankrupt. Yet no one will extend a farthing's credit. I know it was he," Mr. Atkins went on darkly as he drew out his handkerchief and mopped his brow. "No one will say so, but I know it was he."

"Indeed? Well, that must be most disagreeable for you," said Lord Berne, thinking furiously. "What becomes of the manuscript now? Do you admit defeat and return it to Desmond?"

"If only I could. But your father berates me for being superstitious. He is suddenly determined the book must be published, despite everything—and upon the most impossible schedule. Three weeks. Who ever heard of such a thing, even in the cheap paper cover? Does he think I have all the copyists of the *Times* working for me?"

"Pray do not overset yourself, sir," said Lord Berne reassuringly. "My father is a man of influence, which he is bound to exert on your behalf."

"Heaven help me, I wish he would not. The thing is cursed, I tell you, bringing nothing but trouble from the start. But Lord Streetham says we must go forward, and so we must—though I know it is to ruin." Atkins wiped away a tear. "At any rate, I have persuaded him to take it back until the work can begin. I would not have that wretched manuscript in my keeping an instant longer than I can help it."

Lord Berne's heart sank. His father had the damned thing *yet*. Forcing heartiness into his voice, he said, "You must not be cast down, Atkins. My father is a careful man. All will be well, I promise you. You must banish these dark thoughts, and think of your golden future. You will make ten times what Murray has on Byron's *Giaour*."

Mr. Atkins only groaned in reply and dropped his head to his desk.

Lord Berne politely took his leave.

"Naturally they speak of sedition," Lord Streetham impatiently told the son who trailed him into his study. "All the Hunts did was call the Regent names. Desmond has told unflattering tales of half the peerage. He's certain to be tried."

"But if such a matter goes to the courts, will not your connexion be revealed?"

"You know nothing of these matters, Tony, and I wish you would tax neither your brain nor my patience by quizzing me about them."

"You are my parent. I cannot help but be concerned," said Lord Berne piously.

"I had rather," said the parent, glaring, "you concerned yourself with Lady Jane. She is arrived in Town and it would behove you to call on her. Atkins and I can manage our business well enough."

"I don't see how I'm ever to learn anything if you persist in treating me like an ignorant schoolboy," the son complained. "I am trying to understand how you expect to proceed safely in this, when the world is in such an uproar."

Lord Streetham sighed and sat down at his writing desk. While his son watched with suppressed eagerness, the earl took out a key from his pocket and unlocked the desk. "I have a great deal of neglected correspondence to attend to," said Lord Streetham. "But if you must know, it is a question of ownership. We took pains to ensure that the manuscript remained, legally, Desmond's property. It is only his word against Atkins's that the book is published against the Devil's will, and Atkins's solicitor will make short work of that claim, should Desmond dare to make it. If he does, there is not a solicitor in London, reputable or not, who will agree to take up his case."

"I see," said the viscount, not in the least taken aback by this arrogant abuse of power. "But how is Atkins to publis.ı when no one will trade with him?"

"A temporary setback. I'll settle *that* in short order," said the earl ominously.

"And the manuscript? You have it yet? Are you not concerned Desmond will trace it to you?"

"Do you take me for an idiot?" the earl exploded. "The dratted thing is safely locked up with our solicitor. Now will you go and let me do my work? The nation has some claim on my attention, I think."

Much perturbed, Lord Berne went, cursing his recklessness in making so impossible a promise to Miss Desmond. He could not face her now. He could not possibly go to her and admit he was helpless to assist her.

Therefore he did not go to the theatre that evening, because she would be there. Instead he took himself to a gaming hell and, after signing a year's allowance worth of vowels, proceeded to York Place, to a late-night gathering at the cramped house of Mrs. Sydenham, Harriette Wilson's ill-natured sister, Amy.

Restored, no doubt, by a friendly interlude with one of Amy's attractive rivals, Lord Berne awoke the next day with new resolution. If he did not wish to alienate his adored Delilah entirely, it were best to be at least partially honest. He would admit to being delayed—but only temporarily. If he chose his story carefully, she must in all fairness agree to be patient. After all, no one could get at the manuscript now, not even her father.

Which meant that no one else could aid her. Surely, as the days passed, she must come to understand that only the Viscount Berne could protect and care for her properly.

He'd scarcely entered Lady Potterby's parlour when her ladyship was summoned out of the room by an agitated servant. Lady Potterby, whose nerves had over a week ago received a jolt from which they had not entirely recovered, was sufficiently distracted by the servant's panic to hurry out of the room with no thought for her grand-niece's lack of chaperonage, though she did have sense enough to leave the door ajar.

The grand-niece was quick to seize the opportunity.

"You have news of the memoirs, My Lord?" she asked, her grey-green eyes bright with hope.

That brightness, the low, throbbing eagerness in her voice, the sweet vulnerability of her entire mien, was Lord Berne's undoing. How sweet, how unspeakably delicious to have her so, lying in his arms! When Paradise seemed so close, how could he wait days, weeks, and in the end perhaps lose her after all—because of some ridiculous book and a lot of stubborn, greedy men.

He had not only word, he lied, but a plan. "It will be difficult, Miss Desmond, and I hesitate to impose upon you after promising to see to it myself."

"Impose?" she whispered, glancing towards the door. "What do you mean?"

The whisper finished him. He could almost feel her warm breath at his ear as he pictured her, snuggled close to him, murmuring shyly in those same soft tones.

"I need your help," he said. "The matter must be handled discreetly and with dispatch, but it will require two people. I have friends I can trust, but—"

"No! I will do it, whatever it is," she interrupted excitedly. "You cannot know how vexatious it is to be a woman, always forced to wait, being told nothing—except that one's help is not wanted. I'm no empty-headed, helpless miss, My Lord, and I'm not afraid."

"I've seen enough of your courage to know that," he answered. "You've been splendid all this time, when another woman would have been weeping and fainting and making a pitiful spectacle of herself. But there's nothing of the helpless victim in *you*. You ought to have been born in another age, when womanly bravery and intelligence were better appreciated."

Delilah flushed with pleasure. Everyone else had called her foolish and obstinate because she would not run away. He understood. Rake he may be, but he treated her as an equal. He asked her to help, to be a partner in this, while everyone else had only told her endlessly to keep out of men's affairs.

"What must I do?" she asked.

"Can you come away? My carriage is waiting."

"Now?"

"There is no time like the present. Surely you will not wish to remain on tenter-hooks another day."

Delilah jumped up from her chair. "Not another minute," she answered, shrugging off a chill of apprehension as excitement. "Only wait while I get my bonnet and shawl."

The words were hardly out of her mouth when she heard voices approaching. In the next moment, an elegant figure in blue satin sailed through the door.

"Mama!" Delilah cried.

"My love," said Mrs. Desmond, taking her daughter in her arms for a brief embrace. Then she drew back to examine Delilah critically. "Your hair is inexcusable," she said. "What on earth was Joan thinking of?"

In the next instant Lord Berne felt the same critical scrutiny, and was oddly unnerved. One might have taken the two for portraits of the same woman, but in different tints. Mrs. Desmond's dark hair partook more of mahogany, while her daughter's was nearly blue-black, yet the mother's skin was the same clear alabaster, scarcely lined.

It was her eyes, though, that most disconcerted Lord Berne. More grey than green, though also with that exotic slant, Mrs. Desmond's eyes were hypnotic, fixing him as a pin fixes a moth, and piercing straight through his brain. He immediately felt guilty, and to his chagrin, found himself stammering as he introduced himself.

"Ah, you are Marcus's boy," she said. "What a naughty fellow he was. But you must save your own naughtiness for another time, My Lord. I have not seen my child in months, and we have a deal of gossiping to do."

She swept the bewildered Delilah from the room, leaving Lord Berne to find his own way out.

= 16 =

"WHERE IS YOUR papa?" Mrs. Desmond asked as she led her daughter down the hallway towards the stairs. "And what were you doing unattended with that wicked boy?" Without waiting for an answer, she went on, "He is amazingly beautiful. One would think one of Botticelli's paintings had come to life, but I must tell you, when they do so, their sole aim appears to be—"

There was a small commotion in the hall behind them, and the two ladies stopped and turned.

"*Cara*," cried Mr. Desmond, hastening towards them, Mr. Langdon following close behind.

The Devil took his wife's hands and pressed them to his lips.

"My dear," she said composedly, "you are looking well."

"Better now, I am sure. This is a most agreeable surprise. I had not expected you so soon."

"I came by mail coach," said Mrs. Desmond. She turned her attention to her husband's companion. "This must be Mr. Langdon," she said, smiling warmly.

Delilah, baffled, looked from one face to the next. What was Mama doing here? What did she know of Mr. Langdon? And why must this all happen now, when the daughter might be out rescuing the manuscript from the evil grasp of Mr. Atkins?

"Mama," she began.

Her mama did not hear her, being engaged in issuing commands to the butler.

"Aunt Mimsy is overset by the excitement," she explained when Bantwell had exited. "I have sent her to her room to rest, but someone must see about dinner. You will join us, sir?" she asked Mr. Langdon.

He pleaded a previous engagement.

"Then you will have a glass of wine at least." Angelica led the group to the parlour.

"Mama, what are you doing here?" Delilah demanded as soon as the door was closed. "Aunt Millicent must be in paroxysms."

"If this is how you normally behave before company, my dear, then I daresay she is experiencing paroxysms of relief that I am here. Mr. Langdon, you will ignore my daughter's outburst, I hope. She *meant* to say how delighted she was to see me. Sit down, Delilah, and stop fidgeting."

Delilah sat, fuming.

The servant entered with wine. Accepting his glass, Mr. Langdon took up a neutral position by the fireplace.

"You might have explained to her, Darryl," Mrs. Desmond began reproachfully.

"I might," was the unperturbed response, "but there has been no proper opportunity. She is rarely at home when I am, and at those infrequent intervals Millicent is inevitably about. Since she was certain to object, silence seemed the wisest course. Besides, as I mentioned, we had not looked to see you so soon."

Miss Desmond glared at Mr. Langdon. He knew whatever it was that had not been explained to her, else her parents would not have spoken so before him.

Mr. Langdon coloured under the glare and said apologetically, "I beg your pardon, Miss Desmond, but I hesitated to discuss the matter with you before I felt more confident my proposal was workable."

"What proposal?" Delilah cried. "Why do you have all these secrets and tell me nothing?"

"You just heard why," said her mama. "There is no need to raise your voice, Delilah. Count to ten."

Miss Desmond reddened. It was not to be borne. To be spoken to as though she were an ill-behaved child—and before this irritating man. She would like to dash Mr. Langdon's head against the mantelpiece, she thought, automatically focusing all her anger on him. That agreeable prospect soothed her sufficiently to allow her to attend her mother's explanation.

"Mr. Langdon has very kindly undertaken to help us prepare a case against Mr. Atkins," said Mrs. Desmond.

"Not that there's any certainty," Mr. Langdon put in, "we have a case. Yet there seems to be a question of ownership, and as far as I can ascertain, no concrete evidence of your father's consent to publication."

"That is why I am here, my love," said the mama. "All your papa's notes for the story as well as his correspondence with Mr. Atkins were in Scotland with me. I thought it wisest to bring them with me, rather than send them. It is a very large package," she said, turning to her husband. "I believe I have everything."

"I know you have, my precious. Though best of all you've done was to bring yourself. I have missed you frightfully."

Mrs. Desmond smiled. "And I you," she murmured, drawing closer to him.

In a few minutes, they had apparently forgotten everything else in this world but each other, for, arm in arm and talking in very low voices, they soon quitted the room.

They might as well have been in their bedchamber, Delilah thought as she watched them leave. Her cheeks pink once more, she turned to Mr. Langdon and was annoyed by the faint smile on his face.

"You might have told me," she said curtly, oddly embarrassed by her parents' indiscreetly amorous behaviour, which had never bothered her before.

"I didn't want to raise your hopes needlessly, Miss Desmond."

"Well, you've got *their* hopes up, and it is very bad of

191

you," she snapped. "You said yourself it was a weak case, and you know how long these lawsuits drag on. It could be years before it goes to court, and by that time my poor father could be dying in prison. What good is it to sue that odious Atkins after the book is published and the damage done?"

Mr. Langdon very carefully placed his still nearly full glass upon a table.

"I have not observed," he answered stiffly, "that Lord Berne has provided for your parents any better solution. To my knowledge, he has not said a word to your father. At least my plan keeps Mr. Desmond safely occupied. I was concerned he might resort to needless risks—"

"Papa is not in his dotage yet, sir. Furthermore, there are times when risk is exactly what's needed—times when it's wiser to *act*, instead of creeping about cautiously."

She rose from her chair and marched to the window, where she stood, fretfully staring at the passing scene.

"If you had not gotten my mama involved, I might have been gone by now," she went on. "I might even have had the manuscript in my hands." She whirled round to face him. "Lord Berne was just here—and he had a plan—and I was to help him. But you must come and spoil everything—and now the chance may be lost forever."

Mr. Langdon's face darkened. "Tony was here? And you remained alone with him?"

"Yes, and he did not ravish me on the spot, for your information."

"I should think not. Not when he could so easily persuade you to go away with him—to God knows where. Have you taken leave of your senses, Miss Desmond? What sort of scheme could he have that required a lady's assistance?"

"Not all women are helpless—"

"You would be, if you went off with him."

"We were not planning to elope, Mr. Langdon," was the tart reply. "Nor do I see why I should not believe him. Did you not tell me but a week ago that no man of honour would make a promise he couldn't keep? Or do you now tell me your friend has no honour?"

"When a woman is so careless of propriety, even a man of honour may be tempted too far," he said, his voice ominously quiet.

"Indeed!" She tossed her head, heedlessly scattering pins. "You are outraged because I spoke privately with him for scarcely two minutes, yet it is quite correct that you remain here forever. Dear me, I forget. Mr. Langdon is the soul of honour. Wise, cautious, and pure of heart. Everyone knows he would do nothing that was not exceedingly correct, for he is above all temptation."

The words had no sooner spilt from her tongue than she regretted them. This was monstrous unjust and ungrateful, when he was only trying to help, and when he had said nothing that Aunt Millicent had not already told her dozens of times already. What on earth drove one to taunt him so? Delilah could feel the tension in the room. As she met his steely grey gaze, she found herself backing towards the window. He was furious.

"Mr. Langdon," she began as he advanced upon her, "I do beg your—"

That was as far as she got because she couldn't breathe. He stood only inches from her, his face taut with suppressed rage, and her heart was pounding so she thought it would choke her.

"You hell-cat," he growled.

She felt his hands close around her throat, but she was immobilized. She could only gaze helplessly into the pitiless depths of his darkened eyes. Then his mouth crashed down on hers and all was darkness.

Darkness and violence, as his mouth moved punishingly over hers until he'd forced her lips open. She was dimly aware of his hands moving from her shoulders to her back as his tongue pushed itself between her teeth. The invasion made her tremble, and she struggled against him, futilely.

He only crushed her hard against him so she could scarcely move at all.

Then, to her dismay, she felt the heat well up within her, washing over her in wave after wave, and bringing with it a sweeping need, like hunger . . . and a greater need still as his mouth left hers to trail kisses along her cheek and down her neck. She moaned softly, the sound drawn from her in spite of herself.

Dear heaven, she thought wildly, why could she not make it stop? His embrace was gentler now and she might have broken free. Instead, her hands crept up along his coat to his crisp neck-cloth, and on to bury themselves in his hair. She held him so, a moment, then, impatient, drew his face, his mouth back to hers.

She had scarcely tasted his lips again when, without warning, he put her away from him. The world instantly chilled. His gaze flicked briefly over her hot face and he smiled an odd, small, bitter smile.

"Let that be a lesson to you, Miss Desmond," he said, his voice low and harsh. "Even a book-worm can be pushed too far."

Without another word, he left.

Delilah stared blankly at his retreating back, and was still staring as the door slammed behind him.

"Jack?" she said, very softly. Then heat flooded through her once more and she tottered, thunderstruck, to a chair.

She sat for a long while, her eyes wide open but seeing nothing amid the churning sensations assaulting her, nearly as strong as they had been a few minutes before. Once more she experienced the pressure of his hands upon her back, the warm touch of his lips upon her neck, the clean, masculine scent of him . . . and the barely leashed rage that had frightened and excited her at the same time—and against which she had been utterly powerless.

Powerless? That wasn't the half of it. All her will had

turned into craving . . . and she wanted him still, wanted him to come back and torment her again, endlessly.

Yet she could not possibly want him. He was not the dashing scoundrel of her fantasies, the younger version of her adored Papa she'd always hoped for. This was a quiet, provokingly conventional, irritatingly muddled *book-worm!* How could she be attracted to a man who must be thoroughly enraged in order to show a spark of passion?

A lesson, he'd said. Damn, and it was—a humiliating lesson. Book-worm or no, he evidently knew as well as any other man how to stir a woman's senses, and had proceeded to prove it. He'd shown her how little she knew of him, of any man, despite all her so-called worldly wisdom. He'd shown that Delilah Desmond was as susceptible as any naïve schoolgirl to practised lovemaking.

Only it wasn't love, but anger. He despised her. She wanted to weep when she recollected his cold, contemptuous expression when he'd thrust her away. He'd made her feel like a whore—and certainly she'd behaved like one— after, that is, acting like a Billingsgate fishwife.

Miss Desmond had scarcely made a decent start in flagellating herself when she received Lord Berne's note half an hour later. It was filled with apologies. He'd been too hasty, he wrote. His plan was ill-advised. He'd since learned that Mr. Atkins was temporarily prevented from publishing by circumstances too complicated to tire her with. When, however, the time was right, the viscount promised to consult with her. Until then, they must be patient.

Delilah tore the note into very small pieces. Let him get the manuscript himself, if he could. She would not go anywhere with him or any other man—not without a bodyguard. She'd already had one sample of the viscount's ardour. Suppose, today, he'd been the one to kiss her in that violent way? She might not have escaped so easily. She had never imagined how easily-roused a beast lurked within one.

Delilah was not altogether surprised when Mr. Langdon appeared late the next morning to ask her to drive with him. If she'd had second thoughts about her behaviour, obviously the Soul of Honour must have had some fit of conscience as well.

The conversation was exceedingly polite until they reached the park. Then Mr. Langdon slowed the horses and, without looking at her, apologised.

Delilah had not thought she could possibly feel more vexed with herself, but she did. His countenance was so rigidly unhappy that she couldn't bear to let him finish his speech.

"I beg you, Mr. Langdon," she said, flushing, "not another syllable. It's I who ought to apologise. My behaviour was perfectly beastly."

"That does not excuse what I did, Miss Desmond. Nothing would excuse it. I—I am aware," he went on, each word sounding as though it were being torn bodily from him, "of the abhorrence in which you must hold me. All the same, there are certain rules about these matters—"

"Oh, no," she cried. "You're not going to propose, are you? Please don't. You only heap coals upon my head. In the circumstances, that rule makes no sense at all. It would be far more reasonable to beat me, I think."

He sighed—with relief, no doubt. That was not at all flattering, but she could hardly blame him. Anyhow, he'd done the honourable thing and, much as it would cost her pride, she'd prove she too knew something of honour. She would admit her error.

"Actually, you did me a favour," she went on, watching his eyes widen in amazement. "You did teach me a lesson. If the method was improper, it was probably more effective than words—at least in my case," she added ruefully.

"Because you know I always lose my temper first and listen and think after."

He sighed once more. "Are you sure you're thinking now, Miss Desmond? By my count, I have three times crossed the bounds of propriety with you, and you persist in excusing me. Yesterday you didn't even hit me. Aren't you concerned I may interpret this as encouragement?"

"Yes. That's what I meant about learning my lesson. You've made me painfully aware of how ignorant I am. I was utterly incapable of coping with—the situation."

"I see," he said quietly. "No wonder I'm still alive and in one piece."

She winced, but went on determinedly, "Since I'm now acutely aware of my ignorance, you may rest assured I will take great care not to find myself in such a predicament again—with anybody."

He had gone about it all wrong, Jack reproached himself later, putting down his pen and gazing in despair at the heap of papers before him. That he'd never attempted to propose marriage to anyone before in his life was no excuse. Many men did it only once.

He had been reasonably composed. He'd even felt a surge of confidence when he'd first set out for Potterby House. Yesterday she hadn't struck him or even berated him. She'd hardly put up a struggle. She'd actually responded to his caresses, ungentle as they were. She'd responded so passionately that he'd had to thrust her away and flee or else he'd surely have dishonoured her—in her great-aunt's parlour of all places!

Yet he wished he'd not been so maddened. Then he might have stopped it more gently . . . might have even dared admit what was in his heart. He should have offered then, instead of covering up with that insulting bravado. What had possessed him to say such an unforgivable thing—after assaulting her, no less? Why had he been so craven today and allowed the horrified expression in those grey-green eyes to unman him?

Max wouldn't have taken No for an answer. Certainly not before he'd said his piece—or swept her into his arms and banished all her anger with kisses.

But it wasn't anger, Jack thought despondently. He'd humiliated her and lost whatever trust she might have once reposed in him. His ill-worded offer today had only added insult to injury. Why could he not say the right words, he who had read hundreds of volumes in half a dozen languages?

Because he had only to look into that devastatingly beautiful face and Reason and Sense abandoned him altogether. He became an inarticulate, tormented brute.

Amantes amentes, he reminded himself. Lovers are lunatics, as Terence had observed centuries ago. Now there was all this curst paper and ink. And so little time. So little, when it seemed he would need three eternities to learn to woo her properly and another ten to win her heart.

Mr. Langdon would have been much comforted to learn that Miss Desmond was suffering her own harrowing reflections, but as she confided these to nobody, he was denied such solace.

Delilah only told her great-aunt she was overset by the excitement of her mama's arrival and had rather not go out this evening.

Lady Potterby was vastly relieved. Though she prided herself on her fortitude, the shock of Angelica's arrival, coupled with the strain of the days following the newspaper announcement, had been rather more than her nerves could comfortably sustain. Though she was not a timid, weak creature, and though she did not mind a little excitement in her life and had a taste for a challenge, her relatives were beginning to wear on her. The prospect of one quiet evening at home and an early bedtime was altogether delightful.

Delilah did not take to her own bed very early. She tried to read, but the *Giaour* only irritated her with its romantic histrionics. She found herself conjuring up instead one handsome, serious countenance with dreamy grey eyes and one gentle, thoughtful voice. How desperately unhappy and trapped Mr. Langdon had looked today. Trapped by his own chivalry, by the rules that were so important to him, by the Honour that demanded what his very soul must recoil at.

That she'd spared him was not, she knew, entirely attributable to noble self-sacrifice. How could she possibly have allowed him to make his offer—let alone have accepted it?

She put her book aside and rose from her chair to stand by the window. Even in Town Lady Potterby must have her garden, more elaborate yet than the one at Elmhurst—perhaps to compensate for the lack of acreage.

As she gazed out into the shadows, Delilah remembered one late-night meeting in another garden . . . the looked-for kiss that never came and her embarrassed retreat. She shook her head. Of course she could not marry him, she who was prepared to accept the first respectable offer that came her way. Her cynical heart was not quite cynical enough. It was not quite hard and cold enough to bear rejection, regardless how courteous a form it took.

In the following weeks there were few opportunities to be rejected, politely or otherwise, for Mr. Langdon was rarely to be seen. Of a half dozen events, he might attend one, and then came and went so quickly that their conversations were little more than greeting and farewell.

Delilah did not see much more of her parents. They spent a great deal of time away from the house, though they were never seen at any fashionable gatherings. When they were at home, they were generally in the study, poring over papers.

Though for the first time in her life Delilah felt shut out, she was not altogether sorry. Her parents were far too perceptive, and she did not wish to be closely examined by either of them. They would know immediately something was wrong and would not rest until they'd teased it out of her. Delilah did not want to think about what was wrong if she could help it. Certainly she did not wish to voice any of her unhappy thoughts, even to her beloved parents.

Instead she kept busy, which was not at all difficult. When no more was heard of the memoirs, the Beau Monde quickly turned its attention to other matters, while its members assured one another they had known all along the announcement was nothing but a hoax. Even Angelica Desmond's arrival scarcely caused a stir. For one, she was almost never seen; for another, she was old news.

In mid-August, following the breakdown of the Prague conference, hostilities had resumed with Napoleon. Though his army was rapidly dwindling, the allied forces were behaving so indecisively that Britons at home devoted considerable energy to expressing their exasperation.

On the non-political side was Byron, who had recently embarked upon an affair with Lady Frances Webster. These and other current sensations were a deal more interesting than what one woman had done more than twenty-five years ago.

Thus the invitations continued to arrive at Potterby House. In addition to Society in general was Society in particular—that is to say, Lady Rand. She and Delilah spent their days shopping for books as well as more frivolous items, or visiting galleries, or seeing London sights. In the evenings they danced their slippers to shreds or got crushed at routs or stifled their yawns at rather mediocre musicales. Occasionally they went to the theatre or opera, and would rant happily at each other on the way home about the audience's boorish behaviour.

Through all this activity, Lord Berne was very much in evidence, the most prominent of Delilah's beaux. Oddly enough, he had also become the most kind, courteous, and altogether well-behaved of the lot. He seemed to be a changed man, for he behaved with a discretion Miss Desmond would not have thought possible. Though he was frequently at her side, there were no more languishing looks and ardent speeches. Instead he treated her with gentle affection and polite solicitude. He contended himself with one dance of an evening, and though he hovered before and after, he was so amusing and made himself so agreeable that Delilah could find nothing whatever to fault him with. He was so decorous a suitor, in fact, that his mother threw up her hands in despair.

Lady Jane, for her part, had too much pride to acknowledge his preference for another, and soon stopped wasting her hostile looks and innuendos on what everyone had begun to perceive as a lost cause. She took up with Lord Argoyne, much to the delight of that gentleman's mama, who had been in agonies all year because he persisted in throwing himself at nobodies.

Since these two enemies seemed to believe Lord Berne was finally, seriously, in love, Delilah was cautiously inclined to believe so as well. All the same, she was determined not to be overly confident again and made a point of giving all her admirers equal attention. Unfortunately, Lord Berne was so assiduous and so formidable a rival—being, perhaps, the most beautiful young man who had ever been seen in London—that gradually the others withdrew in defeat. While she still had dance partners and riding and driving offers, Delilah soon perceived that no other sort of offers would be forthcoming. Like it or no, Lord Berne seemed to be her only solid prospect.

She did like it, she told herself. He was extremely handsome. He admired her, amused her, and treated her kindly. He actually did seem to love her. That she didn't yet return the sentiment was no great obstacle. If he was a good husband, she would learn to love him. If he turned out a bad one—which was a risk everyone must take—at least he could not hurt her, and certainly she would have every comfort for herself and every means of caring for her parents.

Was this not the reason she had dragged her family back to England? Had she not told her father months ago that love had nothing to do with it?

$=$ **17** $=$

MISS DESMOND SUCCEEDED in convincing herself that matters were proceeding as well as she could have wished—until one morning in early October when she met up with Mr. Langdon as he came out of her father's study.

His hair was as rumpled as an unmade bed and his coat looked as though he'd slept in it. She felt a queer tugging inside as she looked at him, and wished she had a comb at least.

"You are about early, sir," she said, keeping her voice light. "Or have you spent the night with Papa, poring over your papers?"

How odd his eyes looked. There was a peculiar light in their grey depths, a glitter of something, like suppressed excitement.

"Actually, I have," he said nervously. "Please excuse my appearance, Miss Desmond."

"You've been hard at work. You needn't apologise for that, when you work on my family's behalf." Resisting the urge to straighten his cravat, she forced a bright smile. "I only hope Mr. Fellows will understand."

"No, he won't," was the rueful answer. "He's already out of all patience with me. I daresay he'll give his notice as soon as he catches sight of me—or at least when he finds out how little time I can give him to make repairs."

Delilah retreated a step. "I beg your pardon. You're in a hurry and I keep you."

"Not at all," he said. "That is, I am in rather a hurry—

but then it seems I have been for weeks—and I do regret I cannot stop—"

"There's no reason to regret, Mr. Langdon. I'm sure we're all most obliged to you."

"Not at all," he mumbled, turning away.

She meant to turn as well, to let him go his way. Instead she moved towards him and touched his coat-sleeve. "Mr. Langdon—"

He stopped abruptly and her cheeks burned as she met his puzzled look.

"I—I hope you will try to get some rest, sir. Papa is indefatigable, you know," she went on hurriedly, "and because he rarely sleeps, he thinks no one else does." She remembered her hand, then, and tried to draw it away, but his absently closed over it.

He smiled. "In my case, he's quite correct, Miss Desmond—but you're kind to mention it. Thank you." He hesitated an instant, pressed her hand briefly before releasing it, then walked quickly away.

Shortly after noon, a very curious figure was seen making its way down Dean Street. Though the day was mild, the figure was attired in a great coat, round the collar of which was wrapped a thick shawl that covered all but its eyes, and these were shaded by the stove-pipe hat tipped low over its forehead.

The singularity of the figure's appearance was matched by its behaviour. Instead of walking straight on in a forthright manner, it darted from doorway to doorway, glancing furtively over its shoulder from time to time—rather in the way of a criminal pursued by the forces of law and order than that of an honest publisher attempting to do an honest day's business.

This was, nevertheless, none other than Mr. Atkins, who, his heart filled with dread and his teeth chattering like a monkey's, was on his way to the printer with the bane of his existence, Mr. Devil Desmond's memoirs.

Mr. Atkins was so terrified that he scarcely dared breathe the entire way. Fortunately, the distance was short. When, his face nearly blue with strain, he reached the entrance he sought, he drew a badly needed breath and thus had sufficient strength to make a mad rush at the door.

Unfortunately, his hat chose just this moment to fall over his eyes and become entangled with the shawl, which prevented his seeing the obstacle in his path.

The obstacle was a gentleman who was at that moment hurrying out of the shop. The resulting collision threw Mr. Atkins back upon the doorstep.

As he frantically pushed the scarf and hat away from his eyes, Mr. Atkins discerned with no small alarm that the man in his way was Mr. Langdon.

"Good heavens, sir! I do beg your pardon," said a greatly flustered Mr. Langdon. "I was not looking—most careless of me. I hope you have taken no harm, Mr. Atkins."

Mr. Atkins clutched his package to his bosom.

"N—not at all, sir. I—I fear I was at f—fault. Excuse me." He tried to get by, but he could not, for Mr. Langdon had bent over in the doorway to retrieve the parcels he had dropped. When he straightened, he apologised again profusely before moving out of the way.

Mr. Atkins, his face soaked with perspiration, edged through the door . . . and came up short against a large, hard figure. Swallowing, he looked up into the glittering green eyes of Devil Desmond.

Mr. Atkins turned white and began to sway.

Mr. Desmond called for assistance, and an apprentice hastened in to help him lead Mr. Atkins to a chair.

"My dear fellow," said Mr. Desmond after the publisher had been made to swallow a few gulps of gin. "I'm afraid I gave you a turn."

"Don't kill me," Mr. Atkins whimpered. "It isn't my doing, I swear to you. I never wanted—"

"Pray do not distress yourself, sir," came the solicitous

reply. "I have no wish to cause you any trouble. I've only come for the rest of my money."

"Y—your what?"

"The money, sir, you promised me." Desmond glanced around at the gathering crowd of onlookers. "But perhaps you would prefer to discuss these mercenary matters in a less public place."

A short time later, Mr. Atkins was sufficiently in possession of his wits to believe he was not dreaming. This was Devil Desmond, sitting calmly across from him in a cramped room, claiming to be perfectly content to have his work published after all.

"Much ado about nothing," the Devil confided to his stunned listener. "What is Woman if not changeable? My daughter, sir, is bored to extinction with London Society and wishes to go abroad. Immediately, of course. She has no patience, you know. I have been trying for days to speak to you, but you have been unavailable." The Devil's teeth gleamed as he grinned. "Press of business, I daresay. You could not possibly have been avoiding me. You are not so poor-spirited a fellow as that."

Mr. Atkins was sufficiently poor-spirited to tremble, though he still maintained his fierce possession of the manuscript. Even when he had swooned, he had not loosened his grip. His fingers had apparently long since frozen permanently in position.

"My good man," said Mr. Desmond. "I assure you there is no reason for suspicion. Please, do what you must with that package. I shall wait here patiently. I suppose there are papers to be signed?"

"Y—yes," said Mr. Atkins. "But they are at my office."

"Then by all means let us go there. I shall be confounded relieved to have done with this tiresome business."

Not many minutes later, the printer had the package and his instructions, while Mr. Atkins, still nearly speechless with amazement at this turnabout, was accompanying his author back down Dean Street.

When the two had turned the corner, Mr. Langdon stepped out of the nearby chemist's shop and disappeared into the printer's. He re-emerged ten minutes later and glanced furtively about him before hastening down the street.

Lord Berne, who had been watching events unfold from the shadows of a doorway across the street, broke into a smile. No wonder Desmond had got the word so quickly— even before himself. The Devil had had Langdon—innocent, honest Jack—do his spying for him. And Langdon had probably got all his information just by appearing muddled and forgetful. He had likely not paid a farthing in bribes.

"Ah, Jack," he murmured, "How it saddens me to see you take up these wicked ways. Yet I do believe you have spared me a great deal of trouble."

Mr. Langdon managed to restrain himself until he was safely home. He had walked slowly, looking, he hoped, as innocently preoccupied as ever, and suitably inept as he hailed a hackney.

He even managed a semblance of calm as he entered his library. Then he shut the door and began ripping open one of his packages. Not until he'd checked the pages and assured himself this *was* the manuscript did he sit down and allow himself a sigh of relief.

Thank heaven he looked so muddled. Even the printer, harassed as he was, had felt sorry for him. He'd never doubted for an instant that Mr. Langdon had picked up Mr. Atkins's package by mistake and given the publisher his own.

Jack had just rung for a well-deserved glass of brandy when Lord Berne was announced.

"Two glasses, Joseph," said Mr. Langdon. "Only give me a moment before you show him in."

As soon as the servant left the room, Jack slipped the

manuscript back into its wrapper and placed it underneath the other parcels.

"Jack! How glad I am to find you at home," Lord Berne cried as he entered. "One sees so little of you these days. No doubt you've reverted to habit—buried in your books again." He glanced at the stack of packages heaped on a chair. "Are these additions to the collection?"

Jack nodded. "With Madame de Stael in residence, I thought I ought to familiarise myself with her work."

Joseph entered with the brandy. Mr. Langdon poured. His hands were surprisingly steady, considering he was beside himself with impatience. If only he could be rid of Tony quickly, so he might go at once to Potterby House with the book. He should have gone directly, but he could not trust his luck, and had to check his treasure first—without Miss Desmond's scornful eyes upon him.

"Ah, just the thing," said Lord Berne. "For now, that is. Perhaps later today I may return the favour with champagne, when I solicit your congratulations."

Jack paused in the act of lifting his glass.

"I'm going to do it, Jack. I mean to be riveted at last—if she'll have me." Glass in hand, Lord Berne sauntered away from his friend to gaze at a small marble bust of Caesar Augustus that stood upon the mantel. He smiled. "I think she will. She has at least given me reason to hope."

He turned his innocent blue gaze upon his friend. "Will you wish me luck, Jack? Though she has been kind, I find my courage repeatedly deserting me. I have twice set out for Potterby House today and twice turned back. I was so agitated I feared I should be incapable of speaking at all."

"Potterby House," Jack said weakly, his one frail, mad hope that Lord Berne referred to another woman dashed. Then, catching himself, he went on. "You mean to offer for Miss Desmond? Have your parents yielded at last?"

"No, they have not," was the composed answer. "Yet I am no babe, to have my life managed and manipulated by my parents. They would consign me to Hell—to Lady

Jane—which is quite the same thing. 'But when I became a man, I put away childish things.' I've learned there is only one woman I love, can ever love, and that is the woman I will have. No other course bears contemplation."

Jack Langdon was too much in the habit of putting himself in the other's place to leave off now. He had dreamed and hoped for months. He had laboured all these past weeks with one aim. It was not inconceivable that Tony, in his own way, had been doing the same. Less inconceivable was that Tony had been doing so to better purpose.

While Jack was not sufficiently unselfish to keep from hoping desperately that his friend would fail, he knew the hope was not only futile, but absurd. What woman in her senses could ever resist Tony? Countless women had abandoned the path of virtue because he smiled upon them. Though Miss Desmond, unlike these others, had resisted ruin, that was just barely. Certainly she would not decline his honourable offer of marriage.

Jack suppressed a sigh, scarcely attending his friend's impassioned declarations of love, loyalty, fearlessness, and heaven knew what else. Really, it was beginning to grow tiresome. First Max with Catherine, now Tony with Delilah. All in the space of a few months.

This time was worse than the one before, far worse. Jack could not imagine what the next time would be like. Perhaps there would be no next time. Perhaps he would simply withdraw from the world as his Uncle Albert had and spend his remaining days as a reclusive, confirmed bachelor, his sole passion lined up neatly upon the shelves of his library.

Jack swallowed his brandy in one long gulp and raised the decanter once more. He might as well get drunk. He was entitled.

That was the last complete thought he had, for as he was refilling his glass, there came a sharp, blinding pain . . . and then there was nothing at all.

Lord Berne gazed sadly down upon the unconscious form sprawled upon the carpet.

"Frightfully sorry, old chap," he said softly, "but we can't have any more of that misplaced gratitude now, can we?"

He coolly began unwrapping the packages piled on the chair until he found the one he wanted. Then he sat down at his friend's writing desk, scrawled a brief note, and left.

Having had an unsatisfactorily short and not altogether enlightening conversation with her mama, Miss Desmond was at the moment wearing a circular path in the parlour carpet. She was not fitted by nature to endure suspense with her mother's tranquillity. That lady had, to Delilah's utter incredulity, retired to her chamber for a nap. She had been up all night, like everyone else, it seemed, while Delilah and Lady Potterby had slept in blissful ignorance of the plots being hatched below.

Delilah was still not altogether clear on just what the plot was, because her mama had looked ready to drop from exhaustion. Baffled as Delilah had been, she'd tried to be considerate, and refrained from demanding lengthy details. At any rate, Papa and Mr. Langdon would explain when they returned, her mother had promised. For now, it was enough to say they'd gone for the manuscript and had no doubt of success.

Still, that was hours ago. Surely they ought to be back by now . . . unless they had failed. The thought was most alarming. Though Delilah had more than once taunted Mr. Langdon with his excessive caution, she did hope he had not been reckless. Papa was accustomed to skirting the boundaries of the law and adept at wriggling out of awkward situations. Mr. Langdon had no such experience. Oh, where *was* he?

She heard the door knocker then and abruptly sat down. Whatever else happened, she would show Mr. Langdon she had as much poise and self-control as any other lady. She folded her hands tightly in her lap and waited.

To her disappointment, Lord Berne was announced. As he entered the room, she struggled mightily to erase all evidence of vexation from her countenance.

Fortunately, Lady Potterby had accompanied him and, during the interval of greetings and small talk, Delilah took herself in hand. She was pleased to see him, she told herself. How could she not be, when he looked so impossibly beautiful, his golden curls slightly windblown, but all else so elegant, sleek, and graceful.

"Indeed, the weather is fine today," he was agreeing with his hostess. "There is not a whisper of a cloud in the heavens. Since these opportunities will be too rare in the coming weeks, I hastened here in hopes Miss Desmond would consent to drive with me—if she will forgive the short notice," he added, bestowing an affectionate glance upon the young lady.

Lady Potterby was even less informed of the latest memoir-connected events than her grand-niece was, for her family had naturally supposed her nerves could not bear more anxiety. She was, furthermore, waiting for Lord Berne to come up to scratch. There was no other possible way to interpret his behaviour of the past three or four weeks, regardless what Angelica said. At the moment, the viscount looked as though he were about to burst with something, and Lady Potterby was not slow to guess what that was. Today. He'd offer today.

To her surprise, her grand-niece appeared most hesitant. Still, her ladyship reflected, that was the way with girls. Bold as brass one minute, then, when matters grew serious, overcome with modesty. Delilah wanted nudging, that was all.

"You could do with some exercise, my dear," Lady Potterby urged with unusual firmness. "You have been too pale these past few days, which I am sure is because you do not take the air. His lordship is most kind to invite you.

Though I must ask you, My Lord," she added, dropping him a knowing look, "not to keep her long. She has an appointment with her dressmaker."

Lord Berne solemnly vowed that Miss Desmond would be returned in good time for her appointment.

Miss Desmond smiled weakly and consented.

At least, Delilah thought as the carriage reached the park gates, this was something to do. Better than pacing, certainly, and far better than working herself into a pet because her parents and Mr. Langdon had kept secrets from her. Not that she'd given her parents much opportunity to do otherwise. For nearly a month she'd scrupulously avoided them. As to Mr. Langdon, why should he tell her anything, when all she ever did was pick on him?

She was abruptly jolted from these reflections when Lord Berne, who had been uncharacteristically mute, stopped the carriage and found his tongue.

"Miss Desmond, a few weeks ago I made you a promise," he said, his voice low and rather unsteady. "I have kept it."

She turned a baffled glance upon him. "I beg your pardon?"

"The memoirs. I've got them at last."

He shifted the reins to one hand and reached under the seat. As he drew out a thick package, Delilah experienced a curious sinking sensation. More curious still was the reluctance with which she took the parcel from him and began to undo the wrapping.

"I don't understand," she said, as her eye fell upon the title page. "This is not possible. How—" She broke off as she flicked through the pages and saw this was indeed her father's work.

"It was very nearly impossible, Miss Desmond," said her companion. "I'm afraid I've gotten myself in a—a bit of trouble as a consequence."

What was wrong? she asked herself. She'd been certain she'd never know a moment's peace until the work was back in her possession. Here it was, and she felt nearly ill. This was undoubtedly her father's hand—though the lines seemed uncharacteristically shaky. Or was that her vision? To her chagrin she discovered her eyes were swimming. She blinked back the tears and made her belated answer.

"I'm sorry. I didn't know what to say. I was just so—so surprised," she murmured. "My Lord, this is—this is exceedingly kind of you. Thank you. I cannot tell you what a relief it is." Then his last words penetrated. "Trouble?" she asked, making herself meet his gaze. "What do you mean?"

"I had to use my father's name to get them," he answered. "Atkins has dealings with him on occasion, you see. He'll be expecting to hear from my father by now, and when he does not, he'll seek him out—and I shall be found out."

Lord Berne's face seemed composed, but the feverish light in his eyes made Delilah uneasy.

"Your father will be very angry, My Lord," she said. "I never meant—I'm sure I never wished—"

"It's of no consequence, Miss Desmond," the viscount replied with a shrug. "My sire and I have already quarrelled bitterly. He's told me in no uncertain terms that I must cease my pursuit of you." He nodded towards the manuscript. "There is my answer to him." He paused a moment. "It's also my question to you, Miss Desmond," he continued in lower, caressing tones. "Will you believe now that mine is not some fickle fancy? I have stood your friend all these weeks, asking nothing in return. I have kept the promise I made you. Will you believe at last that I love you?"

He reached to take her hand and bring it to his lips. "Because I do love you," he went on softly. He kissed each finger. "More than life, more than honour. Ask me anything and I will do it. Tell me how to go away forever, and I will."

He turned the unresisting hand over and kissed the palm.

213

Then he raised his head, and his blue eyes seemed to burn into hers. "But you must tell me now—and it must be forever," he said, more softly still. "I cannot wait any longer, my dearest."

Miss Desmond knew an ultimatum when she heard one, and like it or not, she had to see the reason in it. She could not expect to keep him dangling forever. However he'd gotten the manuscript, he had done it, and saved her father as a result. To spurn the viscount now would be the height of ingratitude—not to mention stupidity. Where would she ever again find so heartbreakingly handsome, so charming, so compelling a lover? Still, he had better understand he must be more than a lover.

"Before I answer, My Lord, you must be more specific about what you are asking," she said, her own voice as soft as his.

He smiled faintly. "Even now you don't trust me, though I understand your reasons. I'm asking you to be my wife. Will you come away with me—now—and marry me?"

She drew back a bit. "Now?"

"It must be. When my father discovers what I've done, he'll know immediately for whom I did it."

"But you did nothing wrong," she cried, apprehensive now. "The book is my father's. You were only returning his property."

"The book is of no consequence. It's *you*. Are you prepared to tell my sire that after obtaining the manuscript from me, you gave me my *congé*? No other answer will appease him, you know. If you can't assure him you've cast me off, he'll do all he can to be rid of you—even if it means destroying your family."

"I don't understand," she said stubbornly. "I must either marry you at once or never see you again? That makes no sense."

"There is no other way I can protect you from my father's rage. Don't you see?" He squeezed her hand tenderly. "Please, my dear, come with me now. We'll go far away. By the time he finds us—if ever he does—it will be too late. He'll have to accept you then, because the alternative is an ugly scandal."

"What of *my* parents?" she returned. "They'll be beside themselves if I don't come home."

"We haven't time. We'll send a message once we're well upon the road. My love, I beg you, no more delay." He released her hand to reach into his pocket. He took out a document and gave it to her.

"A special license," he said. "After the last row with my father I saw there was no alternative. If you were generous enough to consent, I had to be ready to make it right immediately. I'm ready. Will you continue to delay, when every moment is precious, when every second keeps us from our vows?"

Naturally, Delilah wanted to delay, to ask another hundred questions. This was too sudden. She hadn't had time to prepare her mind and heart to accept him fully. Besides that, she was skeptical. Even though he'd behaved well for weeks, perhaps he'd only wanted to give her a false sense of security. He could not suppress the passion in his voice now, any more than he could mask the hot gleam in his eyes.

Still, lust was not a terrible thing—not to her. She could never be happy with a passionless man, she told herself, thrusting another image from her mind. Even if bedding her formed the greater part of Lord Berne's wishes, she sensed there was sufficient love in him as well. That would serve—so long as he did marry her.

That he would do, she vowed inwardly, whatever he truly intended. She was no green schoolgirl. A special license was all very well, but she had her pistol in her reticule, and that was better.

═ 18 ═

At about the time Miss Desmond was agreeing to run away with her desperate swain, Mr. Langdon was being recalled to consciousness by his valet, who had been summoned by a hysterically babbling Joseph.

Though Mr. Langdon was confused and in great pain, he was in sufficient possession of his wits to know he had not passed out from drink. Nor did Mr. Fellows need to point out that his master must have been struck on the back of the head with the bust of Caesar Augustus. The bust, being made of marble, lay undamaged upon the carpet. Mr. Langdon's head, being made of more delicate material, was in the process of producing a large, throbbing lump.

Mr. Fellows expressed his disapproval. He could not think what the world was coming to when young gentlemen must behave like the veriest ruffians, engaging in brawls in respectable households and bashing one another's skulls.

"Damn it, man, it wasn't a brawl," Jack growled as his valet helped him to his feet. "He came up on me from behind and—" He broke off as his gaze fell upon the disorderly heap of wrapping paper and books on the floor by a chair. Thrusting his valet aside, Jack tore into the heap, flinging away paper and books in a perfectly demented manner and leading Mr. Fellows to observe aloud that his master was suffering from concussion.

"He's taken it," said the unheeding Jack in stunned disbelief. "He knocked me unconscious and *stole* it."

"Inbreeding," Mr. Fellows pronounced. "That is the

trouble with the aristocracy. In another generation, mark my words, they'll all be precisely like His Majesty."

That he was nonetheless moved by the present situation was apparent, for Mr. Fellows immediately set to restoring order himself, instead of requiring the dumbfounded Joseph to do so. The valet picked up the books and placed them neatly on a nearby table—which was when he saw the folded piece of note paper.

He handed it to his employer, saying, "I suppose there is some delirious explanation in it." He turned to Joseph. "You needn't stand there gaping like an imbecile. Go find some ice."

Mr. Langdon staggered to a chair and sat down to read the note, though the letters seemed to dance before his eyes. Fortunately—and uncharacteristically—it was brief. No more than five apologies and a dash of purple prose clouded the main point, which was that Tony had relieved his friend of the manuscript because he had a greater need for it, Love taking precedence over all other human concerns.

When Jack arrived at Potterby House, he found Mrs. Desmond, who'd only moments before come downstairs, standing in the hall upbraiding her aunt.

"Unchaperoned, Aunt Mimsy?" she was saying, her voice deeply reproachful. "With *him*, of all men?"

Lady Potterby was opening her mouth to defend herself when Jack hurried forward.

"She's gone?" he asked, too agitated to remember his manners. "Miss Desmond has gone out?"

Mrs. Desmond's glance took in his ashen face, the wreck that was once his starched neck-cloth, and the ruin of his frantically-raked hair. "The parlour," she said quickly. "Aunt Mimsy, go to your room."

Mr. Langdon spent no more than five minutes in the parlour—only enough time to make Mrs. Desmond promise to say nothing to her husband. Or, if this was impossible, she must at least do all she could to keep him at home.

"Then I must lie to him, Jack," she said, "and I've never done so before."

"This is no time for scruples, ma'am. Tell him she's with me. She will be, I promise you."

From Potterby House Mr. Langdon rode directly to Hyde Park. The hour being relatively early, the place was not yet jammed with vehicles. He did not therefore require too much time to ascertain that Tony's curricle was not there.

With increasing sense of foreboding, Jack left. He had no idea where Tony could have taken Miss Desmond. There was only one hope of discovering a clue.

Not long after he'd left the park, Jack was at Melgrave House, crashing the knocker against the door.

"Lord Berne," he demanded of the stony-faced servant who opened the door. "Where is he?"

"His lordship is not at home, sir."

"Damn it, I know he's not home. Where's he gone?"

The porter retreated a step from the wild-eyed figure before him, though he maintained his frigidity.

"An extended trip, Mr. Langdon," he answered curtly as he attempted to close the door.

Jack pushed him aside and stormed down the hallway. "Where is Lord Streetham?" he shouted.

The shout brought out the butler and several other curious servants, none of whom seemed inclined to cooperate with this madman. That he was not taken up and thrown out bodily was attributable only to his being considered more or less part of the family. Thus, though unhelpful, no one attempted to prevent him as he stomped towards the earl's study, where he met that gentleman at the door.

"What a devil of a noise you're making, Jack," the earl

reprimanded. "Don't tell me you and Tony have taken to quarrelling again as you used to."

"Where has he gone?" Jack demanded. "You would know. You know all his hideaways. Where has he taken her?"

"My dear boy, I haven't the least idea what you're raving about."

"Tony has run off with Miss Desmond," said the dear boy in some heat.

Lord Streetham's lip curled in contempt. "Is that all? He's run off with a wench. What of it? This would not be the first time."

"All?" Jack echoed incredulously. "This is not some ballet dancer we speak of, but Mr. Desmond's daughter. Lord Stivling's grand-niece—"

"I know who her relations are," said Lord Streetham. "Most of them do not acknowledge her existence—and rightly so, if what you announce is true. She has bewitched my son and he has made her his mistress—as she no doubt has schemed for from the first. Well, I wish her joy of the transaction, for not a penny will I give that stupid boy to throw away on *her*."

Upset as he was, Jack could see that pleading Miss Desmond's innocence would be futile. Though certain she'd been deceived—may even have been rendered unconscious, as he had—Jack could never convince the earl of that.

Only one prospect might rouse Lord Streetham from his sneering complacency.

"I think, My Lord," said Jack, "you underestimate how thoroughly 'bewitched' Tony is. Not two hours ago he was at my house, informing me he intended to marry her." He went on to repeat as much as he could remember of Tony's speech, with particular emphasis on his friend's expressed defiance of his parents.

"All talk," said the earl at the end of the recital. "More of his absurd speeches. I am sure he believed himself—for at least ten minutes."

Nonetheless, a flicker of uneasiness had crossed the older man's face. That was the only hint, but it was all Jack had. A few minutes later, he'd taken his leave.

Mr. Langdon waited in the mews until he heard, with unspeakable relief, the summons for Lord Streetham's carriage.

After another endless wait, the carriage was readied. A short while later, it was on its way, with Mr. Langdon following at a discreet distance. Not until night had fallen did Jack feel sufficiently sure of its direction to dash ahead.

They were headed north, which could mean Gretna Green. Unfortunately, it could also mean Lord Streetham's hunting box in Kirkby Glenham. Still, the earl could not be certain either, unless Tony had been unusually confiding in his valet. At any rate, Jack told himself, his lordship must stop to make enquiries along the way, and it would be wisest to precede him.

Darkness had descended and the air, consequently, had grown chilly. Miss Desmond, wrapped in a thick rug her thoughtful spouse-to-be had provided, was only uncomfortable inwardly. The farther they retreated from London, the more she repented her decision, and the harder it became to understand why she had made it, why she had so little considered the pain her act would cause others.

Her parents must be beside themselves with worry—or, in Papa's case, rage—and she hated to think the condition Aunt Millicent must be in. Delilah could only hope her father was not yet in hot pursuit. At least he had no clue to her direction. Though at present she wouldn't mind being caught and taken home, she would mind very much what Papa would do. The Devil was not short-tempered, but even his patience could be tried too far, and the result would be deadly. If he found them, he'd be certain to kill Lord Berne first and ask questions after. Then Papa would be hanged—and it would all be her fault.

If she had been more discreet, Lord Berne would have known nothing about the manuscript but what the gossips said. Then he would not have stolen it. It was a stupid thing for him to do, and so clumsy. Papa would have had a much cleverer scheme, untraceable to himself. Still, she was to blame for the viscount's foolhardiness. She'd demanded heroics and Tony, romantic fool that he was, had performed them.

Even Mr. Langdon had tried, in his way, to be heroic. Only he'd failed, poor man. How embarrassed he must be. She could picture him, his hair all rumpled and his cravat limp and wrinkled and his face flushed . . . and she wanted to weep, because she would have given anything if, at this moment, she might have smoothed his hair and straightened his cravat . . . and covered his flushed face with kisses and told him she loved him anyway.

This last reflection resulted in an urge to weep so violent that she had to focus all her energies upon resisting it. Being so occupied, she did not at first comprehend the sudden halt of the carriage, or the meaning of the hoarse shout, "Stand and deliver!"

Not certain she had heard correctly, Delilah raised her head—to behold a masked figure astride a dark horse. The figure was pointing a pistol at Lord Berne's head.

Delilah's heart seemed to shoot up into her throat, but her brain instantly cleared. Under cover of the rug which wrapped her, she drew her reticule closer and opened it. Her hand had just clamped round the handle of her pistol when the harsh voice rang out once more, making her start.

"No, madam. Throw it down—now—or your lover dies."

"For God's sake, Delilah, do as he says," Tony whispered.

Delilah threw her reticule into the road in front of the robber's horse.

"Now you," he said hoarsely to Lord Berne. "Give the lady the reins and down into the road with you."

Tony scrambled down from the carriage.

"Off with your coat—and your waistcoat—and your boots. And be quick about it."

Though Lord Berne promptly obeyed, Delilah could see, even in the weak moonlight, that his face was contorted with rage. She could not think what to do. She dared not whip up the horses. The highwayman might shoot Tony—not to mention *her*. Her reticule was now far out of reach, and she could hardly expect to overcome their assailant by throwing the manuscript at him—even if she could get to it without attracting his attention.

She wracked her brains for some comparable experience of her father's to guide her. But Papa would never have been so careless. Gad, how could Lord Berne have been so foolish as to continue travelling after dark? Why was he not armed? Why had he not suggested they spend the night at the inn where they'd stopped earlier?

While Delilah was plaguing herself with If Onlys, her companion had completed his undressing.

Keeping his pistol trained on the viscount, the robber dismounted and collected Lord Berne's belongings and her reticule. He tied his horse to the carriage, then climbed up onto the seat beside her.

"Turn the carriage," he growled, his pistol now aimed at her.

"I can't," she lied. "I don't know how."

"Turn it!" the thief hissed.

"Don't argue with him, Delilah," Tony pleaded. "He'll hurt you."

Muttering a most unladylike oath, and certain she would be hurt regardless, Delilah turned the curricle. With the pistol pointed at her, she could do nothing else but drive on as ordered, leaving Lord Berne behind in his silk-stockinged feet, in the dust.

Considering her peril, Miss Desmond ought to have been

frightened out of her wits, but she was too furious to be afraid. To be at the mercy of a common thief—she, the daughter of Devil Desmond—was the outside of enough. At the first opportunity, she vowed inwardly, she'd drive the carriage into a ditch. At worst, they'd both be killed. At best, she might make an escape. In any case, she would not wait quietly to be raped by this low ruffian.

Rape seemed inevitable. Why else had he not left her behind with Lord Berne?

They were rapidly approaching a fork in the road. The highwayman told her to take the right turning—which was odd, she thought. This was the way she'd come from London—but no, there were other turnings. He must be heading for some out-of-the-way spot. His hideaway, no doubt. Some thieves' den.

Her mouth went dry. He must have accomplices. Lud, what would Papa do? The odds. Weigh the odds first. One man, one pistol, versus one woman. Later, who knew how many cutthroats, or how soon she'd be in their midst? It must be now.

Delilah slowed the carriage, ostensibly for the turn, then pulled hard on the reins. As the horses reared in protest, she threw herself at the robber.

The sudden attack took him by surprise, and the pistol fell out of his hand to the floor of the carriage. Delilah lunged for it, but was taken up short when he grasped the hair dangling at her neck and yanked her back.

He tore the reins from her hands. "Damn you," he rasped as the horses settled down. "Are you out of your mind?"

Somewhere in the periphery of her consciousness was a jolt of recognition, but Delilah was in too violent a state to pay attention. Her fist swung towards his face, only to be grabbed and wrenched aside. Then a hard chest pressed upon her, pushing her back hard against the carriage seat. She could scarcely breathe, but with what little breath she had she informed him in Arabic that he was the product of an interesting relationship between a camel and a dung beetle.

As she tried to twist away from the menacing masked face lowering to her own, she thought she heard him snicker.

Startled, she looked at him. Behind the narrow slits of the mask were glittering eyes. In an instant, the glitter turned to darkness as his mouth descended upon hers.

Though she twisted and struggled, she found herself slowly, inexorably sinking back onto the seat under the relentless pressure of her attacker's body. Unable to budge him, she shut her eyes tight and willed herself to be rigidly unresponsive. That much control she had at least.

Unfortunately, her position was awkward and painful to begin with. Maintaining a stiff posture made it more so. Her body ached horribly, and she was badly winded. Even her will was rapidly deserting her. Struggling had done nothing, evidently, but drain all her strength, for her stupid body was weakening, warming, succumbing to the brutal, seeking kiss. Sick and miserable, she gave up battling because she simply couldn't continue. Later, she promised herself . . . later she would *kill* him.

In the next instant, to her astonishment, the weight was lifted off her. She opened stunned eyes to meet her attacker's serious gaze. Serious? It could not be, she thought hysterically.

He'd started to move away from her, but in a flash she caught hold of the scarf covering his face and yanked it down, unmasking him.

"You," she gasped. "Good God, Jack, I nearly killed you. Why didn't you say right off it was you?" Joy, relief, welled up inside her, and she was about to hug him when he moved hastily away and gave the weary cattle leave to start.

"I was about to," he answered irritably, "when you attacked me. What on earth possessed you, Miss Desmond? We might have both been killed. If the horses hadn't been so tired, they might have taken off and overturned us."

Miss Desmond? Delilah squelched a sigh of vexation. "I thought I was being abducted by a highwayman," she said, striving for patience. "What did you expect me to do? It's the middle of the night. You were wearing a mask. How was I to know it was you?" Her lower lip quivered. "I think you're monstrous unfair to scold me," she went on unsteadily, "after you've frightened me half to death. You might at least have said something, instead of—of assaulting me."

"As I recollect, it was you struck first," he shot back. "Since I could not hit back, I tried to restrain you. When that didn't work, I resorted to the only response that ever does seem to work with you. I'm sorry I frightened you, but really, you left me no choice."

She threw him a reproachful glance, but he was staring stonily ahead, his posture rigid. She could not comprehend how a man could kiss one so passionately one moment and be so coldly indifferent in the next.

Yet she did understand. He'd only wanted to subdue her, and he'd succeeded because, as he'd said, that way always seemed to work. Without answering, Delilah turned her mortified gaze to the trees that lined the road. She heard a bird cry somewhere in the distance and another cry answering it. She wanted to cry out too.

They rode on in tense silence for a few minutes. Then he spoke. "You're shivering," he said, his voice gentler.

She pulled the rug up over her.

Mr. Langdon drew a long breath. "Miss Desmond, have I made a mistake?" he asked. "Did you truly wish to go away with him?"

"I don't know if you've made a mistake, Mr. Langdon. You still have not told me why you came," she hedged.

"Why I came?" he repeated in amazement. "I thought he'd made off with you. I couldn't believe my eyes when I saw you sitting so tamely beside him. I'd thought surely to find you trussed up and unconscious. I could not believe you'd go away with him of your own free will."

Delilah's face began to burn. "So now you conclude I was going passively to my ruin—is that what you think?"

"Not *passively*," came the meaningful reply.

"I see," she said, turning away so her face would not betray her. "You thought I was ready to throw my cap over the windmill. Indeed, why shouldn't you assume what everyone else does? Licentiousness is in my blood, of course. I could not possibly be running away to be married."

"If that's what he told you and you were naïve enough to believe him—"

"I did not believe *him*, Mr. Langdon. I believed a piece of paper signed by a bishop." She rubbed away the traitorous wetness on her cheeks, though she still would not look at him. "It's in my reticule," she added with cold dignity, "if you care to read it."

The carriage stopped.

"He showed you a license?" Jack asked, his voice uneasy.

"Not only showed it, but gave it to me for safekeeping. In my reticule—somewhere in that heap with all his things. He'll probably take a terrible chill and die, and he has his friend to thank for it," Miss Desmond continued while her companion bent to search.

He found the reticule and offered it to her, but she shook her head.

"You can't be so careless as to trust me with that," she said. "As you must have guessed earlier, my pistol is in there, too."

He opened the purse and drew out the folded document.

"It's too dark to read it," he said.

"How thoughtless of me not to bring a tinder-box and candles."

Mr. Langdon considered briefly, then drew a sigh.

"I'd better take you back to him," he said wearily. "I won't even attempt to apologise." He paused to gaze at her unmoving profile, then blurted out, "Damn, Delilah, but I'm sorry. Only I thought—well, you know what I thought—but I was so—I was half out of my mind with worry," he went on hurriedly. "I was sure he'd hurt you. He wasn't himself—I mean, he knocked me on the head with Caesar Augustus and ran off with the manuscript and I was sure he'd gone mad—"

Miss Desmond's head whipped towards him. "He *what?*"

Mr. Langdon must have recollected himself, because he turned away from her horrified gaze. "Nothing," he said quickly. "He was beside himself, and I suppose I can understand. His father was perfectly beastly, and Tony must have felt desperate. I mean, he'd *promised* you, hadn't he? He wanted to help you, to be your hero, I expect—only I was in the way."

"*You* had the manuscript?" Delilah asked shakily. "He stole it from *you*—not Mr. Atkins?"

"Evidently, I got there first."

"Are you excusing him? He attacked you—stole the memoirs from you—and you make excuses?" Delilah blinked, but it didn't help. The world was still hopelessly askew.

"I cannot decide," she said slowly, "which one of you is more insane. But one thing is certain. I am not going back to him this evening. You will take me home, Mr. Langdon. I am not in a humour at present to be married—and certainly not to a lunatic."

Nonetheless, the lunatic was not altogether abandoned to his fate. Jack insisted upon leaving messages at the tollgates for Lord Streetham, describing where he might collect his son. Luckily, they were able to pass the earl's carriage unnoticed half an hour later. He had stopped at an inn and was inside, probably making enquiries, when Jack and Delilah drove by.

To neither Delilah's nor Jack's very great surprise, they were received by her parents with complete composure.

Lady Potterby, succumbing to the welcome enticements of laudanum, had gone to bed. Thus, there were no shrieks, tears, upbraidings, nor any other sort of carryings-on. Even after Mr. Langdon had departed, the parents only gazed upon their daughter as though she were an exceedingly intricate and difficult puzzle.

"You and Mr. Langdon were rather cool to each other, I think," said Mrs. Desmond at last, as her husband refilled her wine glass. "Did you quarrel the whole way back?"

"Not the whole way, Mama. For the last two hours we did not speak at all."

"Oh, Delilah," her mother said reproachfully.

"Well, what would you have me do, Mama? He made me feel a perfect fool. I thought—well, I could not believe he'd go to so much trouble—disguising himself as a highwayman, no less. I thought—" Delilah's eyes went to her father then, and she flushed. "I thought he cared for me—but all he did was scold. And then the provoking man must commence to defending his friend. He even offered to take me back to Lord Berne. Can you believe it?" She sighed. "I can do nothing with him at all. It's perfectly hopeless, which I knew it was all along. It's all hopeless," she went on drearily. "I wish he'd never come. I wish I'd gone back and married Lord Berne after all. He at least I can manage."

"Good heavens," said Mr. Desmond. "Why did you not tell me you wanted someone manageable? I might have ordered Lord Berne at swordpoint to marry you at the outset, and spared us all a great deal of aggravation."

Delilah blinked back a tear. "I am not in a humour to be teased, Papa," she said. "I am very tired."

Her father gazed blankly at his wife. "My dear, I am certain she has told me a dozen times at least that she could only be happy with some sort of deceitful, unpredictable scoundrel like her poor papa."

"Indeed, she has said as much to me countless times," the mama agreed.

"Am I manageable, Angelica?"

"Not in the least. There is nothing to be done with you."
Mrs. Desmond sounded resigned.

Their daughter, who had been trudging dispiritedly
about the room in pale imitation of her usual energetic
pacing, now flung herself into a chair. "I had rather be
punished, you know. You might as well scold me and be
done with it. Or lock me in my room for the rest of my
life. I really don't care. I'd prefer it, actually. Obviously
there's no other way to make me behave properly." She
stared glumly at the carpet.

Her father paid her no mind, but went on addressing
himself to his wife.

"I do not understand," he said. "I thought he was exactly
what she wanted. He has a perfect genius for skullduggery.
Who was it finally unearthed Streetham's connexion with
Atkins? Who learned the precise hour Atkins would deliver
the manuscript to the printer? Who suggested exchanging
one package for another, so that Atkins would not know
what had happened until it was too late?"

Delilah looked up. "Are you telling me, Papa, this was
all Mr. Langdon's doing, not yours?"

"Not *all*," the father corrected. "Let me see. It was he
who asked Lady Rand to take you about—but you were
aware of that, I think. He also asked the Demowerys to
help us by denying all existence of the memoirs and
persuading the gossips the newspaper article was a hoax.
Then there was his idea of spreading rumours better suited
to our purposes—such as the legal case I was preparing
against Atkins and the sad state of the man's finances." Mr.
Desmond reflected a moment as he sipped his wine. "Oh,
yes, and the matter of luring away employees, so that
certain businesses could not function with their usual
efficiency. Well, there's more, I suppose, but Mr. Langdon
prefers to keep some matters to himself. Very close he is,
and sly. Not at all to be trusted, now I think on it."

"Certainly he was not open and aboveboard in disguising
himself as a highwayman," Mrs. Desmond concurred. "I'm

afraid he was not altogether frank with Lord Streetham, either. Mr. Langdon must have tricked him into betraying his son's direction. Moreover, though Delilah is too delicate to mention it, I feel certain Mr. Langdon's behaviour this evening offended her modesty."

The delicate daughter flushed.

"She is quite right," said Mr. Desmond. "The fellow is altogether incorrigible."

"We should have paid more attention, Darryl. Poor Delilah is obviously no match for such a scoundrel. He would only run roughshod over her," said Mrs. Desmond.

Mr. Desmond shook his head sadly. "I'm sorry I did not see it sooner. Of course she will do far better with Berne. She will do, in fact, anything she likes with him."

The pair turned apologetic gazes upon their daughter. "We do beg your pardon, dear," said her mama. "We have sadly misjudged the situation."

Delilah glanced from one compassionate countenance to the other. Then she gave an exasperated sigh, rose from her chair, and stomped out of the room.

=19=

BEING A MAN of honour and possessed of a powerful sense of justice, Mr. Langdon knew where his duty lay. He had a most disagreeable task to perform, but he did not shrink from it. He would do what honour required of him . . . and then he would hang himself. It was quite simple, really. All would be over within a matter of hours.

Accordingly, after he had lain in his bed long enough to call it rest, he arose, dressed, and, taking up the neat bundle Mr. Fellows had made of Lord Berne's clothes, took himself to Melgrave House.

Though the butler admitted him with some reluctance, he did admit him, no orders having been given to the contrary, and directed Jack to the viscount's dressing room.

Lord Berne glanced at his friend's face, then at the bundle he handed the valet.

"Leave us," the viscount told his servant.

The valet exited.

"There is no point in calling me out," said Lord Berne before Jack could speak. "If you force me to a duel, I promise to delope. You may kill me if you like. I cannot blame you. You'd be doing me a great favour, in fact. I wish I was dead." He said all this without his usual dramatic vehemence, though his face was white and rigid.

Jack looked at him in incomprehension. "I don't think you understand, Tony. It was I last night—"

"I know. I guessed it when my father told me how he

found me so speedily. He told me you'd been here looking for me earlier."

He turned from his friend's gaze. "I should not have hit you. I might have killed you. I should not have done a great many things, as my father has pointed out at length. He says I'm to offer for Lady Jane today," Tony went on bitterly. "If I do not, he'll cut off my allowance and forbid every tradesman in the kingdom to extend me credit. If he had another son, I'm sure he wouldn't hesitate to have me transported."

Jack thought that if Conscience had been a living creature, it would have risen up and throttled him on the spot.

"This is all my fault," he said. "I misjudged you horribly. You've told me repeatedly how much you cared for Miss Desmond and I refused to believe you. I persisted in thinking this was like every other passing fancy, when naturally it couldn't be. You've never spoken so of other women, never persisted so long."

The viscount smiled faintly. "An hour, Jack. Maybe a day. Certainly I never nearly murdered my friends on such an account. Yes, it was—is—different, but—"

"And you might have been married by now, if I hadn't jumped on my charger. Gad, I shall never forgive myself. Lady Jane—Tony, you cannot do it."

"I must. I am not equipped to live modestly, and, being a perfect gentleman, I have no productive skills by which to earn my keep. I'm not even a good card player." The smile turned bleak.

Jack considered a moment. "Miss Desmond is," he said absently. "Her father taught her a great many things, including how to use a pistol." Noting his friend's bafflement, he added, "You knew she had a pistol with her, didn't you, Tony?"

"No," came the stunned reply.

"That's why I made her throw down her reticule. She would have shot me without turning a hair."

Lord Berne found a chair and fell into it, his face working strangely.

Jack moved to the dresser. Jewelled tie pins, rings, watch-chains, and seals lay strewn about in gay abandon. Idly he began arranging and rearranging these in tidy lines.

"How idiotic I was," he said "to think you could dishon-our her, even if you'd meant to—though I do apologise for thinking you would. You know enough of women to know she's a treasure."

He placed an emerald tie pin next to a diamond ring, frowned, and moved it next to one of the seals.

"There's no one, there never will be anyone like her," he went on. "You saw that, and told yourself you could never settle for anything less."

Lord Berne was staring at the carpet.

"It's more than beauty, isn't it?" said Jack. "Even though it's a beauty that breaks your heart. When she's near, you feel you're in some wild, primitive, very dangerous place. Yet there's something so tender and fragile about her, as well. She *will* strike out and wound you, and even as you're reeling from it, you ache to protect her—perhaps from herself."

He drew a deep breath and moved away from the dresser. Tony looked up, and there was dawning respect in his blue eyes.

"How do you know so much, Jack?" he asked.

Jack shrugged. "She's the Devil's daughter," he answered lightly enough. "She makes every man a little mad, I think, and so to some extent, every man must understand."

"You love her." It was not a question.

"I love quiet and peace, everything in its proper place. When one is forever muddled, you know, one prefers that everything else not be so."

"That's no answer," said the viscount quietly. "But I won't plague you. I've done enough of that—more than I knew. If it's any comfort to you, I shall be paying, all the rest of my life. Lady Jane will see to it."

"In that case," said his friend, "you're a great fool."
And without another word, the friend was gone.

An hour after his conversation with Jack, Lord Berne was at Potterby House. To be precise, he was in the study with Mr. Desmond, under whose withering, green-eyed scrutiny the viscount struggled in vain not to quail. The viscount seemed to be shrinking smaller by the minute under that gaze, until he felt he was looking up at the Devil's boot. At least, the young man thought wryly, it wasn't a cloven hoof.

"Marry her?" Desmond was saying in the most affable way. "Why the deuce should I give my daughter into the keeping of an ill-gotten, lying, sneaking, idle wretch of a pretty boy like yourself? Even if I didn't think you were mad as a hatter—which I do, incidentally. Even if I were not convinced you were a prime candidate for Bedlam, why should I give her into the custody of one whose father has done everything possible to destroy my family?" He turned away and sauntered to the window. "I only ask for information," he added.

"When you put it like that," said a thoroughly crushed Lord Berne, "I really cannot imagine any satisfactory answer."

"Then perhaps you are not quite so deranged as I thought. You are correct. There is no satisfactory answer."

Mr. Desmond continued to gaze out the window. After an agonisingly long minute he said, "She tells me you never touched her. Is that so, or was she protecting you?"

"It is true, sir." The green eyes fastened on him again and Lord Berne, to his horrour, heard himself adding, "I did not have the opportunity."

"That's just as well," was the cool reply. "She would have shot you."

The viscount wondered wildly if what he'd heard was true: that the Devil was a mesmerist. Certainly one could not possibly tear one's gaze from those glittering eyes. No more had Lord Berne been able to keep back his ghastly confessions, for it seemed as though that control too had been given over entirely to the Devil's keeping.

"Moreover," Desmond went on, "it would give me the greatest pleasure to shoot you myself. Unfortunately, that would only play into your father's hands. He would like to see me hanged. He's longed for such a conclusion these five and twenty years. Do you know why?"

Lord Berne shook his head.

"Because my wife would not have him." He smiled faintly. "They say Hell hath no fury like a woman scorned. How little they know. How little *you* know, My Lord. But you have a beautiful face and a fine figure, and perhaps Delilah will take those into account. At any rate, I'm confident she'll provide you a most stimulating education."

Lord Berne required a moment to digest this speech. "I beg your pardon, sir. Are you giving me your permission?" he asked, astonished.

"I have no choice. I am so overcome by your audacity that I have not the strength of mind to resist you."

"But you hate me," said Lord Berne.

"My dear young man, you are scarcely worthy of so much energy. I do, however, pity you, for a number of reasons—your obsession with Delilah being not the least of these. Whether she accepts you or not, she will make you thoroughly wretched, and there is some satisfaction in that. She will make your father even more wretched, and to be perfectly frank, I find the prospect irresistible."

"My father can have nothing to say to this. I explained the situation to you, I thought."

The Devil waved this away.

"You are merely his son," he said. "He does what he likes with you. He will not find me nearly so malleable. If Delilah weds you, it will be in St. George's, Hanover Square, and all the world will be obliged to think it a very good match, indeed. Rely upon it."

Mr. Desmond returned his cynical gaze to the window.

"You may go to her now," he said. "After you've had your answer—whatever it is—my wife and I will have something more to say to you."

Mr. Langdon had proceeded from Melgrave House to that of Lord Rand, in order to see his friends one last time before he hanged himself.

He had devoted the walk to convincing himself he had no need to see Miss Desmond one last time because she would only break his heart again. It was wounded in so many places already that one more blow would surely collapse it altogether, and he did not wish to die in front of her. Hanging himself was more dignified, and certainly more discreet.

All of which he knew was ridiculous, but he was lovesick and his case was hopeless and, in the circumstances, being ridiculous was virtually an obligation.

Peace, he thought, eternal peace. Never again need he struggle to preserve the mask of a civilised gentleman while a ravening beast within fought wildly to overpower him.

In the end he'd be quiet, just as he'd told Tony—in a cool, tranquil vault where she could never get at him and rattle him. Never again would he look upon her maddeningly beautiful face or hold her in his arms. Never again would she run her willful hands through his hair . . . and pull his mouth to hers . . . and moan so softly, her breath warm on his face. . . .

He had just turned the corner into Grosvenor Square and had to stop and lean against a railing because all the breath seemed to have rushed out of his body at once. He stood there, clutching the railing, oblivious to the curious stares of passersby, a long while. Then he straightened, tugged at his cravat, and turned back in the direction of Potterby House.

The butler was just explaining that Miss Desmond was busy at the moment, when Lady Potterby fluttered out, all smiles, and led Jack into the drawing room.

Ten minutes later, Jack was on his way home. He saw no need to linger. Tony was in the parlour with Delilah and they were unchaperoned because Tony was proposing, as Lady Potterby had been stubbornly assuring one and all he would. He had even, her ladyship announced triumphantly, gone about it in the proper way, speaking first to the young lady's papa.

Oddly enough, Jack felt calm at last. This was the end of it. He would not hang himself—not yet. No doubt Tony would want his friend as groomsman, and it would be churlish to commit suicide before fulfilling one's obligations to one's friends.

Meanwhile, Jack would go back to Rossingley. He would not, however, stop at any inns along the way, not even if overtaken by a hurricane.

Lord Berne made the most moving proposal any young lady was like to hear in this century. Following his interview with her father, Tony had decided he'd be wisest to commence with a clean slate. He admitted he'd been driven by lust and had intended only to make her his mistress. The special license, he explained with some shame, he'd had for ages, and had used twice before to deceive his victims.

Delilah did not appear at all surprised. She listened quietly, in a vaguely bored manner that made her suitor feel even more like a worm than he'd been made to feel by everyone else.

Nevertheless, he went on determinedly, "Even today I thought only of myself, and felt sorry for myself because I had failed and would not have another chance. I was even prepared to wed as my father ordered, because I was afraid of the consequences if I didn't. Luckily, I have a friend far more loyal than I deserve, who helped me see my error. I tell you all this to make an end, once and for all, of deception. I only hope you will be more generous than I deserve. Will you forgive me, my dear, and allow me to begin fresh? Will you do me the very great honour and give me the great happiness of consenting to be my wife?"

Delilah was certain she'd meant to say Yes. The words came out as No, however, and she thought her heart would break when she saw the shattered look on his beautiful countenance. More beautiful, she thought, than it had ever been before, perhaps because for once in his life he had told not his fantasy truth but his heart's truth.

Yet as he'd spoken, he'd somehow revealed her own heart's truth as well, and that crumbled all her carefully built defences, her cynical rationales, and her assurance.

"I'm so sorry, Tony," she said. "I really am sorry to hurt you. I meant to marry you, you know. I would have made you do it—you don't know me—and then we would have been so unhappy."

"Why? How?" he asked. "You could never make me unhappy—except now, to tell me you will not be my wife. I love you, Delilah. I would die to make you happy."

Even as he spoke the words, he knew they were futile. Though she sat quietly enough, gazing down at her folded hands, he sensed this was not the world-weary repose it seemed to be. With a jolt he remembered what Jack had said.

Tony lifted her chin so he could look into her beautiful eyes. "It's Jack, isn't it?" he asked. "You're in love with him. That's why." There was no reproach in his tones. He saw it in her eyes, a fact, and like the others he'd confronted today, this would not go away for wishing or pretending.

She smiled, rather cynically, he thought, but that was not the truth. That was pose. What she said was pose as well—pretending, wishing.

"Oh, Tony," she said. "You look for a rival instead of listening to what I say."

"It's what I see," he answered.

"Your vision is clouded," she said, "if you see Delilah Desmond in love with a book-worm."

He'd risen, intending to leave, but something nagged at

him. He struggled for a moment, then sat down beside her on the sofa and, taking her hand, began to speak once more.

"What is this?" Mr. Atkins screamed. "Where did you get this?"

Mr. Gillstone gazed down in bewilderment at the sheets the publisher was clutching in his hands. "From you," he said, wondering if the man had at last gone completely mad. Atkins was too high-strung for the business. It wanted a less sensitive nature.

"This is not the manuscript I gave you," the little man cried. "Do I not know the curst thing by heart? Where did you get it? Who bribed you to take it?"

A heated argument ensued, Mr. Gillstone being much offended by the accusation.

They shouted at each other for twenty minutes. Finally, when Mr. Atkins's face had turned purple and the blood vessels were visibly throbbing in his temples, the printer recollected the muddled, flustered, apologetic young man who'd come to him yesterday. Then he dragged Mr. Atkins to his office, made him swallow a tumbler of gin, and told him what had occurred.

The soothing effects of geneva notwithstanding, Mr. Atkins bolted from his chair, snatched up the manuscript, and dashed out of the shop.

Two minutes later he was back again.

"Print it," he said.

"Print it?" Mr. Gillstone echoed.

"Yes. This is the only book we shall ever get from that fiend without trouble and I shall never see my money again, so we might as well salvage what we can. Just don't show it to me when it's done. Deal with my assistant. I never want to see the curst thing again as long as I live."

= 20 =

MR. LANGDON HAD ordered his bags packed so that he might leave first thing in the morning. He'd had enough of dashing about like a madman in the middle of the night.

All the same, he did not expect to spend the night in repose, so he did not even attempt to go to bed. He sat in the library, staring at a volume of Tacitus for two hours before he noticed he had not turned a page. He slammed the book shut and flung it aside.

Then he put on his coat and went out for a walk. A long walk. Perhaps he would be set upon by ruffians and savagely beaten. That would be a profound relief.

He circled the West End endlessly, passing houses where drawn-back curtains and brilliant lights boasted of festivities in progress. Occasionally a carriage clattered past, but it was too early for great folks to be heading home, and the streets were relatively quiet. At midnight the watchman's voice rang out, informing the interested public not only of the hour, but of the circumstance that the world, at present, was well, the moon in the sky where it belonged, and the sky itself gradually clearing.

That was when Jack's mind must have snapped, because the watchman had scarcely completed his observations when Mr. Langdon's legs, no longer controlled by a brain or anything like it, blithely took him to Potterby House.

The house was dark, in the front at least. Facades, however, can be deceiving, and ever a seeker of Truth, Mr. Langdon slipped round to the back. There on the second floor, one window remained faintly lit. He stood at the gate for a moment. Then he climbed over it and dropped into the pathway leading to the garden.

His eyes went up to the window once more, and his heart began to pound because he saw a movement by the curtains. A figure in a gauzy negligée passed quickly—though not quickly enough to prevent his catching one tantalising glimpse of the form outlined in the candlelight.

" 'But soft! what light through yonder window breaks?' " he murmured, though he had sense enough left to smile at his folly. " 'It is the east, and Delilah is the sun. Arise, fair sun, and kill the envious moon—' "

The light went out.

"Oh, Delilah," he whispered. "You'll be the death of me."

Twenty times in the next half hour he turned to leave, and twenty times he turned back, because the window held him. Though it was painful to remain, he could not go—not while his mind persisted in reviewing every element of her being. The black, unruly hair that fell so easily into disorder and always made him yearn to see her tumbled among thick pillows in the flickering light of a single candle . . . to see the shadows playing upon the fine bones of her face and the soft light reflected in her lustrous eyes, like moonlight on a lagoon. He longed for so much more. To touch her . . . to feel her touch . . . those restless hands in his hair . . . and so much more still. He wanted to scream.

His heart commenced to crashing against his ribs because he knew what he was going to do even as he was commanding himself not to even consider it. He knew what he was going to do because Max had told him how to do it, had described a dozen times how he'd done it himself.

Not to put too fine a point upon it, Mr. Langdon proceeded to scale the walls of the house. The window was open, after all, practically shouting at him. So, like a common thief, he climbed up to it.

One kiss, he promised himself as he paused halfway over

the sill. Just one chaste kiss. He would not even waken her—good grief, he'd better not—and then he would go.

He crept noiselessly across the thick carpet towards the bed. Though there was no flickering candle, there was sufficient moonlight to outline the form: a dark head upon a white pillow. He bent over her face.

Instantly, a hand seized his wrist, jerking him close. Simultaneously hard metal thrust against his chest. Jack cautiously tried to pull away.

"Another move and you'll find yourself a grave man," she whispered.

He froze.

The hand on his wrist tightened, and the pistol tried to force its way into his lungs.

"Don't," he said.

"Jack," she whispered. "Why it's only you."

Nonetheless, the weapon remained where it was. Jack began to perspire.

"Yes," he said edgily. "Will you please put that away?"

"And leave myself defenceless? Certainly not."

"It's only me, Miss Desmond. You know I mean you no harm. And you're digging your nails into my wrist," he complained.

He heard a derisive sniff.

"No harm?" she repeated scornfully. "From a notorious highwayman, an abductor of innocent maidens? Papa was right. You're a blackguard, Mr. Langdon. I really can't understand how I let myself be so deceived in you."

Actually, he thought, it was better to have the pistol jammed into his chest. Otherwise he might mean harm in spite of himself, because he was too close to her. He was acutely conscious of a faint fragrance which reminded him of roses after a rain.

"Miss Desmond, this is an extremely uncomfortable position. In another moment, my spine will snap."

"Just as well. That will be much less untidy than bullet

wounds. The maids would never get the stains out of the bed-clothes."

He tried to shake off the viselike grip. "You won't shoot me," he said firmly.

"I don't see why not. The world rather expects something of the sort, and I should so hate to disappoint them. Why are you here?" she demanded.

There was no point pretending—even if he'd been capable of formulating a single decent excuse. He sighed. "I only wanted to kiss you," he said, though he was embarrassed as soon as he'd said it. "Just once, before I leave. To—to say good-bye."

"Only to say good-bye?" she asked. "Why, you must have had to climb over the gate. I know it's locked. Then up the house—and there is not much foothold because they've cut back the ivy. Really, that was reckless of you, though quite romantic. But you are a desperate villain, and I suppose I have no choice but to let you kiss me."

A kiss? What the devil had he been thinking of? He could never leave contented with a single kiss. He could probably never leave at all—unless he did so now.

"I—I had better not," he said, panicking. He needed to pull away, but he was concerned the pistol would go off. At the moment, he was not certain whether he'd prefer to be shot, but the noise would arouse the household, and that would never do, he thought wildly.

"If you do not kiss me now," she said slowly, "I will shoot you, and you'll never have another chance. 'The grave's a fine and private place,/ But none, I think, do there embrace.' That is Marvell, is it not?"

Mr. Langdon had had enough. He yanked the pistol from her hand and dropped it on the carpet. Being a small weapon, it made only a small thud.

"Not so much noise," she warned. "Do you want to wake everyone?"

"Delilah, don't make a game of me."

"Jack, don't be such a damned, thick-headed fool. Kiss me at once or I'll scream my head off."

He kissed her. It was not the chaste kiss on the cheek he had intended but he knew now that was never what he'd intended. His lips touched soft, cool ones and he was lost, caught, helpless, because her hands came up to caress his face, then wandered into his hair. He wondered if he'd been killed after all and had flown up straight to heaven.

Several devastating minutes later, he drew away. "I can't stay," he said. "You're driving me crazy, and you don't know how much danger you're in."

"I know," she said wistfully. "I hate being respectable. Oh, Jack, I wish you would kiss me forever."

Being an exceedingly courteous fellow, he instantly set out to oblige her, which was a great mistake, regardless how polite. He soon found himself on top of the bed-clothes, and the need to slip under them was becoming painful. He shuddered and pulled himself away.

"You are impossible," he said, his voice rough. "You know I can't stay, yet you do all you can to keep me here." Then an awful thought struck him. "Tony," he breathed. "You're engaged!"

"Not at all. You haven't asked me." Her voice was soft and languorous. "You'd better, you know. There's no getting out of it now."

Jack grasped her shoulders to shake her back into the real world. "Tony," he said. "What of Tony?"

"There's no need to be so ferocious, Jack. I declined his offer. Really, do you think I would be entertaining you now if I hadn't? Though it would have served you right if I had," she went on petulantly. "You and your dratted honour and loyalty and I don't know what else." Her hands reached up to bury themselves in his hair once more. "Oh, Jack, how difficult you've been."

"I?" he answered indignantly. "I've been getting slapped and screamed at and insulted and—"

"How else was I to get your attention?" she interrupted.

"Do you have any idea how hard it is to penetrate that wall of politeness of yours? How frustrating—" She broke off abruptly.

He brought her hand to his lips and kissed the palm. "If you only knew," he said softly, "how very difficult it's been to be polite and gentlemanly. I've wanted you from the moment I knocked you down. Wanted you desperately. And no matter what I did, it only got worse."

"Then you should have offered right off. That would have been the proper thing." She paused. "Or were you appalled at the prospect of shackling yourself to a wanton adventuress with a beastly temper and unspeakable manners? That must be it. You wanted a ladylike, intellectual, sweet-tempered woman like—like Catherine."

He drew back a bit, much surprised. "What about Catherine?"

"You loved her—love her. That's what everyone says," came the rather wistful reply.

Jack considered briefly. "I see," he said. "You're jealous."

"Yes. If I didn't like her so much I would have throttled her long since, I promise you."

He smiled. "Good. I hope you remain insanely jealous of her all the rest of your life. Perhaps that will make you a tad more manageable."

"You are a coxcomb, Mr. Langdon." Her hand slipped to his neck-cloth to pull him closer. "I will not be manageable at all, and I will make you forget her. Rely upon it."

Evidently, she planned to begin this task immediately, for a most passionate embrace ensued.

Mr. Langdon did not wish to discourage his companion's efforts to extract Lady Rand's image from his heart. On the other hand, he had a ticklish conscience and a powerful sense of honour. These won the day, and he managed to extricate himself before he committed any grave impropriety—though he could not help cursing propriety in the process.

"That is quite enough," he said thickly. "I had better go —*now*. Tomorrow I'll speak to your father."

He got up from the bed and turned to leave.

"Jack."

"No."

"*Jack*."

He clutched his head and turned back towards her. "What?"

"You haven't said."

"What?"

She hesitated. Then, "That you love me," she said very softly.

He moved back to the bed. "I love you. I've loved you for ages. I adore you. You make me crazy. Please, Delilah, let me go."

"I love you, Jack," she whispered. "I've loved you forever."

He groaned, and kissed her once, quickly. Then he did go, though of all the difficult tasks he'd ever undertaken, this was the hardest by far.

Having given up all hopes of ever sleeping again in this lifetime, Mr. Langdon's return home was occupied primarily in pacing until the servants began to stir, when he could at last order a bath. Despite the time consumed in having hot water hauled up the stairs, not to mention shaving and then changing his clothes some half dozen times—which elicited a sharp lecture from his valet—it was only a bit past nine o'clock when Jack arrived at Potterby House. Luckily for the aspiring son-in-law, Mr. Desmond was congenitally incapable of sleeping more than three or four hours a night, and was swallowing the last of his breakfast ale when Jack was shown in.

"You had better not do that again," said Mr. Desmond before his visitor could do more than wish him good morning. "There is hardly any foothold at all, and you might have broken your neck."

There was no point pretending incomprehension when one's red, burning face had already given one away. Nor could Mr. Langdon feel in the least amazed at Desmond's powers of perception.

"Sir, I really cannot express to you how deeply—"

"Then don't. You had better marry her while you are still in one piece. As it is I cannot understand how you've survived the courtship—or whatever it was, exactly." Mr. Desmond gestured towards the sideboard, which was heavily laden with covered dishes. "Take some breakfast, Jack."

Jack could not consider anything so mundane as food. He was frantically in love, and he was *loved*, which was inconceivable. All he wanted at the moment was to see his maddening darling. Unfortunately, he could not think of any acceptable excuse for dashing up to her bedchamber.

A swish of soft fabric and light footsteps made him stiffen suddenly, in the way of a setter that has caught scent of its prey. But the figure pausing in the doorway was Mrs. Desmond. As she entered, Jack crushed his impatience and made his bow.

She smiled, then bent to drop a kiss on her husband's forehead.

"I have news for you, my love," the husband said.

"Do you, dear?" She was moving towards the sideboard, but Jack gallantly offered to do the honours.

"Yes," said Mr. Desmond. "Jack is to marry Delilah."

"Are you, Jack?" said she, taking her seat. "I'm glad to hear it. I hope you took no hurt last night." She did not appear to hear the cover crash against the coffee urn. "I cannot think why Aunt Mimsy had all that lovely ivy cut back."

With studied composure Jack placed her plate before her, then took a seat opposite. "I hope Lady Potterby is fully recovered from recent events," he said politely.

"Oh, quite. She is surprisingly resilient. She has managed to confront each catastrophe with a minimum of sal volatile and burnt feathers. Then she immediately puts the

whole matter from her mind. She is a lady to the core."
Mrs. Desmond spooned a dab of preserves onto a small
piece of toast. "Actually, I'm more concerned about your
friend, Lord Berne," she said with a brief glance at her
husband.

"So am I," said Jack, frowning. He met Mr. Desmond's
enquiring look and added, "Not that I intend to make any
stupid sacrifice on his account. He had his chance—and
I've done quite enough for him. Practically ruined my life.
But that's done with." His eyes went to the door.

"Is she never coming down?" he asked plaintively.

Though Delilah had believed sleep quite impossible, she
must have slept nonetheless, for the sun was shining
brightly as she opened her eyes and stretched, just like the
laziest, most self-satisfied feline in the world.

She had a right to be satisfied. She was madly in love
with Jack Langdon and he was madly in love with her.
She'd realised this stunning fact as soon as she'd heard the
rustling in the garden under her window. It might have
been any villain, and she ought to have been afraid, but
villains did not daunt her—not when she had a pistol under
her pillow. Besides, she had known—there was no question—it was he.

Joan entered. "If you please, Miss, your mama sends her
compliments and when will you be down or should she tell
Mr. Langdon to come back I—"

Delilah leapt from the bed, tore off her nightgown, and
flung herself at the wash basin.

Fifteen minutes later, she was in the breakfast parlour,
sublimely unconscious of the fact that her hastily-arranged
coiffure was already tumbling to pieces and one of the
buttons at her wrist was as yet undone.

Jack rose as she entered, then was nearly knocked back
down again, for she threw herself at him and kissed him so
soundly she nearly dislocated his jaw.

"Stop that, Delilah," said her mother. "A young lady

does not leap upon her beau like a savage upon the poor beast he's just trapped."

Delilah reluctantly retreated to the seat her mama indicated beside her.

Mr. Langdon dropped back into his own chair and took a deep, steadying breath. When he dared to look up again, he found a pair of tip-tilted grey-green eyes fastened upon him, conveying a message that set his poor, abused heart thumping like Mr. Watt's steam engine.

"This," said Mr. Desmond, glancing from one to the other, "will never do."

"Certainly not," his wife agreed. "They cannot go out in public together. What would Mrs. Drummond-Burrell say if she saw Delilah wrestling her fiancé to the floor at some elegant society affair?"

"Bother Mrs. Drummond-Burrell," said Delilah. "Jack *likes* to wrestle with me, don't you darling?"

"Yes, I'm afraid I do," said Jack. He looked for a moment as though he would leap over the table to prove it.

"Am I delirious, Angelica?" Mr. Desmond asked. "Are parents not present? Is this conduct—or conversation—at all becoming in a newly betrothed couple?"

"Not at all, particularly at breakfast. I'm certain my digestion will be adversely affected," said Mrs. Desmond. "They had better adjourn to the parlour."

As the couple hastily arose, she fixed Jack with a basilisk look. "I am counting on you, sir, not to abuse a parent's trust. Obviously it is pointless to rely on my daughter's sense of decorum, as she hasn't any."

While the two besotted lovers were struggling to maintain a pretence of decorum in Lady Potterby's parlour, Lord Streetham was having a most disquieting conversation with his son. That son, having apparently lost his mind at last, was demanding a commission in the army. The earl's only offspring was insisting upon joining the military—now, of all times, when the nation was at war on virtually

249

every continent—and promising bitter consequences if h
father would not help him.

Since it is often considered wise to humour the insan
and since moreover the earl was thoroughly alarmed—
though he never showed it—he quietly agreed. When h
son had left the house, Lord Streetham ordered hi
carriage.

"Ah, Marcus," said Mr. Desmond as the earl was show
into the study. "I have been expecting you."

"I daresay," was the curt reply. "Well, what is it yo
want?"

"I?" the Devil innocently enquired. "I rather though
there was something *you* wanted."

"You know what I want—my son. You know what h
plans. I expect it was you suggested it. You are quite in hi
confidence, I understand. His mentor, perhaps," Lor
Streetham said sarcastically.

"Perhaps."

"Very well. I see you have bested me in this—you an
that conniving girl of yours. I must have her as a daughter
in-law or send my only son off to be killed. State you
demands, then. What will it cost to make the young lad
change her mind?"

"My dear fellow, Delilah will not change her mind," sai
Mr. Desmond in mild astonishment. The earl must hav
looked like contradicting him, because he added, "Befor
you say anything you might regret, Marcus, I must assur
you this is no invidious plot. My daughter has fixed on Jac
Langdon, and I should have to sever her arms to pry he
loose."

Though warned, Lord Streetham went on to say a grea
many reckless things. Mr. Desmond, being a patient man
calmly allowed his guest to rant until exhausted, at which
point the earl was obliged to take the chair courteousl
offered him.

"I am aware that Lord Berne is rather distraught a

present, and I appreciate your alarm. All the same, you cannot buy off this trouble from your son," said Mr. Desmond as he seated himself opposite. "Indeed, you have done him a great injury in doing so repeatedly, all his life. My wife tells me she could hardly bear to look at him, for it nearly broke her heart to see what a pathetic, undisciplined creature you have made of your fine, handsome boy."

"It's you who've done this to him," said the earl hoarsely.

"I, to my infinite regret, have done nothing to him. It was you set him after my daughter," Desmond answered calmly. "Really, it is a wonder to me how a man so clever in so many ways can be so blind in what most nearly concerns him. I must give you credit for cleverness, Marcus," he added with a faint smile. "It required weeks to uncover your connexion with Atkins, though I suspected you from the first. However, I must admit I did not exert myself overmuch. You see, I thought you intended to destroy the manuscript."

The colour drained from Lord Streetham's face. Still, he managed to collect himself sufficiently to answer coolly that he hadn't the least idea what his host was talking about.

"Not until the newspaper announcement appeared," the Devil went on, unheeding, "did I suspect otherwise. I had been quite certain you had not even looked at the work before consigning it to the fire. But you did. Were you surprised?"

The earl only glared at him.

"Not a word about your fanatical pursuit of Miss Angelica Ornesby, who had declined your offers some half dozen times. Not a word about the abduction you'd planned, bribing her friends in the theatre company to help you. No mention of the actress who took her place that night, while Angelica and I were in Bristol, being wed."

Mr. Desmond appeared to gaze off into some great distance. "Now I wonder why I left that fascinating story out?" he asked thoughtfully. "Something to do with not kicking a fellow when he's down, I expect. I had won the angel. It seemed base to rub your nose in your failure—especially after all these years."

Lord Streetham drew back ever so slightly as the glittering green gaze flickered to his face.

"But you have not forgotten, have you, Marcus? Your failure still gnaws at you. I suppose that is why you chose to enhance my tales with your own bits of filth. Quite a coup, you must have thought: Confound and humiliate your political rivals, destroy the Devil, break his wife's heart, and ruin his daughter, all at once. Your son, of course, would see to the last. You were certain you could count on him for that, if nothing else."

"This is monstrous," the earl gasped, rising from his chair. "I will not remain to hear another word. You will regret this, Desmond—"

"You will remain, My Lord, and I will regret nothing, because I hold the tainted manuscript. Or actually, Lady Potterby's solicitor has it," Desmond corrected. "In a carefully sealed package. A letter is enclosed, addressed to Lord Gaines, to whom the material is to be delivered in the event of my untimely demise."

Lord Streetham sat down. "Gaines?" he croaked.

"That rings a bell, perhaps? Let me refresh your memory, for you must have somehow forgotten when you were hard at work on your revisions. Perhaps because you were so drunk on that evening long ago, you forgot that I and the others had already retired to our entertainments while you and Gaines continued to dicker with the bawd."

"You—and the others—gone?"

Desmond nodded. "The tale was a revelation to me. I suppose Gaines swore you to secrecy. Certain he disposed of the bawd. She was taken up next day, tried speedily, and transported. She did not survive the voyage to New South Wales, I'm afraid. But then few persons ever do survive Gaines's displeasure."

The earl drew out his handkerchief and wiped his forehead. His hands trembled slightly.

"You know," his host continued, "were Lord Gaines to read those pages, I suspect he would have no difficulty believing you had written them. Perhaps, after so long a time, he would see the humour in the episode, perhaps not. What is *your* opinion?"

A strangled sound escaped Lord Streetham's throat, but for a moment or so, nothing else. Then he put away the handkerchief, and with visible effort, drew himself up. "I should have known," he said. "You made it too easy. You were waiting."

The Devil smiled. "My wife tells me I am patient to a fault. I rather think it is sheer laziness. Once I learned for certain you had the work, I was most curious what you were about. Still, I could not produce one good reason for exerting myself to steal it from you when I might have it from Atkins with no exertion at all. From Atkins's printer, actually. Even then it was Mr. Langdon who did all the planning and all the work. But I suppose your son has told you about that."

"Yes, and I was scarcely surprised," the earl grumbled. "You bend everyone to your will. Why not that poor, muddled boy?"

Mr. Desmond rose to ring for a servant. When he returned to his chair he answered, "I really do not understand why everyone insists Mr. Langdon is muddled. From the moment I met him, I was struck by his sagacity. My most terrifying grimaces were utterly wasted on him. He would neither cower nor be distracted. Quite remarkable. Of course, he could hardly see me for Delilah, but that— Ah, Mr. Bantwell," he said as that personage entered. "You are a miracle of promptness, indeed. Will you be kind enough to send in one of your minions with a sample of the smuggled spirits her ladyship keeps in the cellar?"

"That is not necessary," Lord Streetham said hastily as the butler was leaving.

"Oh, but it is," said Mr. Desmond.

Bantwell left, closing the door behind him.

"We have not yet discussed your fervent desire to make amends," the Devil explained.

"I knew it was too easy."

"Certainly. You have not yet spoken with Angelica."

The earl turned startled eyes upon his host.

"I thought it best," said Mr. Desmond, "that the brandy be near at hand when you did."

== 21 ==

MR. LANGDON'S MAMA, with her youngest daughter in tow, burst upon London a few days after the earl's conversation with Mr. and Mrs. Desmond. She made direct for Melgrave House, where she launched into a fit of hysterical grief that would have done Mrs. Siddons proud.

Lord Streetham, however, knew he had far greater reason for hysterical grief. Her only son was merely getting married, not going off to some filthy battlefield to be killed by barbarous Frenchmen. This made an extremely distasteful task somewhat less offensive than it might have been, and he was able to call her to order with a respectable show of his usual imperiousness.

"My dear Edith," he said coldly, "you are quite absurd. The young lady is—" He paused to clear his throat of some obstruction. "She is utterly charming, beautiful, and intelligent. She will be"—there was another moment of difficulty—"one of the foremost hostesses of the Ton."

"A hostess!" Mrs. Langdon screamed. "The daughter of an actress. Devil Desmond's daughter. The mortification will kill me. Oh, how *could* my son—but I cannot blame Jack," she added with a sob. "What does he know of women—of anything but his stupid books? The minx has tricked him. You must put a stop to it, Marcus."

"Certainly not," said the earl. "I have already given them my blessing."

Mrs. Langdon promptly fainted dead away. When she revived, the world still had not got to the rightabout, for

Lord Streetham only told her to take herself in hand and be sensible.

Thus began the making of amends. In the two months preceding the wedding, Lord Streetham found the amends he was obliged to make not unlike the labours of Hercules, though he was certain that cleaning the Augean stables was nothing to what he had to do.

When Mrs. Langdon's attitudes had been satisfactorily rearranged, the earl proceeded to those of Lord Stivling. This was a more formidable task, but Lord Streetham was formidable himself. Within a week, Lord Stivling had not only condescended to acknowledge his young relative, but agreed to provide her an extravagant betrothal celebration. By the day of this ball, the Baron Desmond had likewise been seized by a fit of Christian forgiveness. By the time the ball concluded, Miss Desmond's position, not only in her family but in Society as well, was as secure as she could have wished.

More important, both a comfortable annuity for her parents and a generous dowry for herself had very recently been arranged by the two families—and miraculously enough, without any prodding from Lord Streetham. Not only need she not ask her prospective spouse to support her parents, but she need not go to that spouse empty-handed. Though Mr. Langdon did not care two straws what she might cost him or what she brought him besides herself, Delilah was half Ornesby and half Desmond, after all, and had all their combined pride.

As it turned out, she also had Gwendolyn Langdon, with whom, to Jack's great amazement, she had become fast friends. Gwendolyn had even agreed to be Delilah's bridesmaid—primarily, the young lady told her brother, to assist Delilah should she come to her senses at the last minute and need to make a speedy getaway from the church.

A few days before the wedding, the two women were

sitting together in Lady Potterby's parlour, inspecting a deck of cards.

"Now, run your hand along the back of the card," Miss Desmond was saying. "Do you feel the tiny pin pricks? It's a stupid trick, not subtle at all, but I promise you Lady Wells had such a deck—and everyone believes her such a high stickler."

Gwendolyn laughed. "Good heavens, no wonder Mama came away so cross from that party. And I had thought you refused to play because you wanted only to gaze at Jack in that perfectly revolting way. You really should not, you know. It makes him conceited, and so high-handed with Mama that I scarcely know him anymore."

"So," said Mr. Langdon, who had noiselessly entered the room. "You are teaching my sister to cheat at cards. That is very bad of you, Delilah. How will you face the minister in two days?"

"With resignation, I daresay," his sister answered. "I have been trying to open her eyes to her error, but she will not attend. She'll learn her mistake soon enough, when she tries to get your attention—for instance, if the house takes fire—and you will not look up from your book. Then it will be too late."

She turned to Delilah. "He'll never notice your new bonnets, you know. And he will not sympathise if the parlour maid is saucy, not to mention—"

"Go away, Gwendolyn," said Jack. "I have something particular to say to my affianced wife."

Gwendolyn eyed the package in her brother's hand. "A present—and you will not let me stay to see her open it. That is very bad of you," she said, though she did rise to leave. "But of course it can only be another book. Really, Jack," she added as she moved towards the door, "you are so *unromantic*."

When she was gone, Delilah reached out to take her husband-to-be by the hand and draw him to the sofa beside her.

"You had better kiss me," she said coaxingly, "or I shall be forced to believe your sister."

"I had better not," he answered, moving primly several inches away. "It always starts as but a kiss and ends by my having to put my head under the pump. Don't pout," he added, as her lower lip began to protrude. "Open your present. Perhaps I shall kiss you after."

Delilah dutifully untied the wrapping, though she declared herself far more interested in the person who had brought it. Then her eyes widened in amazement as she stared at the book in her lap.

"Papa's memoirs," she said, baffled. She looked up at Jack. "How can this be? I gave them to Papa that night when we returned."

"You gave him the manuscript Lord Streetham had 'amended,' " Jack corrected.

"Yes—and Papa gave it to the lawyer, so Lord Streetham could not give us any more trouble. That's why I don't understand—"

"We had to give Atkins something," Jack interrupted. "We might have given him a parcel of blank paper, but we'd have been found out too soon. I thought he might as well get memoirs, since that's what he wanted so badly. So, we rewrote them."

Delilah reflected as she gazed at the book cover. "I see," she said at last. "That's why Mama came with all those notes and letters. It had nothing to do with a legal case. Now I remember—Papa said something about it that night you brought me home—how you wanted people to think—" The gaze she raised to her betrothed was reproachful. "You let *me* think it, Jack."

"Don't look at me that way," he answered uncomfortably. "I suffered agonies of guilt the whole time. Originally, I didn't want to tell you because the plan was so farfetched. We had no idea whether we'd have enough time, whether we could delay printing long enough. Then, when I realised Tony had got you to confide in him, I couldn't risk it, because he might be reporting your conversations to his father. A lawsuit wouldn't alarm Lord Streetham, but what we were truly up to would—and he'd be quick to act."

Delilah flushed. "I suppose you were right," she admitted, "not to trust either me or Tony. Obviously, I was an idiot to trust him—"

"It's hard not to trust him. I've known him all my life, yet I believed a whole pack of lies—but then, he half-believed them himself."

Reflections upon the unhappy Lord Berne could not but be painful, yet they could not be thrust away so easily either. For a few moments the pair sat in silence—until Miss Desmond recalled that she still had not a satisfactory explanation for the book. She pointed out that the crisis had been resolved some time ago. Jack and Tony were bosom-bows again. In fact, the viscount was to be groomsman, before going abroad with his regiment. His father, moreover, had turned all Delilah's relatives up sweet.

"Everything has been tranquil and relatively sane for two months," she reminded severely, "yet you never once said a word about this." She gestured at the volume in her lap.

"Oh, yes. That." Jack fished out a piece of paper from his pocket and gave it to her. "The reviewer is anonymous," he said, "but I can make a guess who it is. A noted bibliophile of our mutual acquaintance. Member of Parliament, closely connected with the ministry, belted earl—that sort of thing."

Delilah swiftly perused the clipping. " 'Charming, lively tales of bygone days,' " she read aloud. " 'Not at all the prurient trash the public was led to expect. A work to be savoured—' " She broke off to gaze at her fiancé with undisguised admiration. "Oh, Jack— you wrote this book?"

"Hardly. Your father dictated, mainly, and we worked on the rephrasing together. I didn't want to cut the heart out of it, you know—so we went for more humour and less bawdiness. Your father is a genius, Delilah. I hope he continues to write—"

"I know he's a genius," she interrupted. "But I see I have a great deal to learn about *you*. You are even more under-handed than I thought."

"Am I?" He took up her hand rather absently and kissed it. The clipping fluttered to the floor.

She sighed. "Oh, Jack." Then she jerked her hand away. "There—you're doing it again. You still have not answered my question. Two months we've been engaged and you never told me you'd rewritten Papa's book."

Mr. Langdon's countenance assumed an expression of abstraction. "Didn't I?" he asked. "I must have forgot. So much on my mind, you know."

"You did not forget," she retorted. "And I will not be taken in by any more muddled looks."

"But it's true," he said gravely. "For two months I have been unable to think of anything but the night on which will finally be permitted to slake my savage lust upon your innocent person."

"Slake your savage lust?" she repeated, turning a skepti-cal smile upon him. "That sounds rather like something you got out of a book."

"Yes. I get a great many things out of books. I got you because of one. I am a book-worm through and through and—" He paused, his eyes very dark now.

"And?" She reached up to brush a lock of hair back from his forehead.

"And I think I am about to mistake you for a volume of Ptolemy." He drew her face closer to his. "Make that Ovid," he said. His lips brushed lightly against hers. "Make that *Ars Amatoria*."

"Make it anything you like," she whispered impatiently as she threw her arms about his neck. "Only kiss me, Jack properly—and *now*."

He did.